Did Sid?

Paul Robins

ISBN:148010342X
ISBN-13:9781480103429

"Did Sid?" is a work of fiction. Any resemblance to any
person, living or dead, is interesting, isn't it? But it's purely a
coincidence. Trust me on this. In cases where references are
made to real businesses, institutions, public offices or public
officials, they are used fictionally.

For Bridget

I love her so,
and she loves me back.

"I am an innocent man."
  -Billy Joel

*"If it looks like a duck,
swims like a duck, and
quacks like a duck..."*
  - Anonymous

CHAPTER 1

There was something about the lawyer's forehead that Sid found distracting. And creepy. There was just too much of it, and the shape was strangely familiar. What was it? Then the light bulb popped on. *Herman Munster.*

Sid thought everybody looked like somebody. The guy who ran the tiny flower shop by the theater on K Street looked like the guy who played the bartender on Love Boat. The people who lived across the street from his mom had a collie that was the spitting image of Candice Bergen. Sid, himself, looked like his father. And his father, unfortunately, bore a close resemblance to Howdy Doody.

Spotting celebrities in the faces of strangers was a lifelong habit— a satisfying, private amusement for an audience of one. Sometimes, in pursuit of this little game, he'd allow his mind to wander off so far that he completely lost track of things that were going on in the real world. And so it came as a complete surprise when the following words left the lawyer's mouth: "Tell your attorney to expect a civil action to be filed by the end of the week."

"You're suing me." Sid snapped out of it.

"Yes," said the mouth below the Munster forehead. "On behalf of Roger W. Matheson."

Uh-oh. Time to pay attention. Sid realized now that the deli had grown quiet around him. At the grill, Joe wiped his hands on his apron, then stood motionless, trying to catch their conversation. In very uncharacteristic fashion, Woody the cop actually put down his fork to listen. Even Eddie the busboy sensed that something was wrong. The sizzle of some sausage links grew strangely loud. The radio by the cash register was on low, and he could just hear "Hotel California" by the Eagles.

Clearly, something important had gone by without Sid catching it. "Do I know this Roger W. Matheson?"

"You've never seen him," replied the lawyer, "But you've caused him significant harm nonetheless."

"And I've done this how?"

"Connie Matheson comes here every day at lunchtime, does she not?"

"Connie who?"

"Four meatloaf sandwiches and four orders of gravy fries."

"Ohhhh..." Sid managed to pull his eyes away from the lawyer with the considerable forehead. "Hey, Joe. Meatloaf Lady's name is Connie."

"Connie *Matheson*," corrected the lawyer. "The woman takes four Meatloaf Sandwiches and four orders of Gravy Fries home to her son, Roger, every day for lunch."

"Just one guy's been eating the meatloaf sandwiches

2

every day?"

"He has, indeed," replied the lawyer. "For at least five years according to my client."

"The meatloaf's awesome," said Woody the cop, to whom the idea seemed completely reasonable.

"Look, pal," said Sid, "I've only had this place for about six months." He turned again to Joe at the grill. "Any chance this guy's been eating four meatloaf sammies a day for five years?"

Joe considered the question. "Been a long time."

"Mr. Matheson currently weighs an estimated 850 pounds," the lawyer pressed on. "He cannot leave his apartment, or even get out of his bed, for that matter." He pointed a finger at Sid's chest. "You are guilty of Contributory Negligence, and as such are significantly responsible for the condition in which Mr. Matheson now finds himself."

Sid noticed now for the first time that Eddie Davis had put down the plastic tray he used for clearing tables and was listening intently. He was smiling as he always did, but the bright eyes set in his handsome, dark face looked like they were brimming with tears. Sid's mind took another shot at wandering off. He'd first met Eddie maybe ten years ago, had never heard him speak a word, and still didn't know exactly what the deal was. "Busboy" was an odd way to describe him, as he had to be close to Sid's own age. Sid's father had clearly cared a lot about Eddie, but you could never tell what the guy was thinking or how much he understood.

Sid picked out a few framed photos on the wall.

Willie Mays. Spiro Agnew. John Wayne. Sid was there the day the Duke had come in for lunch. How old had he been? Eight? Nine? He smiled at the thought.

"Mr. Bigler, did you hear me?" The lawyer was still there.

His father had been gone for six months. The deli belonged to Sid now, and life was suddenly going to hell in a hurry. Woody the cop picked his fork back up. Don Henley sang , "You can check out any time you like, but you can never leave..."

It's 1980. The year Sid Bigler, Jr. would end up on the front page of the Sacramento Bee more than a dozen times. The crazy lawsuit, the ridiculous problem with Jock Bell, and, of course, the shootings would all combine to make him an irresistible, if reluctant, media magnet.

CHAPTER 2

At least the peckerwood attorney had chosen a good time to bring everything to a grinding halt. At 9:45, the breakfast and coffee crowd of mostly state workers had come and gone. Politicians and media types favored Sid's Deli, but people like that generally didn't show up 'til lunchtime. Besides the two employees, it was just Woody the cop holding down his usual stool at the counter and a couple of other customers distracted by the morning paper.

"So it's my fault this guy weighs 800 pounds?" Sid asked.

"850," said the lawyer, and he began to spew legal phrases like pick-up lines at a T.G.I. Friday's. "As a restaurant owner, you have the fiduciary responsibility to care for the health and security of your customers in a way that any reasonable person would. You certainly should have known that your high fat, high calorie foods, when consumed at high levels, pose serious bodily risk."

"Give me a break, pal. Let's just ask the chef." Sid turned for help to his father's oldest friend, who raised an eyebrow at the word, *chef*. "Joe, how much fat would you say is in one of our meatloaf sandwiches?"

As always, Joe Diaz thought before speaking. "A buttload," he said, then shrugged and returned to his grill.

Very helpful.

"Buttload is not a legal term, and therefore not admissible in a court of law," Sid tried to sound Perry Mason-ish. The lawyer stared back at him without expression.

There had to be a way to get rid of this guy. Sid glanced at his best customer—although "customer" may not be the right word, as it implies one who actually pays for their food. Woody Carver was close to Sid's age. Late twenties, and by all accounts a hell of a cop. He was only an inch or two taller than Sid, but he was built like a Rock 'em Sock 'em Robot, and when he gave somebody the *cop look*, it had a paralyzing effect. In a city full of hairspray and sideburns, Woody wore the only crew cut in Sacramento outside the local Air Force bases. Generally about the time the commute was winding down, he'd park his cruiser along the red curb right in front of the deli where he anchored the same stool five days a week. He could put away Joe's Breakfast Special with frightening precision, and Sid never gave him a bill. Cops at the counter were good advertising, and one free breakfast every day was a cheap price to pay for added security. Besides, he generally left a tip that would've covered the meal and then some.

"Hey, Officer Carver, any law against serving delicious food to happy, hungry customers?"

"Not in the U.S.A." Woody wiped his chin and smiled.

Sid opened his hands and gave the lawyer a shrug. "Looks like I haven't done anything wrong," and Sid smiled, too.

The lawyer paused with a disturbing confidence.

"No, Mr. Bigler. Despite the keen legal insight of your muscle-bound policeman friend, you are culpable in the tragic decline of my client's health." So much for Woody's intimidating cop act. "Tell me, what else did Mrs. Matheson pick up every day with her lunch order?"

The guy sounded like he was practicing his closing argument. Sid thought about playing dumb, but what was the point?

"Banana cream pie," he admitted.

"Only *one* pie, Mr. Bigler?" Damn. The guy was good. "As I said, your attorney can be expecting to hear from us very soon. Good day." With that, the man handed Sid his business card, turned, and walked out. Sid read the name on the card. "Vince Headley, Esq." No kidding.

Sid took a moment to wonder just exactly how big a problem this whole thing was going to be. The timing couldn't be worse. Woody was the first to speak.

"You got an attorney, Sid?"

"Yeah, Woody," he replied. "I got an attorney."

One of the other customers approached the register and paid his bill. Sid thought in passing that if the guy wore a wig he'd look a little like Jane Hathaway from the Beverly Hillbillies. Ordinarily the thought would have amused his inner self more, but he was suddenly a tough audience. Before the guy headed out the door, he dropped the newspaper on the counter and said, "You're mentioned in the paper again today."

Sid looked at the newspaper. This article was smaller than the last few, and there was no photo. But even with no new developments, the story was still front page news. The headline read: "No Leads In Landmark Shootings". There was nothing more to say than that really, but the Sacramento Bee managed to squeeze about six column inches out of the nothing. The police had held a press conference the previous day to say that they had collected more clues regarding the bizarre series of shootings, but could give no details and they had no suspects. They'd appreciate it very much if anyone in the public who knew anything about the crimes would contact them. Blah. Blah. Blah. Sid's name did, in fact, appear about two thirds of the way down. The last line of the article read, "The city holds its breath waiting for more bullets to fly, wondering what the next target will be." Sid rolled his eyes.

By now the story had started to make the national news, and certainly everyone in the Sacramento area knew all about it. Twelve days ago, someone had fired a gun at the State Capitol building. No one saw anything, but several people heard the gunshots. It happened shortly before midnight, and there were conflicting reports about just how many shots had been fired. The paper had reported that some earwitnesses claimed they heard at least eight shots. Sid strongly suspected that "earwitness" was not really a word, and was considering writing a letter to the ombudsman. Others said there were five at the most. Police only managed to collect physical evidence from three shots, but that was fairly impressive given the size of the stately building and the grounds surrounding it. A golf ball sized chunk of concrete had been chipped off one of the north steps, a small caliber bullet hole was found in the beautiful state seal on the north side of the building, and one shot had broken a north-facing window. Following some of the city's most impressive detective work, the Police Chief said, "We're confident the shots came from the north side of the Capitol."

Sid Bigler, too, was confident that the shots had come from the north. And he was certain that there had been exactly five shots. He had been less than a block away when it happened.

Sid put in an average of seventy-five miles a week training. When the weather started to warm up, he did most of his running after the sun went down, and it wasn't uncommon for him to be out well past midnight. He often included a few laps around Capitol Park. Even in the dark, it was one of the most beautiful places in town, and it gave him the added advantage of being able to check up on the deli. On the night of the first shooting, Sid was running up L Street just approaching 12th when he heard the shots behind him. Bang-Bang-Bang-Bang-Bang. In his mind he could still hear them almost two weeks later. There had been five.

So it turned out that Sid was one of the earwitnesses, and he was clearly the local media's favorite. He was the owner of a Sacramento institution and he had a big mouth. Perfect. He was interviewed by the Bee, the Sacramento Union, and all four local TV stations. The camera loved Sid Bigler. His fifteen minutes of fame proved to be fun and interesting. Nobody had gotten hurt, and it had been a nice plug for the deli.

Three days later City Hall was targeted. Same thing all over again. Late at night, five shots at a government building, nobody injured and nobody saw a thing. One bullet recovered this time. No suspects, no motives.

Another two days went by. This time the target was Lew Williams Chevrolet on Fulton Avenue. Five shots. Odd target, but to some this was the most villainous crime so far. Two pick-ups, a Caprice Classic, and three Corvettes were hit. Corvettes. Oh, the humanity. The media was really beginning to salivate.

And then the story exploded. Exactly eight days after the initial incident at the Capitol, somebody popped off five shots at Sutter's Fort. For those who have never taken the elementary school tour, Sutter's Fort was the first attempt by the white man to set up shop in California's heartland. Back in the 1840's, John Sutter was a Swiss gentleman who got permission from Mexico to take land from Indians. Perfectly logical. In an odd twist of history, Sutter was responsible for the mill in the foothills where gold was discovered, and the discovery of gold was responsible for the abandonment of Sutter's Fort. Rather than being given back to the Indians, the run-down fort was eventually restored by the Native Sons of the Golden West and the land ended up becoming a small State Park at 27th and L Streets in midtown Sacramento, surrounded mostly by laundromats. Hardly anyone ever set foot on the grounds, but Sacramentans considered it their own and strongly resented anyone shooting at it. It was clearly those five shots at this most treasured historical landmark that elevated the crimes from "news story" to "spectacle."

Reason number one: For the first time more than just property was damaged. A homeless guy sleeping next to the fort had a bullet pass through the big toe of his left foot. And reason number two: The only witness to the crime was Sid Bigler.

It was a clear, cool night that had followed a day in the mid-nineties. The delta breezes came up just about every evening and made for perfect running weather. Sid was out for an easy run, clicking off six minute miles as Van Halen's "Runnin' with the Devil" played in his head. He had cruised past the Capitol ("the scene of the crime," he thought) and was approaching Sutter's Fort when he heard the shots ahead. He may have seen some flashes. He thought he saw a figure dash across L and disappear around the corner at 27th. Sid actually had the thought, *"I can catch that guy,"* and his pulse jumped from 140 to 200 in an instant. But the long, terrible wail of a bum with a big toe that was suddenly hamburger caused him to pull up short. He ran to the fort and comforted the wounded until the cops arrived.

Being the prime witness to a juicy crime was an adventure the first time around. But now it was something different. He was like the guy who'd won the lottery twice in a row. Sid was the center ring attraction of what was the most extravagant media circus the city had ever seen. The headline of the Sacramento Bee read: "Deli Owner Hears Shots Again." The Union, perhaps

because of trailing circulation, tried even harder:
"Sandwich Specialist Spectator in Second Shooting!"
Hard to believe Mark Twain once worked for that paper.
Sid went from being a soundbite on the evening news to
a live, in-studio guest. Channel 10 actually had him wear
make-up. Reporters asked him questions as he came out
the door of his house in the morning and as he arrived at
the deli for work. He was called a hero repeatedly, which
he found more embarrassing than flattering. But there
was also some jerk on a local radio station who went on
and on about how suspicious it was that one guy would
be at the scene of two different *random* shootings.
Implying what, exactly? Prick. It all began to taper off
fairly quickly, but for a couple of days he had a brief
glimpse of what it must be like to be Wayne Newton—
famous, with a hint of criminal suspicion—and he didn't
like it.

As he stood in the deli staring at the newspaper,
enjoying the post-breakfast lull and the absence of Mr.
Headley the lawyer, Sid took some comfort in the
thought that at least he was all done with the madness
surrounding the shootings. Sid was wrong about that.

CHAPTER 3

Sid's Deli was an American success story. The original Sid Bigler came of age as the country went to war. He'd spent his youth in Stockton, California, where idleness and opportunity produced a nineteen-year-old who was a pain in the ass for just about everyone he encountered. In fact, it was only a very timely attack by the Japanese that kept young Sid Bigler, Sr. from his first trip to prison. A grouchy but sagacious judge thought the boy could be of more service in the Navy than behind bars, and he was right. World War II took a lot of lives, but it made a good man of Sid Bigler.

It was aboard the USS Texas that Sid met Joe Diaz. Sid wrestled 14-inch shells into the battleship's big guns, and Joe wrestled pots and pans in the galley. The physical difference between them was close to comedic. Sid was five feet, four inches tall and built like a jackrabbit. Joe was nearly a foot taller, as powerful and purposeful as a glacier. But this physical disparity was only the tip of the iceberg. Sid talked enough for two men and Joe hardly said a word. Sid was loud— a friendly kind of loud that was infectious . Joe was quiet— an imposing kind of quiet that made people lower their voices around him. Sid was impulsive and had a short fuse, a fact the insightful judge in Stockton had been quick to point out.

Joe, thankfully, was slow to anger. Sid was messy, impetuous, optimistic. Joe was organized, reserved, a little melancholy. And so it went. Sid liked coffee and Joe liked tea. Sid had many friends and Joe had only one. Sid.

The Texas wasn't a shiny new ship that was cranked out for the purpose of joining the battle in WWII. She was commissioned in 1914 and was perhaps the most powerful weapon on earth during the first World War. By the time Sid and Joe came on board in 1942, the ship was getting long in the tooth. But it, and they, served admirably. The battleship's history sounds like a highlight's reel of the war, from supporting the invasion of North Africa, to the D-Day landing at Normandy, to action in the Pacific at Iwo Jima.

Sid and Joe had promised themselves that they'd go into business together if they survived the war, and the plan from the very beginning was to open some kind of restaurant. Sid would schmooze the customers and Joe would cook. It was not a terribly sophisticated plan, but it was a good one. Mostly because of the fact that Joe was something of a genius in the kitchen. In general, the food in a Navy galley was better than what you found in the other branches of the service. At least, that's what they told the guys in the Navy. Regardless, Joe's chow was legendary in the Pacific Fleet. When the war ended, it was said that the USS Texas was the only ship in the Navy where the sailors didn't want to go home because they'd miss the food.

When the two friends were discharged from active

duty, they headed west. Joe had very little family and even fewer friends back in Philadelphia, and Sid had filled his head with glamorous stories about Stockton. That Sid was able to convince his friend that Stockton was a desirable destination is a testament to his power of persuasion. It was Sid's parents who not only put up some money to get them started, but suggested that they consider Sacramento for their new business. "It's a bigger city with more opportunity," they said. "The state capital!" The fact was that Sid's parents were less than convinced their son had turned over a new leaf, and were only happy to spend some of their money to get him back out of town.

It was Spring of 1947 when they opened for business at 1028 K Street, and dumb luck smiled on them twice. First was the location, chosen for the sole reason that it was the cheapest rent they could find. If they'd looked twice as long and spent three times the money they couldn't have done better. From the corner window they could actually see the Capitol dome. Second was the improbable identity of one of their very first customers. In the days leading up to their grand opening, Sid met and became quick friends with a fellow veteran who had ended up with the California State Police working security at the Capitol. The state cop was friends with a guy who was dating the Governor's personal secretary, and the Governor's personal secretary mentioned to her boss that a couple of boys returned from the war had opened a little deli just a block from the office. And that's why, on the first Friday they were open, Governor Earl Warren

ate his first Pastrami Deluxe at Sid's Deli. Joe's secret
was a little molasses and Tabasco in the mayo, and the
governor pronounced it "the best dang sandwich I ever
ate." It was a time when the governor of California could
walk to lunch without much hoopla, and that's what
happened two or three times a month for the rest of
Warren's term. And every governor after him made it a
point to occasionally grab lunch at Sid's. Five governors
in all, including the movie star Ronald Reagan. One by
one, their photos went up on the deli walls, along with
anybody else notable. Legislators, lobbyists, all those with
an inflated image of self-importance loved the place, and
Sid knew them all by name. The deli was fairly small—
eight tables and a lunch counter. Nothing on the menu
was over seventy-five cents when it opened. And it was
one of the top places in town for a political power lunch.

One note about the name. Some may wonder why it
wasn't "Sid & Joe's Deli". That's what Sid wanted to call
the place, but Joe would have none of it. As usual, for
Joe it was simple. "You and your folks put up the money.
It belongs to you." Despite the fact that Joe's food was
the main attraction, it was, in fact, "Sid's Deli."

The early years were ones of professional and
personal success. Open only for breakfast and lunch, the
place was surprisingly profitable. Sid paid Joe as well as
he paid himself. He purchased the building they were in
at 11th & K and stopped paying rent. In 1949, a stunning
redhead came in to buy a Greek salad, and before the end
of the year Sid was married to Rose O'Brien. Gloria
Bigler was born in 1950 and Sid, Jr. was born in 1953. It

was upon the birth of his son that Sid, Sr. became "Big Sid" Bigler, and that's what everybody called him from that point on. At his height, occasionally someone meeting him would think the name was a joke. But to those who knew Big Sid, the name was a perfect fit.

Big Sid's wife introduced her cousin to Joe on his 38th birthday. He and Theresa were married in 1962 and they never found out why children never came along.

After years of operating the store with only two people, Big Sid hired Eddie the busboy to help out in 1970. It was a remarkable thing to do at the time, because the disabled were usually kept out of sight in those days. No sense making all the normal people feel uncomfortable, right? Interesting thing about Eddie— when you first saw him, you had no idea he was different. A great looking African American kid with a friendly smile and an analytical look in his eye. But after a while, you realized that the smile never left, the look in his eye never changed, and he never talked. Something was missing. He seemed to understand a lot of what was said, but it was hard to tell. Nobody ever asked what was wrong with Eddie Davis, and nobody seemed to care. He was a hard worker, he was always in a great mood, and everyone liked him. He was just 17 years old when he started at the deli. Over time, Big Sid and Joe grew to feel very paternal toward Eddie. With no children of his own, the feeling was especially strong for Joe. A few years back a customer referred to Eddie as "that retard." It was the first time anybody besides Big Sid had ever seen Joe get angry, and if Big Sid hadn't gotten in the way,

Joe might have killed the guy.

Eddie showed up just about the time Sid, Jr. went off to college. Older sister Gloria was already in law school and would go on to become a brilliant attorney. Sid, Jr. was not quite as brilliant and his grades always showed it. But he was funny and gregarious like his father, and he could run like the wind. He accepted a Track & Cross Country scholarship to Humboldt State up near the Oregon border where he spent the next four years surrounded by redwood trees and hippies. Humboldt wasn't exactly Harvard, but they had a killer track program. Sid, Jr. somehow managed to graduate and returned to Sacramento in 1975. In the pursuit of his Communication Studies degree, Sid had learned exactly nothing, and so began a career in radio ad sales.

The rest of the seventies were smooth sailing for everyone whose lives were connected to Sid's Deli. Jerry Brown was elected governor and he loved the Vegetarian Taco Salad. Almost every Sunday evening Big Sid and Rose hosted dinner at their house for the whole gang— Joe and Theresa, Gloria and her family, and Sid, Jr. Life was good. That's why it came as such a shock when, in the fall of 1979, Big Sid put a gun to his head.

CHAPTER 4

It is not malicious to say that Sacramento is not the most beautiful city in America. It's just a fact. It's like saying that Ringo is not the most handsome Beatle. But what California's capital lacks in aesthetics it makes up for meteorologically. Yes, it's inexcusably hot sometimes in the middle of the day during the summer. And you'll occasionally hit a three or four week stretch in the winter where a thin layer of clouds sits on top of the valley like foam on a cappuccino— it never rains, you never see the sun, and the locals go a little nuts. But otherwise, the weather is pleasant and predictable.

Sid was thinking about the weather as he was closing up the deli. It was 2:45, Joe had just left for the day and, as usual, had given Eddie a lift home. The temp was topping out at close to ninety degrees— warm, but not unusual for early May. He and his girlfriend had talked about having a light dinner, catching a movie, then going out for a run together around 10 o'clock. It should be back down in the sixties by then. Perfect.

Keys in hand, Sid flipped the "Open/Closed" sign in the window around to announce that Sacramento's Best Deli (as voted by the readers of both major newspapers) had called it quits for the day. He then hit the light switch and pulled the plug on the Coors sign, causing the amazingly realistic waterfall to freeze in place. His dad had loved that sign and would stare at it endlessly, trying to figure out how it worked. Sid was reaching for the doorknob when someone began to open the door from the outside.

"Sorry, we're closed," he announced, and looked up to find himself staring into the face of Jock Bell. Just about everybody in Sacramento knew who Otis "Jock" Bell was, and most would describe him as a *character*. That's because most people had never actually met him. If you knew Jock Bell, you knew he was a jerk.

The old guy had operated the pawn shop right across K Street from the deli for almost three decades. He also ran a bail bonds business out of the same location. His "Jock Will Set You Free" TV commercials had been a staple of late-night television for years. But the pawn shop and bail bonds operation was just the centerpiece of a uniquely *Sacramento* business empire. Just a part of the Jock Bell mystique. He'd made a name for himself by being willing to try out any crazy business idea that occurred to him. He was the first and only person to offer mini-submarine rides in the Sacramento River to tourists. The Sacramento River is a solid brownish color, and there's nothing to see on the bottom anyway, but the damned sub was quite a sensation for a while. It was still docked at the Miller Park Marina with Jock's name painted on the side, though nobody had gotten inside the thing for years. Jock Bell opened the area's first comedy club in an empty restaurant banquet room in Old Sac. It only lasted six months, but The Smothers Brothers and

Fred Travelena both played there before it went belly up. At various times, Jock sponsored fireworks shows, sold ad space on hot air balloons, built a year-round artificial snow ski slope, and operated a school for aspiring professional wrestlers. Most of his ventures fizzled quickly, but everybody heard about them. And the curious thing was that the spectacular failure of some of his enterprises only served to make his successful businesses more famous. His two waterbed stores had combined annual sales of nearly a million dollars. He started the first whitewater raft rental operation on the American River and sold it for a huge profit. He opened a singles bar called *The Phone Company*, with in-house telephones at each table so horny singles at one table could call up horny singles at another table to introduce themselves. It was cheesy, but horny singles packed the place nightly.

In addition to this strange variety of businesses that came and went over the years, there were the real estate deals. Jock Bell bought and sold more downtown real estate than anyone else in the sixties and seventies. That may sound impressive, but keep in mind that, after the State Capitol, the most notable building in Sacramento in 1980 was the DMV on Broadway. Still, he had a knack for buying a commercial property or apartment building that nobody wanted, getting a zoning change or variance, and doubling or tripling his money in a matter of months. Most considered him extremely lucky, but those in the business community suspected that more than luck was involved in the favors he was shown by city government.

21

And Jock Bell had managed to accomplish all this while treating people like crap. Oh, if you had something he wanted, there was an oily charm about him. But if he perceived that someone was not valuable to him, he was quick-tempered, intimidating, and dismissive. Diana Ross on steroids.

This was the man Sid came nose to nose with as he went to lock up the deli. Sid had seen him downtown on numerous occasions, and lots of times on TV, of course. But he'd never actually spoken to him. Never been close enough to smell his breath. Sid tried to stay focused. Tried to ignore the still, small voice that was already beginning to make quiet observations about the famous Jock Bell. *My God, how old is this guy?*

It was a fair question, and a tough one to answer. This was the most deeply tanned, deeply lined face Sid had ever seen. There was an ancient, yet well preserved quality to his skin, like leather seats in an old, expensive car. A catcher's mitt with eyes, nose and a mouth.

And the thing that really threw Sid off, the thing that made the man's age so hard to guess, was Jock's hair. Sitting on top of this ancient face was the hair of an eighteen-year-old. Too much, too dark, too carefully styled. The hair had the same effect as a chubby streaker at a ballgame— he didn't want to stare but he couldn't make himself stop. It wasn't a wig. He could see the individual hairs going right down into the leathery scalp. Did Jock steal it from one of the guys in Air Supply? Whatever it was, it made him look like a Muppet. Sid fought back a chuckle.

"Hello, Little Sid." The voice was deeper and softer than it sounded in the commercials.

It wasn't Jock's appearance but his opening line that started Sid down the road to detesting this man. He hated the name "Little Sid." It may have seemed like a natural thing to call him, since his dad was "Big Sid," but he hated it. He was five feet, eight inches tall. A very average height, and a full four inches taller than his old man. It was probably inevitable that he be called "Little Sid" as a baby, but from the time he was old enough to express a preference, he made it very clear that he found the name insulting. Through the years, the only people who called him that were some punks in junior high and high school who did it for the express purpose of making his life miserable. The Dunlop brothers, in particular, had a way of pronouncing "Little Sid" that conveyed the deeper message: "You're a pussy." Unpleasant moments from his youth began to play in Sid's mind like newsreel clips. He forced himself to focus and consciously decided to give the man the benefit of the doubt. Jock Bell couldn't have known how he felt about being called "Little Sid."

"Mr. Bell, I was just closing up."

"Call me Jock," he said, and slithered past Sid into the slightly darkened deli. "I've been meaning to stop by and wish you luck with the place ever since your father passed away." The man ran his hand along the counter and glanced around the small restaurant.

"Thank you, Jock." The name just felt wrong coming out of his mouth. "It's been tough on my mom,

23

but we…"

"How long's it been, couple of months?" Bell interrupted.

"Six months. My father died in November."

"November." Half question, half statement. "Before Christmas. I didn't realize. That's tough." Hard to tell if this was an act or not. Jock sat down on one of the stools.

"But, uh, things are going pretty well now," said Sid.

"Yeah, I see you got a line out the door at lunchtime again. Almost as long as it used to be before. That's nice."

"Look, I was just closing up for the day."

"Sure. I could tell."

In normal, everyday life, if Guy #1 expresses an intent to close and lock a commercial establishment and Guy #2 acknowledges the intent of Guy #1, it's at that point that Guy #2 gets up and leaves. But Jock Bell didn't move a muscle. He looked at Sid, and Sid looked at him.

What was this guy's deal? Jock had obviously been perfecting the quiet, confident bully routine for years. For a few, brief moments, it had actually been working. But as he sat there on the stool with his bizarre explosion of hair, wearing tight Ditto jeans and a white turtleneck on a warm May afternoon, Jock Bell began to deeply amuse Sid Bigler. Sid drank in the sight. He noticed some small details that had escaped him at first. The bracelet wristwatch caked with gold nuggets. The James Brown looking sunglasses in his hand. The gold rope chain on the outside of the turtleneck. Nice touch. He clearly didn't mind modeling some of the stuff he took in at the pawn shop. Sid sat down, too, two stools away.

The long, uncomfortable silence ploy probably worked with most people, but it was a mistake for Jock to have tried it today. Sid couldn't have been happier, sitting quietly and looking at Jock. He was like Jane Goodall, silently observing every little aspect of the appearance and habits of the great apes. How long would the man sit there without speaking? Had it been thirty seconds yet? More? Fascinating.

"You know I wanted to buy this place from Big Sid." Jock's voice interrupted Sid's reverie. Both men knew that this round was probably going to the man who had been able to hold out the longest, but you keep punching 'til the bell rings.

"Did you? When was that?"

"Starting maybe two years ago. Made him a couple of offers. Good offers."

"Really? I didn't know that."

Sid knew. His old man was a great storyteller, and there were a several times when Big Sid had the whole gang dying over dinner on a Sunday as he told of his latest encounter with Jock Bell. Sid realized now what a good impression of this creep his dad did, and it made him smile.

"Well, my dad loved this place. I'm not surprised he didn't want to sell it."

"What about you? You love the place?"

For a moment, the posturing ended. The question

hit Sid out of the blue, and it didn't matter who had asked it or why. This deli had been the center of the Bigler Universe since before he was born, but how important was it to him? To his mom and his sister? There would be time to sort out his feelings later. Time to move forward or give up the advantage.

"Oh, I don't know... Business is good. I enjoy the people." He tried for casual. "And, of course, I'd hate to give up the building. You know this is the only building on this entire block with access to the old underground?"

Sid let that last line slip out as if it were an afterthought. He watched Jock closely. The man's saddlebag face showed only the tiniest reaction. Just a flick of the eyes, but it was there.

"No. No, I wasn't aware," Jock lied. "Look, son, I've worked a lot of real estate deals in this town. I'm sure you know that. Big Sid bought this place a long time ago. You might be surprised what it's worth now."

"Yeah? How much?"

Jock paused and tried on a smile. "You're trying to close up and go home. We can talk about this later." He slid off the stool. His shiny black zipper boots clicked on the linoleum as he made his way to the door.

The encounter almost over, Sid made the mistake of dropping his guard. Jock Bell paused before stepping into the sunshine, and his final words caught Sid unexpected. Made his head spin.

"Stop by the shop sometime," he said. "You know your dad pawned some stuff the last few months he was alive? Bet you'd find it interesting, Little Sid."

CHAPTER 5

Out of the corner of his eye, Sid caught Amy trying to read the numbers on her watch as they passed under the streetlamp. He grinned and flashed back to his competitive days. He'd never worn a watch in training or competition. It was one of the main tenets in *Sid's Rules of Running*. When you push hard it makes you uncomfortable. Lactic acid builds up in your muscles, your lungs fall behind your body's demand for oxygen. You look at your watch to confirm that your speed justifies how much you're hurting. And it's that glance at your watch that informs the runners around you that you're vulnerable. A runner looking at his watch is a runner that's about to get his butt kicked, so Sid never wore a watch. If he was dying, he just told himself that the other guys were dying more and he dug down deeper. The words of Coach Armbruster floated through his head: "If you're not barfing, you can run faster."

"You doing okay?" Sid asked.

"Yeah. Good." The words came out in puffs.

"Let's back off some."

"Yeah. Good."

They shortened their strides a little and Amy's relief was almost immediate. As hard as Sid was prone to push himself, he never thought it was his place to push others.

Amy had been setting the pace tonight, and he was just along for the ride. Her breathing steadied.

"Thanks," she said. "I'd been wanting to slow down for the last couple of miles, but I was trying to impress you."

"You impress me standing still."

Sid Bigler and Amy Solomon were the exact same size. 5'8", 135 pounds. It was amazing what a difference allocation of resources could make. He was stringy, all elbows and knees. She was lithe, all curves and curls. And the legs were unbelievable. A guy that wasn't blinded by love might have noticed her front teeth were a little too big. And with her hair pulled back, it was true that her ears stood out a little more than average. But in Sid's eyes even her imperfections were just right. And then there was her stride. Smooth, but with enough bounce to make her brunette ponytail do a hypnotic dance. Yes, Sid was attracted to her stride. It was the first thing he noticed about her. If fast was sexy, Amy could be Charlie's fourth angel. Almost three years older than he was, she'd turned thirty the day after Big Sid died.

They'd met a year ago at a local 10K race hosted by the Buffalo Chips running club. Sid had come in second behind some college kid. It didn't matter that he'd won his age division. Second is second. Amy had won her age division, too, and didn't care at all if some college girls came in ahead of her. A win is a win.

Here's how the weekly *Movie and a Run* date worked: Sid would pick up Amy around six o'clock and they'd have a quick dinner. Nothing heavy because they'd be running later, and nothing expensive because Sid was paying. After the movie he would drop Amy off at her apartment in the Pocket Area to change. Sid would then drive exactly three miles to his house in Old Land Park, throw on his shorts and a t-shirt and head out his front door. He'd push pretty hard for the three miles back to Amy's, then the two of them would take off together. It was about an eight mile loop to run from her place down Riverside and circle the park twice before returning to her apartment. Sid would drop her back at her front door and end with three more hard miles home.

This night it had been Taco Bell and *Friday the 13th*. Sid Bigler knows how to treat a lady. It was now 11:15, and they were maybe an easy ten minutes away from her place. For the fifth time that night Sid suddenly screamed, pointed at some bushes and yelled, "There's a guy in a hockey mask!" Again, his post-movie scare tactic produced no visible results.

"So, tell me about Jock Bell." Amy had been waiting all night to hear the story. Over bean and cheese burritos at dinner he had casually mentioned that one of Sacramento's most colorful citizens had paid him a visit that afternoon. He had promised to give her the details during that night's run, and over their last miles together he recounted the story. The dramatic entrance, the bizarre combination of ancient face and adolescent hair. The head games. He omitted Jock's departing comment. If there really was some of his dad's stuff in that pawn shop, he thought he'd keep that news to himself. But he told her the rest, including his casual remark about access to the old underground.

"Why would Jock Bell give a rip about what's beneath the deli?" Amy asked.

"You don't know about this?" Sid was genuinely surprised. "You're not gonna believe it. He thinks there's hidden treasure down there. Gold."

"Get outta here."

"I'm serious. Some guy who works at the pawn shop snuck over and told my dad last year that they'd taken in a box of old books. One was a leather-bound diary from the 1850's. One of the entries talked about a stash of gold hidden under the floorboards of the mercantile at 11th and K. Right where the deli is now."

"You're making this up."

"I swear. Jock Bell thinks there's gold down there. The guy's a crackpot."

A lot of Sacramentans had no idea that, as they strolled the sidewalks downtown, they were actually about ten feet off the ground. Like Seattle and Portland and a number of other cities, California's capital raised the street level of the whole city over a century ago to solve a regular flooding problem. As a result, there were blocks and blocks of a dark, forgotten city underground. Bricked up windows, doorways that lead to nowhere, dry, broken water pipes and tangles of electrical wires. Not exactly the Paris underground, but interesting. Fifty percent creepy and fifty percent cool.

"Is there any chance he's right?" Amy asked.

"What? About the gold?"

"Yeah."

"No way. I used to play down there as a kid. Mom said it was dangerous and off limits, but dad knew there was no way a boy could resist. He'd let me sneak down there with some buddies every once in a while. I walked and crawled every inch of the place. There's some old furniture, some neat old bottles and other junk. But no hidden treasure. Unless you include a small stack of magazines filled with, uh, artistic photos of attractive young women."

"Sid, I'm shocked." Amy smiled as they slowed to a trot approaching her apartment.

"They weren't mine," Sid sounded for a moment like he was twelve years old. "Clark Halvorsen took 'em down there. I'm not sure I ever even looked at them."

"Right." They stopped at her door and Amy retrieved the key that she'd tied into her shoelaces. "Thanks for running my slow pace again."

"No, you were awesome tonight. Great run."

"You're very sweet. I'd kiss you, but you smell."

With that, Amy flashed the smile with the big front teeth, and she was gone.
"Lock your door. There's guys with hockey masks and axes all over the place." Sid waited until he heard the bolt click on the other side of the door, then turned and headed for home.

Time to crank it up. Sid would cover the last three miles at close to a five minute pace. There's lots of talk about the *runner's high*. He had no idea what that was. Wouldn't know an endorphin if it poked him in the eye. But Sid had discovered in junior high that when he pushed himself hard, he got to a place where he liked how it hurt. He could feel his heart beating not just in his chest, but in his head. It became a drumbeat that replaced any other sound. Eyes fixed straight ahead, the ground disappearing under his feet. This was flying, not jogging. Often a song would creep into his head, keeping beat with his pulse. And there was always that pleasant pain that was somehow a part of the package, reminding him that he was doing something hard.

Sid never consciously thought about running, the mechanics of what he was doing. In fact, he never intentionally tried to think at all. Anything and everything went through his mind at times like this. It was kind of a mental free-for-all. A brain potpourri. He made the turn onto Land Park Drive and snapshots of the day ran through his head.

What could his dad have pawned at Jock Bell's shop? And why? Big Sid wasn't loaded, but it seemed like they were never hurting for money...

What a ridiculous movie. Did Betsy Palmer get her head chopped off? There'll never be a sequel...

No word in a few days from Mr. Headley the lawyer and his super-fat client. Maybe that's just gone away...

Where did I leave that Rubik's Cube? I had two sides done...

Such were the thoughts of Sid Bigler at 11:39 p.m. as he entered beautiful Land Park and ran past the entrance to the Sacramento Zoo. It was quiet. No traffic. No moon in the sky. Off to his right was Fairytale Town. When was the last time he'd been to Fairytale Town? Had to be 20 years. Cinderella's Coach was in there.

King Arthur's Castle. Jack's Beanstalk. Humpty Dumpty sat above the entrance and silently watched him glide by.

Bang-Bang-Bang-Bang-Bang!

The sound cut through the drumbeat in Sid's head and stopped him dead in his tracks. It was behind him. Five shots just like before. No doubt about it. He turned and scanned the wide, dark street. He strained to see something moving between the trees in the park. Nothing. No one. Long, slow seconds ticked by.

Sid was standing still, but his mind was racing wildly. *Where's a payphone? Did he have a dime? How could he be a witness to some nutcase shooter for a third time?*

He'd run by here a thousand times. It had never been this quiet. This empty. *Had it been a minute now since the shots? Would the cops possibly believe him again?*

He remembered giving statement after statement to the police after the last time. He remembered the reporters coming to his house and clogging up the deli. He remembered the articles in the paper and the endless questions by customers. And he remembered the jerk on the local radio station.

What do I do? What do I do? What do I do?

Sid glanced around one more time and saw only dark, empty streets. Moment of truth. He took a deep breath, turned toward home, and ran harder than he had in a long, long time. He wasn't sure exactly how fast he was going. He wasn't wearing a watch.

33

CHAPTER 6

There were really only two things that Sid was any good at, and neither was particularly useful or potentially profitable. One was running and the other was sleeping. And although he was very good on his feet, he was even better flat on his back. He could go from awake to asleep the way most people could go from standing to sitting. Like turning off a faucet or flicking off the lights. There was no trick to it. It required no special effort. He simply had the gift. Lay down. Close eyes. Done.

In 1961, when Sid was eight years old, his dog was hit by a car in front of their house. Buster was half German shepherd and half beagle— a bizarre combination that came about when the Patterson's German shepherd went into heat at the same time the Walker's beagle learned how to climb a chain link fence. The result was a remarkably agile, dopey looking fifty-five pound dog whose life revolved around the game of fetch. Specifically, Buster loved chasing a half-sized rubber football. The unpredictable bounces produced by its odd shape were evidence enough for Buster that the thing was alive and therefore, once caught, must be shaken vigorously until it was dead. On a gorgeous afternoon in late July, young Sid Bigler threw the little football, it took an odd bounce, and went into the street. The dog never saw the station wagon and, more importantly, Mrs. Vaughn never saw Buster. Only Sid saw what happened, and that night was the first night in his entire life he couldn't go to sleep.

Since then, there had only been two other nights where he laid awake— the night before he asked Jennifer Pinkney to the Prom (she said "no") and the night after his father died.

That made this sleepless night number four. Sid had covered the distance from the zoo to his mom's house in just under four minutes. On a normal night, he'd grab a quick shower, have his traditional bowl of Sugar Frosted Flakes, and be asleep moments later. His pulse at the end of a hard run might hit 180, but within a couple minutes of stopping it would be a third of that. Tonight, Sid stared up at a black ceiling, his heart still beating twice per second. What the hell was going on?

On three separate occasions he'd been in the vicinity of the *Capital Shooter*. That's what the media had recently taken to calling the crackpot who was blasting his way to celebrity status. This weird episode in his life was purely the product of chance, right? Whoever this nut was, he was getting his jollies by randomly shooting up Sacramento landmarks at night. Sid ran at night, and he happened to live fairly close to some famous Sacramento landmarks. It was dumb, unfortunate luck. It was that simple.

Or was it? Honestly, what were the odds? This was the fifth shooting, and Sid was within a hundred yards on three of those occasions. And he'd been out running on the nights of the other two shootings as well. If he'd chosen a different route, he might've been there for those, too.

It was this line of thought that eliminated sleep as an option that night. If his proximity to what had become the most celebrated crime wave in memory was not the product of chance, that meant somebody was including him in their bizarre, felonious rampage on purpose. The idea was completely nuts, but he couldn't shake it. And it made his skin crawl. He cycled back and forth between the certain knowledge that the shootings had nothing to do with him, and the terrible, persistent notion that somehow Sid Bigler was a part of the story. It was impossible, of course, but the thought wouldn't go away.

The minutes grew longer and longer, and Sid's sleeplessness became an exercise in déjà vu. Gradually, the night merged with the last night he'd laid awake. In this odd, not-sleeping state, the recent shootings and his father's death somehow swirled together. He found himself thinking again about that night last November. Grieving again, asking the same questions again…

Six months ago, he and Amy had been out for a bike ride on a Sunday morning— two and a half hours enjoying the paved trails along the beautiful American River Parkway. They rolled up to his cheesy bachelor apartment near the college just before noon. He didn't know it at the time, but in the coming days he'd end up moving back into his parents' house. The phone was ringing as he opened the door.

"Dad's dead."

It was his sister, Gloria. Two words and nothing else. They had absolutely no impact on Sid. They meant nothing. It was as though she'd said "monkey pajamas" or "tango macaroni." They were two words that simply didn't belong together and they made no sense at all. Seconds went by.

"Gloria?"

"Oh, God, Sid. I'm sorry. I should've said something else, but I don't know what. Mom and I just got back from church. Dad's dead."

Yes, it was definitely Gloria. And there was enough information now to begin to grasp what she was saying, though it would be a long time before Sid fully felt the weight of the news.

"You're at the house?"

"Yeah."

"I'm coming."

Big Sid went to church with his wife on Easter and Christmas Eve. That was it. If you included weddings and funerals, that was more than enough trips to church for Big Sid. His son shared his lack of passion for things ecclesiastical, but Rose and her daughter had always been enthusiastic church goers. Westminster Presbyterian was on L Street across from the Capitol. A beautiful building—part California mission and part cathedral. It played an important role in the lives of the Bigler women. In adulthood, it became a tradition for Gloria to pick her mom up on Sunday mornings and they'd go together. After Gloria got married and the girls came along, there was hardly a week when her whole family didn't give *Grammy* a ride to church. Thank God, it must be said, that on this particular Sunday, Gloria had dropped Marty and their daughters off at their house before taking her mother home.

The tires made a squeal and one wheel hopped the curb as Sid stopped the car in front of his parents' house. Gloria stood on the porch of the beautiful, craftsman style home where he'd spent so much of his life. If Sid hadn't already known something profound and terrible had happened, one look at his big sister would have told him. Arms not just crossed, but reaching around to hug herself. Eyes wide and searching. And she was white. Yes, Sid's whole family was very, very white to begin with. Ozzie and Harriet looked like Cubans compared to the Biglers. But Gloria was the color of skim milk.

Amy followed as Sid ran across the lawn he'd mowed a thousand times. He took all three steps in one stride, and had to fight off the urge to dash past his sister and go inside to find Big Sid. For the moment he was nursing the conviction that Gloria had to be wrong. His dad was 53 years old and healthy as a horse. He might have fainted or hit his head, but he wasn't dead. Sid made himself stop, put his hands on Gloria's shoulders and looked her in the eye.

"I'm waiting for the police," she said.

For the second time that morning, Sid heard his sister's words but couldn't make sense of them. He searched her face, trying to understand. Gloria's eyes were focused on something miles away.

The police? Why would the police be coming?
Something icy ran down his spine.
"Where's Mom?
"With Daddy."
The living room was empty and neat as a pin. Of course. Sid checked the kitchen next. Then bedroom, bathroom, bedroom. Nothing. Then he walked into his father's office and saw, for the first time, an image that would play and replay in his head for the rest of his life. He would flash back to it without warning in moments when his mind was at rest. Waiting at a stop light. Riding an elevator. Sitting on the can. It would stay just as vivid as it was that first moment.

"Amy, don't come in here," he heard himself say.
This had been young Sid's bedroom. His dad had converted it to an office the day after Sid moved out. "*Converted.*" That was the word Big Sid had used. The sum total of the conversion had been the removal of Sid's bed and the addition of a desk. His old dresser was still there and his old posters were still on the wall. On the desk was the big dictionary and the ridiculous old typewriter that his father loved. Big Sid was seated in his chair, body slumped forward, head resting on the typewriter keys. A puddle of blood covered half the desk. It dripped onto the carpet and had spread into a stain the size of a hula hoop. His mother, Big Sid's precious Rose, was on her knees beside him. Her arms were around his waist, her head resting on his shoulder, her eyes closed. The yellow dress she'd worn to church was half red now.
And there was a gun on the floor that Sid had never

seen before.

The rest of that day went by with Sid feeling as though he was watching it on TV. The police arrived within minutes to find him and Amy with Gloria on the front porch, all silent. It was one of the cops that found the note still in the typewriter. How could they not have noticed it?

As a boy, Big Sid had been much more than simply a lousy student. He had elevated "unmotivated snotty kid" to an art. He didn't just avoid homework, he relished not doing it. Or doing it very badly. His counselor told him he had the worst grades of any kid who had ever actually managed to receive a high school diploma. The two main consequences of his delinquency were dreadful handwriting and an inability to spell almost any word longer than six or seven letters. As an adult, this proved to be a great embarrassment. Big Sid was ridiculed repeatedly while in the service, and swore to himself that he'd take care of his penmanship problem once he got out. The solution came in the form of a used 1937 Royal typewriter, and it became something of a trademark for Sid Bigler, Sr. Except for signing checks and tax returns, just about everything Big Sid wrote for the rest of his life came out of that typewriter. Shopping lists, notes for the paperboy, everything. When he bought somebody a birthday card, he'd open the thing up, roll it into the old typewriter, and add his personal message. The clack of the keys was a happy sound in the Bigler house, and a symbol of Big Sid's determination to make something of his life. And so it's ironic that the last thing the typewriter produced was this note:

I am so sorry. This is nobodies fault but mine. I have detts that I cant pay and I cant live with having every thing taken from us. This is the only way I can solve the problum. You know I love you. Every thing will be ok now.

Apparently Big Sid hadn't taken the time to proof read his last note before pulling the trigger.

In the weeks that followed, the things that he'd written made more and more sense. Gloria took care of settling the estate. A close examination of the books at the deli and activity in Big Sid and Rose's bank accounts showed that he'd managed to make at least five thousand dollars disappear every month for the last six months. There was no way he could've gone much longer without it becoming obvious. Big Sid had been a good husband and father. It was hard to find anyone who'd say a word against him. But maybe some of the recklessness of his youth never left. No indication of exactly where the money went, but everybody knew he enjoyed gambling occasionally over the years— cards, horses, sports. It always seemed like recreation to him, and no one suspected that the stakes had gotten so high. The cops said they found records showing that he'd purchased the pistol just a few weeks earlier.

Big Sid's only son finally dozed off about an hour before sunrise on the night he heard the shots by the zoo. His alarm would go off twenty minutes later. For twenty minutes he dreamed of Rose's yellow dress and his dad's old typewriter, buried gold and Buster the dog. And guns firing in the darkness.

CHAPTER 7

The Bleubird Sandwich was one of the deli's main attractions. Invented by Joe in 1954, it was a spicy grilled chicken breast on a hamburger bun topped with bleu cheese dressing and three slices of bacon. Sid did the math on a paper napkin. They sold an average of ten a day. Twenty-six years times two hundred sixty-one days (not open on weekends). Factoring leap years, he figured the Bleubird Sandwich he was just finishing was somewhere around number 67,930. Delicious.

He felt surprisingly good for having hardly slept at all the night before. And despite this being one of the busiest days since the deli re-opened, it had gone smoothly. Sid had actually arrived a little earlier than usual, about ten 'til six, and discovered that Joe and Eddie were already at work. In fact, they had the place mostly set up and ready to open before Sid got there, so it had made for a relaxed start to the morning. But once the doors opened, there hadn't been a quiet moment. The breakfast crowd was big and lunch had been crazy. Now the deli was about half full at 1:30. Sid had been starving for the last couple of hours, and finally allowed himself the luxury of sitting down at the counter and enjoying his favorite sandwich.

He watched Joe Diaz at the grill. The great ones

make it look easy. Prefontaine. Sinatra. Chamberlain.
Sid considered adding Don Knotts to his list. Funniest
man alive hands down. Still, probably not in Wilt's
league. The place had been jumping almost from the
moment they opened, but Joe was in the zone. The
busier it was, the calmer he got. Sid had an image of the
Millennium Falcon going to warp drive or light speed or
whatever they called it. You knew he was going fast, but
there was a slow motion quality to it. If Joe ever retired,
Sid would just close the place.

As usual, Joe's apron was dirty enough to draw a
warning from County Health. Puzzling man. This was
Sid's godfather—the only other person in the world
who'd known him as long as his mom and sister. And yet
he felt like he didn't really know him at all. To be
completely honest, there were times when he wondered
what his dad had seen in Joe. Yes, he'd surprise you
occasionally with a good one-liner. But the great majority
of the time he was unreadable. A cigar store Indian. Sid
thought he might have detected a small change in Joe
since his father died. A little quieter, if that was possible.
A little more withdrawn. But it was hard to say for sure.
Like when the optometrist gave him that eye exam,
flipping back and forth between lenses—"Which is
better? This one or this one?" Hard to tell.

"Joe, this was the best Bleubird ever." Sid chased
some bleu cheese dressing drips around the plate with a
french fry.

"Yeah. Didn't drop that one on the floor." Just
when you least expect it.

Sid was thankful for how busy the day had been. At times he got lost in the relentless stream of customers and managed to briefly forget about the events of the previous night. He hadn't told anyone what had happened and had resolved to keep his mouth shut, but much of the time he couldn't avoid the subject. The place was buzzing with news of the latest shooting, and many of the customers had asked him about it. Of course they brought it up. Sid was an expert on this kook. He was famous. He'd almost seen the guy on two separate occasions. *Right... Two.*

The headlines of both papers announced that Fairytale Town was the latest target, and two of its most beloved characters had fallen victim to the Capital Shooter. Mother Goose's bonnet had a big piece shot off and Humpty Dumpty took a bullet squarely in the crotch.

The Union had a side article with quotes from a forensic psychologist. The "expert" seemed absurdly certain of a lot of things about the shooter. The target selection indicated a boldness on the part of the Capital Shooter bordering on egomania. So arrogant he thinks he can't be caught. He probably works in a trusted profession. *Where did they get this stuff?* The shooter probably won't be able to keep from boasting to someone about his crimes. Most importantly, according to the psychologist, you could tell by the symbolic choice of targets that the shooter is someone with an irrational hatred for tradition and authority. *Or maybe an irrational hatred for Sid.* Hey, there's a thought. Sid's stomach knotted and every crazy idea that had kept him awake last night came rushing back at once.

Sid hadn't noticed the man in the bad suit standing next to him until the guy called out to Joe, "Hey, pal, you own this place?"

Joe turned from the grill, took his time to appraise the man, then pointed at Sid with his metal spatula.

The bad suit looked at Sid. Sid looked at the bad suit. Pause. *Oh, God. He had to be a cop. Busted.*

Mid-thirties, the man had a bushy yellow moustache and an immovable golden helmet of hair. His mouth was too big for his face and his teeth were too big for his mouth. Even with palms sweating and his heart suddenly pounding in his ears, Sid couldn't help but notice that the guy was a blonde Tony Orlando.

"Donut, officer?" Not bad, considering he was very close to crapping his pants.

The man smiled and dropped a card on the counter next to Sid's plate. Det. Benjamin Stokes, Sacramento Police Department.

"Thank you, no. I always pack a lunch. Don't trust restaurants."

Det. Stokes wore an artificial *friendly* like a coat that didn't quite fit. If you just snapped a photo, the smile looked pretty good. But he sent out a vibe that said amusement was not really in his repertoire. Just about the time Sid expected the smile to fade and the man to get down to business, the smile grew slightly broader and he raised an eyebrow. It was kind of weird, like he was expecting something. Sid didn't know what to do next, but figured he should talk.

"Sid Bigler." He extended a hand to shake.

"Like in *Sid's Deli*," Stokes deduced aloud. The detective drew a notepad and pen from somewhere inside the bad jacket to make a note.

Sid left his hand out for several seconds while the detective scribbled. He had no idea what the man was writing, but it was taking a lot longer than the time required to write "Sid Bigler." He eventually wiggled his fingers a little and then dropped the hand to his lap.

Det. Stokes finally looked up from his notes, the smile turned down about fifty percent. "You're the guy who witnessed a couple of the shootings."

"Yeah, that's me." Suddenly the Bleubird was feeling like a very bad decision.

"I just have a few questions for you."

"Look, I've already talked about all this with some other officers."

"Right, Detectives Fidrich and Kaminski. Fidrich's appendix popped a couple days ago. I'm just helping out."

"Oh. Tell him I'm sorry."

"Yeah, I'll do that." Det. Stokes' smile clicked down another notch. "So, your crackpot was at it again last night."

"Hmm?" Sid tried for casual and innocent.

"The shooter. *Your shooter.* He went off again last night at Fairytale Town."

"Oh, yes. I did hear something about that."

"But you weren't around this time?"

"Around the shooting last night? No."

There it was. Sid had just lied to a cop investigating a felony, and he didn't even appreciate the moment as it went by. It just happened. Other than the several times he denied he'd been speeding, he had zero experience lying to the police.

"Can I ask where you were last night between 11:30 and midnight?"

"Gee. Last night." Sid blew out a breath and scratched his head and generally overacted a little. "I guess I was out running."

For the second time, the detective paused to scribble in his notebook. Again, he took way too long to write whatever it was he was writing. Sid glanced around. It looked like none of the customers realized he was being grilled by The Man. That was good. Joe made eye contact with him. Sid raised both hands and gave him an "I don't know" look.

"Running. Talk to me about that," Stokes continued. "Fidrich and Kaminski tell me you were out running on the two nights you heard the shots. The Capitol and Sutter's Fort."

"Yeah, that's right."

"And why were you running?"

"Well, because I run. About six days a week. I'll go anywhere from five to twenty-five miles."

"Jesus, you're kidding me. What for?"

"I like it. I'm good at it."

"What, like bowling?"

Sid shrugged. The whole idea of it seemed to have

derailed Stokes a bit, and Sid liked that. A little ray of hope. His initial reaction had been one of blinding fear. Now that they had a little conversation going, his head was beginning to clear some. Stay cool and you'll be fine.

"Yeah, I guess."

"So, when you go out running—at night when people are shooting guns—do you run with anybody else who can corroborate your whereabouts?"

Stokes kicked the smile back up a little, and Sid decided maybe he wasn't derailed at all.

"Sometimes." Sid heard himself sounding like a guy who was guilty of something.

"Last night?"

"Yeah, last night I was running with my girlfriend, Amy Solomon."

"You were with her last night at 11:40."

Uh-oh. Time for some quick thinking, and Sid had very little experience at that. He wasn't sure of the exact time that things happened last night. No watch. But he remembered looking at the clock after he'd been home for five or ten minutes. It had been almost midnight.

This was ridiculous. He had nothing to do with all this, and here he was figuring if he could get away with lying to the cops. Again.

One thing was certain, he didn't want Amy mixed up in any of this. Stokes was sure to talk to her, and Sid had no intention of having her cover for him. While he was fairly determined to ride out this lie with the cops, he decided that, at least when it came to Amy, honesty was the best policy. Hell, Stokes was going to find out anyway.

Now it occurred to him that he didn't know how long he'd been sitting and thinking about this while the detective stood there. Again, Stokes raised the eyebrow, waiting.

"Uh, I dunno. Maybe not. I might've left her place around 11:30."

"Okay. Where's her place?"

"Pocket Area, Seastone Way, just off Riverside."

"Address?"

"I'm not sure. They're big gray apartments on a corner."

Stokes went back to writing on his notepad. Eddie the busboy came up and cleared away Sid's plate and wiped down the counter in front of him, unaware of the fact that the world was spinning off its axis. Sid decided that he was doing the stupidest thing he'd ever done in his life. Stupider than the time he let Larry Vogt talk him into jumping off the roof into the wading pool— He had tried a cannonball and ended up missing the rest of baseball season. He should just wave the white flag, apologize for having forgotten to report the shooting last night, and promise his fullest cooperation in exchange for not being thrown into prison with a large, tattooed man. That's what he should do.

Stokes looked up and asked, "You left her place and you drove home?"

"No, I ran home." The truth shall set you free.

The detective flipped a few pages, scanning for something. Found it. "And you live at 1928 3rd Avenue.

Old Land Park."

"It's my mom's house."

"But you're living there. You ran there last night."

"Yes."

This whole time, Sid had been thinking of Det. Stokes as a glorified high school principal—an authority figure who could give you some grief if you screwed up. Now he realized that this was a man with the ability to gaze into your bare soul and snatch away everything you held dear. *This really was The Man.* It was definitely time to start telling the truth.

"Running from, uh, Ms. Solomon's apartment to your mom's house, that should've taken you right by the zoo and Fairytale Town last night."

"Yes."

"Yes, what? Yes you ran through the park last night? Ran by Fairytale Town?"

"Yes."

"Well, I don't know how fast you run, but if you left her apartment around 11:30, you could've been somewhere near Fairytale Town when the shots were fired."

Days later Sid would look back at this moment and wonder how things would've turned out if he'd actually told the truth. Would the whole mess have ended sooner? Would it have kept him out of jail? Could he have saved a life?

"Were you there last night, Sid? When the shooting happened?"

"No," said Sid. "No, I wasn't."

CHAPTER 8

Sid looked Det. Stokes right in the eye and waited. At the moment he had opened his mouth he really intended to tell the truth, but somehow that's not what came out. So now all he could do was wait and see what happened next. Stokes reached up and scratched his chin with the end of his pen. Sid saw Tony Orlando with a microphone and it broke the tension a little. Maybe the guy had something, but maybe he was only fishing.

"Well, I'm sorry to hear you say that, Sid."

"Sorry?"

"Really sorry. 'Cause if you didn't see or hear anything, we got nothin'. A nutjob pops five shots in the middle of the park and nobody sees a thing. I knew it was a longshot that you would've been around a third time when something like this happens, but I figured, what the hell. Couldn't hurt to check."

It took everything Sid had to suppress a giggle. "Yeah, this whole thing is crazy. Go figure."

Stokes reached down and patted his business card on the counter. "You keep this, call me if something comes to you, okay?"

"You bet I will." Sid pocketed the card.

"Thanks," said the detective and he headed for the door.

It was over. Sid took in a deep breath, let it out and slid off the stool feeling like he'd gotten a lucky roll and just missed landing on Boardwalk or Park Place with hotels. Times ten.

"Oh, one more thing." The voice surprised him. Sid turned to see the same simulated smile that Stokes had first shown him. "The nights of the other two shootings, the ones you didn't see—" He glanced at his notes. "May 3rd, that was City Hall, and May 6th, that was the Chevy dealer—any chance you were out running on those nights, too?"

"Oh, uh, maybe."

"Okay, maybe you could check on that for me. I know a lot of serious runners keep a log of their runs, you know? Like a diary. When and where they ran, total miles, stuff like that. You keep one of those?"

"Uh, yeah, I do."

"Yeah, I thought you might. I used to do a little running myself, not that you can tell anymore." The detective smiled, patted his belly. "You check your runner's log and call me. And tell me if anybody else was running with you those nights."

For the second time in less than a minute, Stokes headed for the door. Sid had been worked. His home address. His route. The runner's log. In his head, he heard Stokes say *What, like bowling?* again. Sid was way out of his league and now he knew it. Everything this guy had said and done had been orchestrated.

Not only that, but all along there had been something about this whole scene that had been nagging at the back of his mind. Something familiar. It would've hit him a lot sooner if Stokes had looked like Peter Falk instead of the "Tie a Yellow Ribbon" guy. Sid had never missed an episode of Columbo. Now he was living it. He watched as Stokes stopped again, turned back around and said, "Oh, I'm sorry to bother you, but could I ask one more favor?"

"Sure, detective. What can I do for you?"

"You mind if I have a look around?"

"The deli? What for?"

"You got some reason I shouldn't look around?"

"No, of course not. Knock yourself out."

Stokes pivoted slowly in one spot, 360 degrees, took in the place. "You got a storage room in back? Maybe an office?"

"Yeah, sure."

"Show me."

Sid gave his eyes a little roll and turned toward the door to the back. Everyone else in the place still seemed to be oblivious. Everyone except Joe, who was watching with a hard face.

Stokes followed him into the room that served for both storage and food prep. Here was everything you'd expect to find in the back of a deli. Sid folded his arms and leaned against the door frame as the detective tooled around the room. Stainless counters and shelves. A door to a small bathroom was open. A much bigger, metal door in the corner led to a walk-in refrigerator. Eddie's bicycle leaned against one wall. Since the weather turned warmer, he'd pedal into work one or two days a week when Joe couldn't give him a ride. There was a deep sink, a slicer, a rolling rack of bread in plastic bags, a couple of cardboard produce boxes that probably should have been in the walk-in. An old payphone was on the back wall where it had hung for as long as Sid could remember. All the regular customers knew they could head back there and make a call if they needed to. The business phone out front was off limits, but the old payphone was fair game. And there was one old metal filing cabinet. It had some paperwork in the top drawer, but the remaining drawers held jars of pickles and olives, big tin cans of mustard and mayo, stuff like that. It looked like it was military surplus, and it probably was.

Det. Stokes stopped at the filing cabinet and pulled out the bottom drawer. Sid couldn't see in from where he stood at the doorway, but he knew what was in there and had no objection to the police examining his canned sauerkraut and pancake syrup. Stokes glanced at him and, for the first time that day, gave him what appeared to be a genuine smile. The hand with the pen reached inside the drawer. The hand with the pen came back out. There, hanging from his pen by the trigger guard, was a revolver.

Three o'clock. Det. Stokes had left more than an hour ago, the large brown envelope with the gun tucked under his arm. The deli had cleared out at the usual time, Joe and Eddie were gone, and he sat alone in his locked-up restaurant, lights out, trying to figure what had happened. The figuring wasn't going well. He was mostly just stunned. Jerry Quarry clocked by Muhammad

Ali. A girl kissed by Elvis.

There was a tapping at the door, and Sid looked up expecting to see his sister, Gloria. Instead, he saw a woman, maybe fifty, with big blonde hair. *Great. Stokes has sent his mom to ask some more questions.*

Sid wasn't feeling the old Bigler charm at the moment. On any other day he'd hop up, unlock the door and politely explain that the deli was closed, maybe hand her one of the paper menus and a "Free Soda & Chips w/ Sandwich Purchase" coupon for her next visit. But in his current state, he simply called out loudly, "Sorry, closed!" And he waved his arms in front of his face, palms out, like the airplane should back up and find another hangar.

The woman nodded as though Sid had said something encouraging and tapped on the glass again. She pointed at the doorknob.

Sid sighed, got up and headed toward the door. He noticed as he got closer that the woman's breasts were pressed lightly against the glass. It wasn't that she was standing particularly close to the door. She simply had a lot to work with. Sid knew absolutely nothing about the architecture and engineering of women's undergarments, but this woman clearly had some device on under her blouse that said "up and out." There didn't seem to be anything provocative or intentional about the breast-pressing. Sid got the impression she used them like bumpers to tell her when to stop at the door. Sid approached his side of the glass and tried again.

"Sorry, closed for the day!" He said it loudly,

exaggerating the words with his mouth.

"I have to talk to you," Sid faintly heard her say.

"Come back tomorrow!"

"It's about Eddie Davis."

That was unexpected. Because he couldn't think of a good reason not to, Sid reached down, unlocked the door, and swung it halfway open. Before the woman could make a move to come in, he stepped up enough to block the doorway. It wasn't subtle, but he really didn't feel like company.

"Did you say this was about Eddie?"

Up close, the second most obvious thing about her was that she was short. Maybe five feet if you included the heels, and the heels looked too tall to be comfortable. Denim top, denim skirt, spangly belt that matched the shoes. If Sid was twenty years older and lived in a trailer park, he'd be pretty interested. Without making the conscious choice to do it, his mind began to play the game. Who did she look like? Dolly Parton was way too obvious. And besides, from the neck up she was much more a middle-aged Sandy Duncan.

"... to find him, but it's no big deal."

Oops. She'd been talking.

"I apologize. This has been a tough day. Who are you again, and what about Eddie?"

"Yvonne Wilcox. I'm Eddie's social worker."

Sid's vacant look was not an act. "I'm sorry, maybe I should know about this. I've only been running the deli about six months, and it's Joe that mostly looks after Eddie."

"Right, I've been with Eddie since Big Sid hired him. This place has been great for him. I was just hoping to catch him and have him sign something for me. Tell him about a change they're making at his group home."

"He can sign something?"

A broad smile lit up Yvonne Wilcox's face, and Sid was surprised to find himself rather charmed. Maybe he would go for her if he was older. There was a warmth. One he supposed would have to be there for somebody to do what she did for a living.

"You don't really know him yet. Eddie probably understands a lot more than you think. He's actually quite good with numbers."

"Yeah, I didn't mean..." Sid stammered.

"It's okay. Really. I assume he's gone for the day." Sid nodded. "Joe took him home."

"That's fine. I'll stop by his house later. Very nice to meet you."

Sid almost didn't notice her tiny hand as it reached out from somewhere beneath her boobs to shake. He took her hand, a surprisingly firm grip, and smiled. The door made its usual rattle as it closed.

Sid bolted the door, turned and leaned back against the glass and closed his eyes, feeling his energy drain away. He had the vague, unpleasant sensation that he wasn't the main character in whatever story he was living in. Somebody else was the central figure. Somebody else knew what was going on. Sid was just... what? Comic relief? Innocent bystander? Fall guy?

He opened his eyes and surveyed the deli. *His father's*

deli, he thought. Black & white glossy faces looked at him from the frames on the walls. Ronald Reagan. Pat Brown. Joey Bishop. Richard Bradley. Barbara Eden. The eyes of a hundred people, famous and once-famous, stared at Sid. Their unblinking gaze made him feel small. Insignificant. Whose story were they watching? And what the hell was happening to his life? He hadn't asked for any of this. Hadn't asked for anything at all. C'mon, he was just the fastest kid at McClatchy High School plus nine years. He'd never tried to be more than that.

Sid closed his eyes again, and kept them closed until there was a tapping on the glass door behind his head.

Chapter 9

Gloria Farrell dropped her briefcase on a table near the door and gave Sid the look that big sisters have been giving stupid little brothers since before the Pyramids.

"Sid, what is going on? I just talked to Carter at the D.A's office. I can't believe what he's telling me."

Sid couldn't help but notice the difference between his two consecutive female visitors. If Yvonne was a cheerleader, Gloria was valedictorian. And president of the chess club.

"It's crazy, Sis. It's ridiculous."

"They found a gun here?"

"Yeah."

"You keep a gun here?"

"I didn't do anything. I swear to God."

At this point, the typical lawyer with the typical client would simply take that last statement at face value. Oh, maybe with a grain of salt, but what did it matter? Attorneys sell what their clients give them whether or not it's true. But in this particular instance, the client was the attorney's little brother. The first time she heard him say *"I didn't do anything, I swear to God"* was 1959, and who knows how many times she had heard it since.

"Sid, tell me what you've done."

Sid had been so anxious for Gloria to get there.

Now he was beginning to wonder which interrogation was going to be worse—his sister's or the cop's. Gloria had always been the smart one and the responsible one. It occurred to Sid that he didn't know which *one* he was— The *average* one? The *other* one?

Gloria had met Marty Farrell attending UC Davis and married him while Sid was still in high school. After college, Marty went from checker to produce manager at Albertson's and Gloria went to McGeorge School of Law. Her favorite professor now sat on the U.S. Supreme Court and they still kept in touch. Niece Nicky was a wonderful accident, arriving a week after Gloria's last exam in her final year of law school. Niece Nellie arrived on purpose three years later.

Gloria was unquestionably the most sought-after thirty-year-old litigator in Sacramento. She didn't do much criminal work, but her firm had quickly discovered she was a gold mine in the courtroom in civil cases. Two years out of law school, she had been second counsel in a case representing the California State Employees Association against all fifty-eight counties in the state. The lead attorney—a name partner in her firm—picked a very unfortunate time to wrap his vintage Harley around a tree, and Gloria ended up with closing arguments at the last minute. She was brilliant, the CSEA made a killing, and a star was born. Now Marty stayed home with the girls and Gloria billed a hundred forty dollars an hour.

"Sid, talk to me."

And Sid talked. Like everyone else in Sacramento, Gloria knew all about his fortuitous presence at two of the first shootings, so Sid started at the part where Det. Stokes arrived at the deli. No sense bringing up the previous night's encounter if he didn't have to.

He walked her through the whole thing. Stokes' questions regarding Sid's whereabouts, his sneaky tactics and his background knowledge of Sid's habits, his casual inspection of the deli. And the bizarre way he went straight to the filing cabinet. Straight to the gun.

"You should never have let him just look around like that." Gloria was exasperated.

"I didn't have anything to hide."

"You had a gun, Sid!"

"No, it wasn't my gun!"

Gloria gave him *the look* again. "Okay, so it was Dad's."

"No. No, listen. There was never a gun. Ever. I'd been in that filing cabinet just yesterday."

That stopped Gloria in her tracks. They stared at each other, Gloria trying to figure out what that could possibly mean, and Sid hoping that she would. This made no sense at all.

"The cop—Det. Stokes—goes right to the bottom drawer of the old filing cabinet," she talked through it slowly, "and finds a gun that wasn't there the day before."

Sid nodded.

"Well, that's really bad," she said.

"Gee, when you talk like that it makes me wish that I'd gone to law school, too."

"It wasn't like he was looking everywhere, turning the place upside down. He zeroed in on the filing cabinet?"

"Yep."

"So he knew in advance."

"Either that or the guy could really kick ass at Easter egg hunts when he was a kid."

"Don't talk like that," Gloria scolded.

"Sorry."

When it came to coarse language, Gloria was just like her mother. There was no place for it. "You should never have let him look around," she said again.

Gloria furrowed her brow and chewed the left side of her lower lip. It was the same look she always had when she was studying for a test in school. She had a gift for collecting information and putting it together in a way that made sense, and doing it quickly. It's what made her a good student and a good trial lawyer. Problem was, at the moment there was very little info to put together.

"Did you ask Joe if the gun was his?"

"No, but he didn't say anything. And it's never been there before."

"Well, ask him. Anybody else have access to the back room?"

"Besides Eddie? Not officially, but it'd be fairly easy for somebody to sneak back there."

Gloria furrowed and chewed some more. Sid waited. Two siblings that were not alike, each doing what they'd always done. Gloria confident she could figure it all out, and Sid assuming it was over his head. She would work through it, find a way to get the answer. He would do nothing and hope for the best.

"I thought for sure the guy was going to lock me up," Sid interrupted her thoughts.

"No. That wouldn't happen. You had an unregistered gun on the premises. There's no proof it was yours. No proof it was used in any crime. Your fingerprints are not going to be found on that gun, right?"

"Gloria, I'm not lying. I'd never seen it before. How could I have touched it?"

"Okay. Then you should be fine. You don't get arrested because they found a gun that has no connection to you. Not yet."

"Yet?"

"Well, I'm going to keep trying to assume that this is all just a big mistake. Maybe there's a simple explanation for all this. Maybe you're just Mr. Coincidence. But I don't like it. Sid, it feels like you've been set up. This detective wasn't just lucky. Somebody's fed him some information."

"Right. But who?"

"Well, that's one of the questions we need to answer."

Gloria stopped short. It was obvious she'd had a new thought. She gave a serious, concerned look at her brother. One Sid had never seen before.

"Are you in some kind of trouble? Like Dad was, I mean?"

"No. No, what are you talking about? I told you, I haven't done anything wrong."

Gloria seemed about seventy percent convinced, but she was ready to move on. "I'll try to look into this. Not much we can do until the cops and the D.A. think they have enough to bring charges, and hopefully that'll be never. In the meantime, here's your homework assignment— think hard about who'd want to make your life miserable. Make a list. I mean it."

"Okay."

"Good. And here's the only rule you need to remember: Don't talk to anybody about this. Any strangers or reporters come around asking questions, you don't know anything."

"That'll be easy. I *don't* know anything."

"Okay. Stay out of trouble. I care what happens to you."

"Thanks, Sis."

Gloria picked up her briefcase and pulled the strap over her shoulder. She was never big on wasting time. They hugged briefly. There had been typical sibling bumps in the road over the years, but their relationship was better than most. They loved each other and weren't embarrassed to say so. Sid was feeling much better. Nothing had really been settled, but Gloria was on the case, and everything would work out.

She had just reached the door when the *Big Sister Radar* went off. Something was not quite right. Her hand still on the doorknob, she turned and looked at Sid. Pause. He squirmed.

"Sidney." Oh, this was trouble. "When the detective asked if you saw or heard anything last night, at the park— you told him no, right?"

"Yeah, I told him no." He looked as sweet and

innocent as a baby seal. Anybody else would have
believed him.

"Sidney!"

"What?"

"Sidney, you were there, weren't you?"

"No."

"Were you there?"

"No."

"Is that the truth?"

"No. I mean, yes."

By now Sid was surprised to discover that Gloria had
dropped her briefcase by the door and had grabbed him
by the shirt. He had no doubt she was prepared to slug
him for the first time in thirteen years. She lowered her
voice.

"I think you're lying to me. If you're lying to me, I'm
going to hit you as hard as I can. And you'll lose the only
attorney you can afford. Last chance, little brother. Did
you tell the detective the truth?"

Sid took a breath, prepared to take the shot, and said,
"No."

"*No*, as in *you lied?*"

"Yes."

"You lied to the cops."

"Yes."

Another pause. Gloria socked him in the right eye.

"Ow!"

"Shut up, I could've hit you a lot harder, but juries
are biased against defendants with bruised faces." It was
true, Gloria had slugged him much harder in the past. It

had been a long time since she was wound up like this. She let go of his shirt.

"You punched me."

"Hey, I don't charge you a penny. Consider that payment for legal services. How could you be so stupid, Sid? How could you lie to the cops?"

"I don't know." His hand was covering his left eye now. "I was scared. I'd been up all night. He'd found that gun."

Gloria gave him the stink-eye. "He didn't find the gun 'til after you lied to him."

In the middle of this disastrous conversation, Sid consciously wondered as he had many times before how Gloria caught stuff like that. Just about anybody else, in the heat of the moment, would never have noticed his little fib— that he'd lied to Stokes well before the gun was found. But Gloria the lawyer would never let something like that slip by. Geez, it was irritating. How many times had she gotten him in trouble through the years just because she was paying attention? And how come things like that never occurred to him?

"Sorry, Sis."

"Aaaaaaah!" The frustrated yell that sounded just like their mother. "We're not kids! You're in real trouble, Sid!"

The two stared at each other for a moment. Gloria picked her bag back up.

"I can't talk to you anymore about this. Do you remember what the only rule is?"

"Don't talk to anybody."

"Good. And think really, really hard about who might hate your guts. Who besides me, that is. Something must have happened before that first shooting— before two weeks ago. Got it?"

"Yes."

"Okay."

Gloria opened the door and started out. Sid called out to stop her, a hand still over his eye.

"Hey. Have I been talking to my sister or my lawyer?"

"What's the difference?"

"If you're my lawyer, you won't tell Mom."

CHAPTER 10

Sid savored the quiet and emptiness of the deli. The hectic breakfast and lunch followed by the visits from Stokes and his sister added up to a lousy day, and it was only half over. He got himself a Coke and sat at the counter for a few minutes. Full glass, no ice. Serious drinking. The throbbing of his left eye reminded him that he should start on that list Gloria wanted— his homework. But he just spaced out. He even dozed for a little bit, elbows on the counter, head bobbing.

At 3:45, the Coke was drained and Sid was heading out the door. It had only been fifteen minutes or so since Gloria left. He realized as he locked up that he'd never given much thought to security at the deli before. Had there ever been a break-in? Not that he could recall, but he found himself double-checking the door before starting the hike to his car on P Street. He could park closer, but it was free on the street. Besides, the bright green 1971 Dodge Duster had ceased to be cool several years ago and he didn't mind keeping it out of sight from the customers.

"Hey! Hey, Sid!"

He turned around, but he didn't need to. He recognized the voice. Jock Bell was calling to him from across the street.

"Hey, c'mere for a minute!"

"It's been a long day," Sid called back. "Maybe tomorrow!"

Jock held up a hand in the universal stop sign and began making his way across the intersection. Against his better judgment, Sid waited. Jock was, once again, making a distinctive fashion statement. White polyester pants, black polyester jacket, black and white checked polyester shirt. Perhaps the hair was polyester, too? Jock had most of the buttons on the shirt undone, wiry white hair and gold chains peeking out from the open collar. Maybe it hadn't occurred to Jock that there was a serious disconnect between the color of his chest hair and the color of whatever that was on top of his head. Sid tried to decide if this was an improvement over yesterday's outfit as he began quietly humming the theme from Saturday Night Fever.

"Sid, how are you?" Jock asked, sincerity as genuine as his hair.

"Uh, not so good. This has been a tough day for me."

"Really? Tell me."

"No, it's fine. I'm gonna just go home and relax a little."

If Jock Bell noticed that his left eye was red and a little puffy, he didn't let on. He kept pushing the phony concern.

"Anything I can do to help?"

"No, no thanks." Sid started to step away.

"Listen, Sid," Jock stopped him with a hand. "I was

hoping maybe now's a good time for you to stop by and see the stuff I have that was your dad's."

Hmmm. That was tempting. It had crossed his mind a dozen times in the last day.

"No, maybe another time," Sid said, but Jock had sensed his hesitation.

"Sure. That's fine. But I have to tell you, a guy came in this morning interested in some of your dad's things. Out of courtesy I told him I really should let the original owner's son see what I had before I sold 'em."

Sid looked hard into Jock Bell's eyes and wondered if it was true. Probably not. His distaste for the old guy clicked up a notch as they headed across the street.

He'd never set foot inside Jock's Pawn Shop before, but he'd been in plenty of thrift stores and he wondered exactly what the difference was. To be fair, he'd never seen a pearly red accordion in a thrift store. Same with the moose head and the bust of Richard Nixon. But otherwise, except for the absence of used clothes, the place screamed *Goodwill*.

"Give me a second, Sid," Jock said as he disappeared, like the guy in a shoe store going to check if he could find a size eight. "I set your dad's stuff aside," he called from the back.

As he waited, Sid took the opportunity to cruise the glass cases by the cash register. Watches and other jewelry. Coins. Baseball cards. Then he spotted something else you can't get in a thrift store. Guns. Four black pistols lay side by side, two revolvers and two automatics, each with a dull shine and a little white tag attached by a small string. The white tags were blank. Sid figured the prices must be face down. He leaned closer.

"Beautiful, aren't they?" Jock's voice made Sid jump.

"I didn't know you could sell these in a pawn shop." He tried to sound composed.

"Oh, sure. I'm a registered firearms dealer in the great State of California." Jock said it like he found it amusing. He pointed to his dealer's permit on the wall behind him, hanging next to a framed Picasso that Sid assumed was not an original. "It's not a big deal for me. I just have these four right now. I bet I haven't moved one in over a year. For some reason they don't sell as well here as other pawn shops, so I don't keep a lot of 'em."

"Oh."

"You know, your dad wanted to sell me a pistol last year, but I had to tell him I just couldn't use it."

The two made eye contact. All the air was sucked out of the place. Either this guy was the most insensitive SOB on the planet, or he had just earned himself a special place in the Faux Pas Hall of Fame. Sid noticed that he was wearing contact lenses. Jock blinked and he saw them slide up and down slightly. He blinked again. There may have been a tiny look of remorse. Just enough for Sid to give him the benefit of the doubt on this one.

"Um, here's the box I put your dad's stuff in," Jock broke the moment.

He set the box on the top of the glass case above the guns, and Sid was surprised to see it was cardboard.

Surely his dad's things deserved a more dignified resting place. It said "Keep Refrigerated" on the side, and he couldn't help but wonder what the box had originally held. Sid realized he was nervous as he leaned forward to look inside.

He didn't know what he was expecting, but what he saw broke his heart. There was only a handful of things in there, but almost every item he looked at caused a flood of memories. Two folding straight razors with carved ivory handles sat on top. Sid hadn't seen those since he was a kid. They'd belonged to his great or maybe great-great grandfather, and Big Sid had kept them in the top drawer of his dresser. There was a quart-sized Baggie filled with buffalo nickels. His dad had always referred to it as his coin collection. Sid saw a woman's ring with what looked like a modest diamond set in it that was only vaguely familiar. And there was his grandpa's watch— a rectangular gold Hamilton wristwatch with a black face and black leather wristband. Gordon Bigler had been awarded the brand new watch in 1938 when his store won the Retailer of the Year award for selling the most Maytag washers & dryers in California. Sid used to wind it for him when he was little. He never saw his grandfather without it right up until his death in 1967.

And there was a felt box with a metal edge that Sid recognized immediately. He carefully lifted it up and opened the lid. Big Sid's military medals. There were three of them, smaller than he remembered. Each was bronze, a little over an inch in diameter, hanging from a multi-colored ribbon. As he looked at the medals, Sid thought about the fact that he was already several years older than his father was at the time of the war. He didn't feel anything like the kind of man that could have earned these. Sid remembered trying them on when he was eight or nine, pinning them to a Levi's jacket and showing them off to his friends. He missed Big Sid at that moment more than he had at any other time in the past six months.

"You can just have the military stuff there. Doesn't do me any good. Nobody's gonna buy that junk. No offense, that's just the way it is."

"So why did you take it in the first place?" Sid asked. Sticking up for the old man. The word "junk" had stung.

"Well, he just seemed desperate. Look, I was doing him a favor. He'd already sold me everything he had that was any good. That's a beautiful watch there, gave him four hundred for that. Pretty nice stone in the ring, three seventy-five, I think. By the time he got to the medals and ribbons, I dunno. I wanted to help. I gave him fifty and told him he really oughta give up the gambling. I felt bad for him. I figured I was helping."

Sid ran his fingers over the medals. It was bad enough to have lost his father, and in such a senseless way. But to have this parasite talking about Big Sid like he was a loser, a charity case...

"I told your dad he could solve all his problems if he'd just let me buy the damn building. Again, I was just trying to help. Told him I'd be happy to let him keep the deli there. I'd lease him the space for whatever's fair, y'know? I think he was really ready to sell the place right there at the end. It's too bad it didn't work out."

"How much to get all this back?" Sid had heard enough. He picked up the box, holding it with his arms around it.

"Look, Sid, I feel bad about this. I wasn't out to take advantage or make money from Big Sid's problems. Like I said, I wanted to give him a fair price for..."

"I'll pay you whatever you gave my father for all this. How much?"

Jock Bell looked Sid over. Sid had the feeling he was being appraised, in the same way Jock might judge the value of a camera or a wedding ring that some down-on-his-luck customer had brought in. It only lasted a few seconds, but it was unmistakable. Jock gave a little grunt, like he'd reached some decision.

"Your father was into me for about twelve hundred," he said matter-of-factly. No more Mr. Fake Nice Guy.

"I'll have the money for you tomorrow."

"Well, Sid, the way this business works, it's more than twelve hundred by now. It's two percent a month interest, plus fifty bucks a month for storage and insurance. Probably close to two grand now, but like I said, I was just trying to do a favor. Let's call it eighteen."

In his head, Sid was reeling at the thought of coming up with eighteen hundred dollars. But on the outside he managed quite a sarcastic "thank you."

"I'm happy to help. You got three days." Bell took the box from Sid and set it down behind the counter.

Sid turned and headed out the door, closing it hard

behind him. He was pissed, and that didn't happen often. He stood for a moment, fuming, replaying the conversation with Jock in his head. He thought of a couple of zingers he would have said if they'd come to him in time.

And then he had a thought that would have made Gloria quite proud. It was one of those little things that should have gone by unnoticed, but his big sister would've jumped on it right away. He opened the door of the pawn shop and went back in. Jock was gone, probably in the back.

"Hey! Hey, Jock!" Sid was loud, and he liked how it sounded. Confident.

"Yeah, what?" Jock said as he reappeared in the doorway to his back room. Any pretense of compassion was gone. The box of Big Sid's stuff was still in his hands.

"Earlier you said you told my dad he should give up the gambling."

"Right."

"How'd you know about his gambling?"

Jock's leathery face went blank for moment.

"Just a sec. Lemme set this down."

Jock turned and was gone. Sid was surprisingly calm. He was unaccustomed to having the upper hand in anything and it felt good. Whatever Jock said next was most likely going to be a lie, but just the fact that he'd caught Bell's mistake was enough to make him briefly feel worthy of being Gloria's little brother. Big Sid's son. Jock reemerged from the back and it was obvious that

Mr. Warmth had returned with him.

"Sid, I know this has all been very tough on you. I don't know who else Big Sid had that he could confide in. I don't even know if those of you in the family knew much. But the first time your father came in looking for a loan, he told me about the gambling. It's a terrible thing when it gets a hold of someone like that."

Was he lying? Sid was pretty sure he was. No way Big Sid would've poured out his heart to this dirtbag. Then again, no one in the family saw the suicide coming. What was going on inside Big Sid's head in those last months before he died? Did this jerk know a side of his father that he didn't? Sid paused for a moment, hoping some great exit line would occur to him. One didn't, so he turned and left in silence, deciding as he did so that it was a classy choice. The door closed behind him again, even louder this time.

Sid began walking toward his car, thinking there was more to Jock Bell than just what met the eye. And when you consider what met the eye, that was quite a claim. He was moving faster than most of the people on the sidewalk, weaving occasionally to avoid state workers or bums. He moved with confidence. He was onto something, though he was unsure of exactly what.

Yet his confidence was tempered by a little melancholy. How could he have forgotten? How could he not have noticed? The things in that cardboard box in Jock's shop were important. They were pieces of his father's life. And nobody had said a word. Nobody had missed them when Big Sid died.

CHAPTER 11

Sid had done something he'd never done before and it had him rattled. It wouldn't have seemed like much to the casual observer, but it was important.

He'd gotten home in the late afternoon and checked phone messages. Big Sid had given the machine to Rose for her birthday last year. First one on the block. The cassette tape rewound to play just one message—Woody the cop saying he wouldn't be able to meet him at the gym. He dropped his keys on the coffee table and headed for the couch. Ever since he had taken over the deli, Sid found himself often grabbing a quick nap when he got home. He was generally the first one at the deli in the morning. Getting up before 5 a.m. seemed ridiculous the first time he did it, and it hadn't gotten any better. So the after-work nap had become a familiar and even favorite part of the day. It was usually about half an hour, and Sid would wake up recharged.

But today was different. His mom woke him up on the sofa at 8:15 and scolded him for leaving his shoes on. She'd been out shopping when he got home, and had tip-toed around the house for three hours before waking him. He'd slept through the phone ringing three times. Once it was Amy. She'd left a message that she was going out with some girlfriends, and she'd said something about a police officer talking to her. Sid's mom wondered if he knew anything about that, and he played dumb.

"Siddy, you have no idea why a policeman would be talking to your girlfriend?"

Sid raised his shoulders and his eyebrows in a well-practiced gesture that said, *Who knows?* His mom pressed once more.

"Your girlfriend Amy who's three years older than you?" To Rose, older woman equaled "hussy." Well, at least it appeared as though Gloria hadn't blabbed to their mom. Yet.

Sid made and ate half a peanut butter and jelly sandwich, put on his shoes and shorts and went out for a run. It was just past nine o'clock. He figured he'd make his way down Freeport to Sac City College and run some intervals at Hughes Stadium. He liked the history of the place. Jim Ryun had just missed a four-minute mile there as a senior in high school back in 1965. Running on dirt. The guy was a god.

Sid wasn't far from home, cruising down the sidewalk, when a car pulled too quickly from a driveway out onto the street. He had to jump to get out of the way, letting out an involuntary yell. The driver hit the brakes hard, making the tires chirp as the car lurched to a stop, blocking both the sidewalk and part of the road. The car's windows were down, and Sid found himself looking at a dopey kid, maybe seventeen, zits and a ballcap.

"Sorry, mister. I didn't see you."

"It's okay," Sid said between breaths. "I was probably speeding."

Dumb joke, and a line he'd used countless times through the years. Things like that happened. You pay attention and you go with the flow.

"You be careful," he said to the kid, because he felt obliged to sound like a grown-up.

It was then that Sid did what he'd never done before. He watched the car pull away, stood there for a few seconds, then turned around and started walking home. Not a conscious decision, really. He just started walking. This was like Yastrzemski sitting out a game because he didn't feel like playing. For Sid, not finishing a run he'd started would be like Raymond Burr not finishing a pizza. It had simply never happened.

He was a very, very good runner, but he wasn't the best and he knew it. The best would've gone to Wisconsin or the University of Texas, El Paso. The best would be preparing for next month's Olympic trials in Eugene, Oregon instead of working at a deli. So even in the one thing that Sid was good at, he still felt like he always came up a little short. To make up for it, he never allowed himself to let up, never missed a workout, and never, ever failed to finish a run once he'd started. There had been plenty of races where he'd beaten a more talented runner because—he was sure of it—somewhere in the past the other guy had cut himself some slack. That's why Sid had never given up on a run. Until Now.

He sat alone in the spare bedroom of his mom's

house, in a funk over bailing out on his run, with a sheet of paper and a Bic pen. Sid and his mom both called it the "Guest Room" and they always would. He couldn't have gone back to his old room. That room's door had been shut for six months. The carpet had been replaced, the furniture removed, and now it was simply not a part of the house. The elephant in the room that no longer existed.

Sid was doing his homework assignment. *"Think really, really hard about who might hate your guts,"* Gloria had told him. The instructions seemed a little rough and simplistic, and he wasn't getting anywhere. He honestly couldn't think of a single person who would have reason to hate him. Sid was nothing if not harmless. He thought a person should have to be a lot more motivated and pushy to earn someone else's contempt. Having made no progress, he broadened the parameters a little.

He chewed the end of the pen and ruminated on the phrase "motive and opportunity." Sid the Private Eye. Why would someone want to set him up? And without hating his guts, of course, because, really, how could they? The sheet was very nearly blank.

At the top of the page he'd written "Jock Bell." It had seemed like the obvious place to start, given the conversation he'd had just hours earlier. It had been twenty minutes since he wrote down Jock's name, and now he struggled to think of someone else. There had to be another name he could add to the list.

He decided to focus on the word, "opportunity." Regardless of their feelings about him, who would have had access to the back room to place the gun there? He wrote "Joe Diaz" an inch or so below Jock's name, and below that he wrote "Eddie Davis." He smiled, almost laughed, and put a line through Eddie's name. Then he did the same with Joe. Then he stared at the paper for another five minutes. He was never any good at homework. He circled Jock's name. Then he made a smiley face out of the "O."

Jock had known about Big Sid's gambling. What difference did that make? Why would that cause the guy go to the trouble of making it look like Sid was some kind of psycho sniper? And that presumed that somebody was, in fact, really trying to frame him. No, Jock was a freaky old creep, but it was hard to imagine he was some criminal mastermind.

Then again, he'd been bitten by the gold bug. According to Big Sid, who heard it from some guy who probably no longer worked at the pawn shop—reliable huh?—Jock was convinced that there was gold somewhere below the deli. Seemed ridiculous, but it was right in keeping with a guy who'd put a mini-sub in the river or open a school for wrestlers. He was desperate to get his hands on the only access to the underground, and the only thing standing in his way was the Bigler family.

This time Sid did laugh out loud. The whole thing sounded so absurd. Still, he circled Jock's name again, and underlined it this time.

He thought about Det. Stokes and that surreal lunchtime encounter at the deli. He saw him walking toward the back room, seemingly knowing exactly where the gun would be. And he remembered the look on Joe's face as Stokes was heading there. It was a look that said what? That Joe was concerned? Angry? Worried? About what?

Sid wrote Joe's name down on the paper again, then drummed absent-mindedly with the pen. It was ridiculous, of course. Joe had plenty of opportunity, but what was the motive? Sid thought hard, wanting to make progress, but came up with nothing. He should just scratch off Joe's name again. But he left it there. And that was the end of Sid's homework assignment. Two names, but no solid proof that either one was out to get him.

Eleven o'clock, and Sid stared at himself in the bathroom mirror as he brushed his teeth. Less than twenty-four hours since he'd heard the shots in the park. The cop, the busty blonde, his furious sister, Jock and the pawn shop, the zit-faced kid trying to run him over. Could it really have been only one day? Sid realized that he hadn't been paying attention and couldn't remember if he'd brushed his top teeth yet. He made himself concentrate, tooth by tooth, until the job was done.

As he reached for the light switch, he allowed himself one more long look in the mirror. Again, he heard his sister's voice from earlier: *"Something must have happened before that first shooting— before two weeks ago."* That made sense. But what was it? Who could possibly have it in for Sid Bigler, and why?

"What did you do, Sid?" he asked his reflection.

Sleep had played hard to get the night before, but it

swallowed him up this night. In spite of his three-hour nap, Sid was out before he knew it, and he slept deeply and sweetly.

CHAPTER 12

Friday morning, May 16th. For the first time in a while, Sid was feeling pretty good. It had been a couple of days since the Fairytale Town shooting. If you didn't know that Gloria had punched him in the eye, you probably wouldn't have noticed. The previous day there had been no visits by the cops, no phone call from his sister, no reason to think he'd be moving to Folsom Prison anytime soon. The Capital Shooter had, of course, come up a few times in conversations with customers, but so what? Business at Sid's Deli was still up, thanks to curiosity spawned by the articles in the paper, and that was fine with Sid. He was more than happy to chat with strangers, or just be gawked at, as long as they ordered something.

"No, I can't make it this afternoon," Woody the cop said as he mopped up the plate with his usual raisin bread toast.

"Jeez, Woody, that's twice in a row. You're getting flabby."

Woody and Sid had become unusual workout partners. Woody could snap Sid in half with one hand, but hadn't run ten feet since his last day at the academy. Sid could run, of course, but struggled to bench press a pack of light bulbs. For several months now, the two had met twice a week in the afternoon—Woody's shift ended at four. One day they'd go to the gym and lift, one day they'd go for a run. They'd both shown rapid improvement in their weaknesses, and their friendship had grown just as quickly.

"No can do, buddy. Sorry." Woody stood and began going through his pockets for some money.

"Okay, but we're back on next Tuesday. I'm thinking about entering Mr. Universe." Sid flexed.

"I dunno. Maybe."

Sid couldn't tell if Woody's lack of eye contact was because he was counting his change or because he lied as badly as your average third grader.

"What do you mean you don't know? What's up?"

Woody the cop closed his hand on his money, glanced up and away for a moment, then looked Sid in the eye.

"Sid, I've been told not to talk to you."

"By…?"

"People in the Department."

If Sid had taken a moment to think about it, he wouldn't have been so incredulous, but he didn't.

"Oh, god, what for?"

Woody stared at him. Waiting. Finally he said, "Look, you're not officially a suspect or anything. But you are involved in a big investigation."

It was like a guy who'd briefly forgotten he had cancer. In a flash the world was once again a gloomy place. Sid tried to not look like he'd been punched in the gut, but he failed.

"Look," said Woody, "I've told them the whole thing is ridiculous. You got nothing to worry about."

"Yeah."

"I'll see what I can do about Tuesday, okay?"

"Yeah, okay."

Woody clearly wanted to say something else, but nothing came out. Just as both of them were getting good and uncomfortable, he grabbed his cap off the counter and turned for the door. Sid stared straight ahead into the space that his friend had formerly occupied. The sound of the door closing seemed to be his cue to glance down and pick up Woody's empty plate and coffee cup. No tip.

"Can I ask what's up?"

The next stool down was still occupied. A forty-something guy in a Hawaiian shirt was about half-way through a stack of blueberry pancakes. He'd asked for extra whipped cream when he ordered, then had proceeded to eat all of it off the top before pouring syrup over the cakes and digging in. All that and a 7Up for breakfast. Health nut.

"Oh, it's nothing," Sid answered. He didn't feel like chatting.

"This something about the shootings?" Hawaiian shirt guy was a talker. "I've read about you in the paper. The cops don't actually think you had anything to do with it, right?"

The guy wasn't a regular. When he had come in earlier, Sid hadn't given him a thought—assumed he was another sightseer taking a look at Sacramento's most famous witness. Now Sid was thinking maybe the guy looked familiar. He set the dishes back down, wiped his hand with a towel and extended it.

"Sid Bigler."

"I've seen your picture. I'm Jack." The guy shook firmly and flashed a smile. "Pretty wild ride, huh?"

Jack looked like he'd lost the battle with teenage acne twenty-five years earlier. He could stand to drop about forty pounds, and he had a light sweat going before 10 a.m. Still, there was something likeable there. An aging, hefty Potsie Weber.

"Yeah, wild. I'm ready to return to obscurity, thank you." Sid picked up the guy's soda and gave him a refill.

"I bet. So what's with the cops?"

"Oh, nothing, I'm sure. They're just doing their job."

"Sure," Jack agreed, "But they can be a pain in the ass all the same. I was a witness to a bank robbery once. Between the investigation and testifying at the trial, I missed about ten days of work."

The trial. Sid hadn't even thought of that. Assuming they eventually caught this nut—and assuming it wasn't Sid himself on trial—this whole mess wasn't going to be over anytime soon. Damn.

"I bet I had different cops ask me the same questions on four separate occasions. Do they ever talk to each other? And before the trial there's meetings with the D.A. and depositions…" Jack and his Hawaiian shirt wasn't making Sid feel any better. Over the next few minutes Sid got the whole story of Jack and the Bank

Robbery—the blow by blow of the actual crime, the repeated questioning by the cops, the trial (and the woman in the jury with the incredible body who kept looking at him), his critical testimony, everything. Thankfully, Jack was a good storyteller.

"…and this wasn't a big, famous case like yours," Jack concluded. "I'm afraid you really stepped in it, my friend."

"Well, so far it's just been me talking to police."

"More than just your uniformed buddy?"

"Oh, yeah." Sid thought for a moment. "Three guys."

"Detectives?"

"Yep."

Jack let out a whistle. "And your cop friend, what's his name? Woody? He sounded like maybe somebody thinks you might be more than just a witness."

Now Sid was getting uncomfortable. "Look, I've gotta get some stuff done," he said and started to make an obvious move away from the counter .

"Hey, Sid, I only brought that up to tell you don't worry about it. It's standard procedure."

"Yeah?" Sid stopped.

"Sure. Basic cop work. Anybody present at the scene of a crime has to be eliminated as a suspect. Happened with me and the bank robbery. Don't worry about it."

Maybe it was wishful thinking, but Sid actually found himself being comforted by this. It made sense. Just because Stokes was asking questions didn't mean he really suspected that Sid had done anything wrong. Just following all the leads.

"You don't have anything to worry about, do you Sid?"

"What?" Sid barely heard the question.

"I was just saying, you had nothing to do with the shootings, right? So you don't have to worry."

"Right. That's right." Sid didn't like how the conversation was turning and decided it was time to end it. "Like I said, I've got some things to do. It was nice talking to you, Jack." Sid quickly picked up Woody's dirty dishes again and headed off to put them in the bus tub. He made a point of keeping his back to Jack, so the guy couldn't start talking again. He looked to the grill hoping he could use Joe as a distraction, but Joe had stepped away, so he busied himself wiping off a couple of salt & pepper shakers with a damp towel for a minute.

When he did turn and look at the counter, Jack was gone. There was a five dollar bill by the plate. Sid cleared those dishes, too, noticing that the plate was now cleaner than it was before Joe had put the food on it. Impressive. As Sid was popping open the register drawer to put the five away, another customer came up to pay his bill, a newspaper folded and tucked under his arm. A tall, skinny John Ritter with gray hair.

"How was everything?" Sid asked.

"Delicious, as always."

"Thanks, glad you enjoyed it."

Restaurant Schmoozing 101. His dad would be proud. He thought their little conversation was over, but the guy had one more thing to say, and it gave Sid a lousy feeling in the pit of his stomach. The guy nodded in the direction of the stool where Jack had been sitting and said, "Nice to see members of the press have discovered how good this place is."

The guy turned and headed out the door as Sid let the meaning of his last words slowly sink in. And he thought of Gloria's only rule: Don't talk to anyone.

"Hey! Hey, excuse me!" Halfway out the door of the deli, he saw the tall John Ritter guy about half a block away and called out as he jogged to catch up to him. The man turned, mildly surprised.

"Uh, who was that guy I was talking to in the deli? The guy in the Hawaiian shirt."

"Jackson Dexter. Writes for the Bee. Talk of the Town."

The man handed Sid his newspaper and continued walking. Sid stood in the middle of the sidewalk, people walking past him in each direction, and opened the paper to the Metro Section. There was the column he'd seen a thousand times. "Talk of the Town." A one-inch tall photo of Jack smiled back at him. The first item today was about a high profile Sacramento couple whose son had been kicked out of Stanford after being caught in a sexual encounter with a young lady while wearing the Cardinal mascot costume. That was followed by some not-so-veiled references to a local TV sports anchor and speculation that his eleven o'clock news appearances were often made under the influence of alcohol. Yes, Jack was a good storyteller.

What might this schmuck write about Sid's Deli and the interest the police were taking in its young owner? Standing on the sidewalk, he decided that a pre-emptive phone call to Gloria might save him from another sock in the eye. He turned and headed back towards the deli.

As he came through the front door, he saw a couple at the register waiting to pay. Eddie was clearing their table and Joe was nowhere to be seen. He didn't want to make such a sensitive call on the telephone out front, so he slipped behind the counter without slowing down, headed for the payphone in back.

"I'll be right with you two," Sid said to the customers as he flashed by. "I got a little emergency."

As he passed through the doorway, Sid stopped short. Joe was at the payphone, facing the wall. Since his back was to Sid, his face couldn't be seen, but something about his posture was tense. He radiated anger, though his voice was so low Sid couldn't make out what he was saying. On any other occasion, Sid would've hung a U-turn and given Joe his privacy. After all, the guy hardly ever took a break. But something made Sid hold his ground for a moment, and then quietly move forward, straining to hear.

Sid stopped in his tracks as Joe stopped talking. For a moment he thought Joe would hang up and turn to find him spying, but the phone call wasn't over. Joe was listening, phone to his ear with his left hand, his right hand clenching and unclenching a fist. When he spoke again it was louder, and Sid had no problem hearing.

"You shut up! He doesn't know anything, so you

just stay the hell away. We are done talking about this!"

Sid could see that the phone call was ending. His mind raced, trying to figure out what Joe was talking about, but his prevailing thought was to get out of there before he was caught. He turned and headed for the door as quickly and quietly as possible. Sid heard the phone slam behind him and he didn't know if Joe had seen him or not.

CHAPTER 13

Someone had a gun, and they were firing it five times. Bang-Bang-Bang-Bang-Bang. Whose hand was the gun in?

One of the rules of dreaming is that there are no rules, and anybody's allowed to shoot a gun if they want to. It's Jock Bell. Bang-Bang-Bang-Bang-Bang. It's Jackson Dexter, the newspaper guy. Bang-Bang-Bang-Bang-Bang. It's Gloria or Amy—hard to tell in the dark. Or is it Yvonne the buxom blonde social worker? Now it's Mr. Perryman, Sid's old high school auto shop teacher. Bang-Bang-Bang-Bang-Bang.

Even though his eyes were still tightly shut, the Saturday morning sun was pushing hard, trying to put an end to Sid's jumble of dreams. He began to stir, and the "Bang-Bang" of a gun slowly became a "Knock-Knock" at his front door. He sat up in his bed, eyes squeezed shut, and tried to give the situation his fullest attention. Yes. Someone was definitely knocking at the door. He cracked one eye open and took a peek at the clock. 7:20 a.m.

In his usual briefs and a t-shirt, Sid made his way down the hallway. He heard the front door unlatch, and his mother's voice saying "Hello." There was a man's voice, low. As Sid entered the living room and got a clear view of the entry, he saw the front door swing open wide and his mom stepped back to welcome Det. Benjamin Stokes. The cop looked at Sid, taking him in from head to toe, and Sid wondered if maybe he was underdressed for the occasion.

Sid was sitting on the couch in the aforementioned t-shirt, but now he had jeans on and a pair of Adidas. Stokes sat in an armchair across from him, and Sid's mom was just entering the room with three cups of coffee. Rose Bigler was, as the song said, five foot two, eyes of blue. That made her just a little shorter than her husband had been, but with her hair done she had him by three or four inches. She had worn the basic Lady Bird Johnson-Ann Landers-Betty Crocker hairdo for as far back as anyone could remember. Over the last ten years the beautiful red was increasingly giving way to silver, but the shape had never changed. Between Det. Stokes and his mother, Sid guessed there may have been over a pound of hairspray in the room.

Rose was, to put it plainly, a little ditzy. Those who knew her well understood that it wasn't a lack of intellect on her part, but a lack of interest in most things that gave the impression that she wasn't the sharpest knife in the drawer. The necessary, mundane things in life—like paying the bills and feeding the cat—completely failed to capture her attention. When things like that went undone, which was often, it looked to the world like she was Edith Bunker come to life. On the other hand, if Rose was interested in something, an entirely different person emerged. She was among the most capable and ruthless bridge players on the planet. She had a devotion to the game of baseball that had matched that of her husband, and an ability to remember sports statistics that was amazing. Big Sid used to challenge his friends to try and stump her. And, fortunately for Sid and Gloria, Rose was deeply interested in her children. Which meant that, even if she was ditzy, she was an extraordinary mom.

Rose set coffee cups on coasters in front of Det. Stokes and Sid, and kept the third one for herself as she sat down on the couch next to her son. While she had been in the kitchen making the coffee, Sid had managed a quiet, private conversation with the detective, letting him know that his mother knew nothing about Stokes' visit to the deli and the discovery of the gun. Sid had shared his concern that his mom was still a little fragile from her husband's death and that he didn't want to worry her. It wasn't true, of course. Rose was the Rock of Gibralter. But it sounded good. Stokes had seemed very understanding.

"Mom, I think Det. Stokes wants to speak to me alone," said Sid.

"Oh, no, it's fine with me." There was a gleam in Stokes' eye. "Is there some reason you shouldn't be here, Mrs. Bigler?"

"I don't know. Is there a reason I shouldn't be here, Sid?" Rose asked the question without guile. Completely sincere.

"Yeah, anything you can't say in front of your mother?" Stokes asked with a grin. It's nice when someone enjoys their work.

"Uh, no. No it's fine. What can I do for you, detective?"

"Well, I was just following up, Sid. Lot of pressure at work to solve this crazy Capital Shooter case and I'm tying up loose ends. Have you heard about the Capital Shooter, Mrs. Bigler?"

"Well, I should say I have, detective. It's all over the news. And did you know my son was a witness? He was on television." Rose sounded like a mom whose son had scored the winning run in a Little League game. "And that last shooting was just down the street, not a mile from here! Just a few days ago!"

"Yes, I heard about that," Det. Stokes flashed Rose the teeth. "And I understand your son was out running that night, is that right?"

"Well, I don't remember," Rose said. "Siddy, were you out that night?"

"Yeah, mom. I was out."

She perked up. "And you didn't hear anything?" Again, Rose asked the question with absolute innocence. Stokes had to be loving this. Sid swallowed, knowing that lying to your mother is a substantially greater sin than lying to a cop who looks like Tony Orlando. But the die was cast.

"No, mom."

"Well that's a shame. It would've been very exciting."

For the first time, Stokes pulled out the familiar notepad and scribbled for a moment, then flipped through some previous pages. Rose sipped her coffee and gave Sid a little wink.

"Let's see," said the detective. "Did you check your runner's log—your little diary—for me? About those other dates?"

"Yes. Yes I did."

"And?"

"I was out running both nights. The third and the sixth."

"Really? How 'bout that?" Stokes said it like he found Sid marvelous and fascinating. If his goal was to irritate Sid, the plan was working beautifully. He turned to Rose to explain the significance. "It turns out that your son was out running around on the nights of every one of the shootings. Isn't that something?"

"Yes, he's a very good runner." The proud mother. Rose grabbed a small framed photo off the end table. "Here he is on the college track team. He was the captain."

"Well, look at that." Stokes oozed a fake enthusiasm that Sid's mom was buying hook, line and sinker. "He looks fast in those tiny little shorts."

"Oh, he was very fast. He still has the school record in the 1500 and the 5000. Isn't that right, Siddy?"

"I don't know, mom. I haven't checked in a while."

"I bet you do, Sid," said Stokes, and he pointed to the photo. "Love the shorts."

"Thank you."

"So, any chance anybody was out running along with you on the third or the sixth? Or any one of the other nights?"

Sid shook his head. "No. Just me."

"Does he always go off running by himself like that, Mrs. Bigler?"

"Oh, I don't know, officer." Rose thought it over. "Seems like he's out with that Amy girl quite a bit. And there are a couple of other boys he runs with from time to time."

Sid's mom appeared to be thoroughly enjoying the morning conversation. If it had occurred to her that her son was a suspect in a felony, she didn't show it. It just seemed like this nice man was interested in her son, and she'd always been proud to talk about him.

"Well, I think it's just amazing. Sid here was out running on the nights of all five shootings. Each time he was running alone."

"And he was a witness twice!" Rose added, happily. "He was on television."

"Yes, twice," said Stokes. Then he turned and looked Sid squarely in the eye. Serious. "And you're positive you didn't see or hear anything four nights ago at Fairytale Town?"

"Wasn't that awful?" Rose chimed in. "Did you see what happened to Humpty Dumpty? There was a picture in the paper. Terrible."

Neither man acknowledged Rose's comment. Neither man blinked.

"Didn't see a thing, detective." There was a pause. Sid thought his denial sounded pretty convincing this time. What's that saying about telling a lie often enough?

"Hm." Stokes was both amused and puzzled. "I was really hoping I'd find a second witness."

Rose blew on her coffee and took a sip. Stokes gave Sid a curious smile.

"Second witness?" Sid asked.

"Yeah, we found a guy who lives on 13th Avenue that was just starting out to walk his dog when the shooter did his thing." The detective took a sip, too. "Delicious coffee, Mrs. Bigler."

Where was Stokes going with this? If they found somebody who saw the shooter, then they knew the shooter wasn't Sid, right? So what was this cop doing here on a Saturday morning?

"You found somebody who saw what happened last Thursday night? Somebody who saw the shooter?"

"Well, that's the thing." Stokes set down his coffee. "Maybe yes, maybe no. This guy hears the gunshots, right? He looks, can't see much in the dark. So he just stands there and waits, watching."

Stokes paused and picked his coffee up back up. Took a nice, long sip. Sid noticed he could feel his own pulse pounding in his neck. He allowed himself to hope that maybe someone got a look at the real shooter. Maybe he was off the hook.

"After a few seconds, the guy sees somebody pass under a street lamp right by the park entrance. Didn't get a real good look at him."

"Did they see a gun? Did you get a description of the guy?"

"Well, my witness was a couple of blocks away. Said

he couldn't see a gun, but what do you expect? It was dark. We figure it was just a small caliber pistol. So, maybe he just missed it."

"And what did he say the guy looked like?"

"Oh, this is the interesting part." Stokes flipped through his little notebook for a moment, licking his finger once as he tried to find the right page. "Let me find the note. I want to get this right. Uh, here we go... He said the guy was wearing dark shorts and a white t-shirt, and he was running." Det. Stokes flipped his notebook closed and dropped it on the coffee table. It made a surprisingly loud smack as it landed. He laced his fingers together and leaned forward, elbows on knees, staring at Sid. "Man said he couldn't give us a better description, 'cause the guy was running really fast."

Ten seconds went by in silence. Rose spoke up.

"Anybody besides me want a cookie?" With that she scooped up her coffee cup and headed towards the kitchen. Sid let out the breath that he just realized he'd been holding.

With Rose out of the room, Stokes lowered his voice and dropped any pretense of friendly. He spoke very quickly. "Okay, I didn't say anything about the gun in front of your mom. She seems like a nice lady. But it's the gun. I know it and you know it. Raven .25 caliber revolver. Almost every other .25 pistol out there is an automatic. Very few revolvers. But an automatic would leave casings at the scene, and we didn't find any casings, so it had to have been a revolver. Am I going too fast for you?"

"Yes!" Sid cried, somewhere between a shout and a whisper. Whatever Stokes had said about revolvers and casings had gone by way too fast for Sid, who had never gotten past the BB gun stage. But it had made his head spin, and the anxiety that he'd first felt when he saw Stokes at the door had blossomed into full blown panic. "This is nuts! I don't have any idea what you're…"

"Save it, pal. Ballistics tests will be back in a day or two. I've got your ass."

Det. Stokes grabbed his notebook, stood up and headed for the door. Sid was feeling desperate. "Wait!" he called out as he stepped quickly, catching Stokes by the arm before he reached the door. The detective turned, glanced down at Sid's hand on his arm, then glared at him.

"I'm not the guy you're looking for." Sid's voice quivered, barely audible. "I'm not the guy."

"Thank you for the coffee, Mrs. Bigler," Stokes called out. The voice was friendly but the glare never changed. He lowered his voice once more. "Why don't I believe you, Siddy?" As the front door closed behind him, the clock in the entryway said 7:40.

CHAPTER 14

The weekend that began with a visit from Det. Stokes didn't show a lot of improvement after that. Sid spent much of it feeling like an innocent man on the fast track to the slammer. And he would learn before the weekend was over that the Capital Shooter, whoever he was, was affecting his relationship with all of the women in his life: his mom, his girlfriend, and his sister.

Rose had returned from the kitchen and was surprised to discover that the nice detective was already gone. She didn't seem particularly worried, but she did wonder why the police were asking him about all this again. Sid gave her the answer provided by Jackson Dexter the day before— basic cop work. Anybody at the crime scene has to be interviewed. Blah, blah. Rose had seemed satisfied with that, but then she said something that had continued to haunt him. She put her hands on his shoulders, making sure she had his complete attention, and said, *"Siddy, you know you can talk to me about anything."*

The stab of déjà vu was intense. They'd had that same moment—not one vaguely like it, but the very same moment—sometime in the past. It didn't hit him until later that morning. When Sid was fourteen he set fire to the neighbor's sofa. It wasn't inside their house. This was one of those once-a-year special deals where the garbage men would take away anything you put out by the curb, and the whole neighborhood looked like a very, very bad garage sale. When Conrad Balzer held up a Zippo lighter and called young Sid a chicken, the salmon colored sofa's fate was sealed. It was just after 10 p.m. and it was an awesome fire, made even more enjoyable by the appearance of the neighbor, Mr. Cavanaugh, in his boxers with the garden hose to put it out. The next day, for some reason that was a complete mystery to young Sid at the time, Mr. Cavanaugh came to their house and asked if the boy had anything to do with the incident. Sid's father called him into the living room, asked him point blank if he was responsible for the fire, and Sid promised both men that he was completely innocent. Case closed. Big Sid walked with Mr. Cavanaugh out to the front yard. That's when Rose, who had been watching quietly from the kitchen door, walked over, put her hands on his shoulders—they were standing in the very same place—and said, *"Siddy, you know you can talk to me about anything."*

Moms of fourteen-year-olds have special powers to know when their sons are full of crap. And now Sid had to wonder if they ever lost that power.

In the afternoon, Amy called to break their date for that night. He hadn't seen her since their run together on Tuesday—the night of the shooting. Nothing unusual about that, weekdays were busy for both of them. They'd spoken on the phone twice. Sid had called her Wednesday night after he got the message that Stokes had been to see her. Amy had seemed fine. In fact, she'd found the whole thing quite exciting, and it apparently hadn't even crossed her mind that her boyfriend might be a big, fat liar. Then Amy had called him on Friday just to say hello and that she was looking forward to Saturday night. But now she had pulled the plug on their plans, and that was very unusual.

Saturdays were a big deal for Sid and Amy. She was one of the few people he knew who owned a VCR—they were new and expensive—and it had become the focal point of their weekends. Amy was a receptionist in a real estate office, but she was working on getting her license. She took a night class on Fridays, so she'd record the show "Dallas" on the VCR, and they'd watch it together on Saturday night. The show had been in re-runs since J.R. had gotten shot a couple of months ago, but the weekly date continued because, in truth, it had always been just an excuse to spend a Saturday night curled up together on Amy's sofa. So when she called to cancel their date, it came as quite a surprise. It turned out that Stokes had headed over to her apartment after he left Sid's place that morning, and Amy hadn't found her second conversation with the cops nearly as entertaining as her first.

"That detective really got me scared."

"Oh, c'mon, Amy. He's not gonna do anything to you."

"No, Sid. *He's* not the one I'm scared of... "

It had taken a moment for what she was saying to sink in. Whatever Stokes had said to her, Amy was really upset. Upset enough to think that Sid might actually be dangerous. And at that point, he got pissed. Sid was mad at Amy for even thinking he'd have anything to do with the shootings, and mad at Stokes for going to his girlfriend's place and saying... what exactly? I think your boyfriend is a psycho criminal? Before the call was over, they both ended up raising their voices, and when Sid said "Yeah, well Dallas is a stupid show, anyway," Amy screamed and hung up.

Sid had fumed silently for a couple of minutes before he remembered that he was the one who had lied to the cops. And to his mom. And to Joe and his sister and his girlfriend and that guy from the newspaper and pretty much everybody else he'd spoken to in the last few days, which sort of took all the wind out of his indignation. He sighed and picked up the phone to call Amy's number back, but it went to her answering machine. Sid thought about confessing everything and begging her forgiveness on the machine, but reconsidered. No sense bringing Amy into this mess now. *It's best that she doesn't know anything. Then there's no way any of this can be her fault.* And so Sid the liar hung up the phone, convinced he was doing the noble thing.

Sid went out for a run on Sunday morning. The weather was starting to heat back up, and it felt great to get out the door early and put in ten miles. He had coasted in the last few, trying unsuccessfully to get that Pina Colada song by Rupert Holmes out of his head. When he got back home, Rose was off to church with

Gloria and her family, so he pulled on a sweatshirt and flipped on the TV. The news had reports of a volcano erupting in Washington. He'd never even heard of Mount Saint Helens. The images were spectacular.

About 11:30 the front door opened and Rose came in, followed closely by his sister. The three of them chatted politely for a while until Gloria grabbed Sid by the arm and announced to their mother that they were going for a walk and would be back in a little while.

"Before I talk to you as your lawyer, I'll say three words as your sister." The two walked down the sidewalk toward the park, Sid with his hands in his pockets. "You're an idiot."

"You know, if I was paying you I wouldn't stand for that."

"Boy, good thing I work for free," Gloria replied.

They took a few more steps in silence. Sid remembered his mom's comment. *Siddy, you know you can talk to me about anything.*

"Hey, did you say anything to mom about all this?"

"Not yet. Why?"

"Nothing."

Somebody emerged from a nearby house walking a dog that looked like a giant white floor mop. They exchanged a wave and "hello."

"Okay, little brother, here's the latest on your legal troubles. First of all, I finally talked to Vince Headley and I think you've got nothing to worry about there."

"Vince who?" Sid asked.

"Headley. The fat guy's lawyer."

"Oh, yeah. Don't you think he looks like Herman Munster?"

"We only talked on the phone, but thanks for the warning. The bottom line here is that there's no precedent for an action like this, and if they're gonna let the fat guy sue you over meatloaf sandwiches, they'll have to shut down every McDonald's in America. This is just a lawyer fishing to see if you'll pay him to go away. Probably read about dad's death last year, figured you'd want to avoid any bad press."

"Hard to believe a lawyer would do something like that."

"Yeah, it's a shame that ninety-five percent of attorneys give the rest of us a bad name."

"So what do I say if Mr. Munster comes sniffing around again?"

"Well, he shouldn't. Completely out of bounds for him to approach you directly, especially after he's spoken with me. Of course, you never know. The guy's a low-life."

"Hey, speaking of low-lifes, I have big news about a certain slimeball and what he has inside his pawn shop…"

For the next few minutes, Sid recounted his recent visit to Jock Bell's establishment and the collection of things their father had pawned. Gloria listened with interest, then offered to come up with the eighteen hundred dollars. Sid accepted.

By now they'd arrived at the edge of the park. Like

most Sundays, the place was packed. Families spreading out picnics everywhere, Frisbees and the smoke from barbecues filled the air. Gloria led them to an unoccupied bench and they both sat.

"Okay, about your bigger legal problems," Gloria said, "After you called me yesterday, I talked with my friend in the D.A.'s office."

"What did he say?"

"He said he doesn't like it when I call him on the weekend. And he said he thinks that my baby brother might be the Capital Shooter."

"And you told him I wasn't, right?"

"I didn't tell him anything. Good lawyers listen more than they talk. Anyway, there's a big difference between them *thinking* you did something and *proving* you did something. Right now all they've got is that gun, and it looks like the gun doesn't prove anything."

"But Stokes said it's the same gun from the shootings."

"Oh, God. Stokes." Gloria almost laughed. "He acts like Mr. Tough Guy, but he screws up. He testified in one of the few criminal cases I've worked, and he was a disaster. We ate him up."

"He looks like a blonde Tony Orlando."

Gloria paused. "You're usually wrong about those things, but that's a good one."

"Thank you."

"Look, the gun they found at the deli was a .25 caliber Raven revolver. Not a common gun."

"Yeah," said Sid, "Stokes said something like that

109

yesterday morning and I was completely lost."

"Most .25 pistols are automatics. Yours was a revolver."

"It's not mine. And so what?"

"Automatics eject the spent shell when you fire the gun. With revolvers, the shells stay in the cylinder until you reload."

Sid stared at her for a moment. "Okay, let's pretend that I understand what you just said, and tell me why this matters."

Gloria sighed. "If the Capital Shooter had used an automatic, they would've found casings—spent shells—laying on the ground. They didn't." She was sounding just a little like their mother when she was impatient. "So either the nut stuck around to pick up the shells, which he didn't, or they figure that somebody used a .25 caliber revolver. And there aren't very many .25 caliber revolvers. So when they find one next to the pickle jar in your filing cabinet, they start to think that maybe you're a bad guy."

"But you said the gun doesn't prove anything."

"Right. Two reasons. Number one—if it proved anything for sure, you'd be wearing an orange jumpsuit right now, and we'd be having this conversation at the county jail."

"And number two?"

"Ballistics is gonna come up empty. There were a grand total of seven .25 caliber slugs recovered from the five shootings. I have it from a very reliable source that every one of them was badly deformed from an impact with something hard, like concrete or metal. Even the one that hit the bum in the toe went all the way through the shoe and into the wall at Sutter's Fort. No way they can be one hundred percent certain they came from your gun."

"It's not mine. And how do you know all this stuff?"

"I'm a good lawyer, Sid. And I care about my baby brother. It's like I said, if Stokes had solid evidence, he'd have arrested you already. He just came by the house to scare you—to see if he can get you to make a mistake. It's typical."

"So, what do I do?" he asked.

"Just remember your one rule, Sid."

"Don't talk to anybody."

"Perfect. If Stokes shows up again, don't say a thing unless I'm present. Don't talk to Jackson what's-his-name at the paper, don't talk to mom, don't talk to your girlfriend, nobody."

"Yeah, well, the girlfriend part will be easy. I'm not sure, but we might have broken up yesterday."

"Aww. That's terrible." Gloria's lack of sincerity was as intentional as a poke in the eye.

"Why don't you like Amy?"

"'Cause Mom doesn't like her."

"Okay. Why doesn't Mom like her?"

"Because she's thirty."

"So? *You're* thirty."

"Right." Gloria paused, only briefly. "And Mom wouldn't like it if you dated me, either."

Sometimes it sucks when your sister's a lawyer.

CHAPTER 15

Mondays had always been the busiest morning of the week, and this one was no exception. It was the only day of the week that Joe made Brown Sugar Cinnamon Rolls, and the things seemed to always sell out no matter how many they made. Joe had to come in two hours early to get the dough started, which is why they only made them once a week. Dubbed "BS Rolls" by Big Sid, it was a recipe Joe got from his mom in 1954. They were tasty the first time he made them, but once he decided to double the brown sugar and the butter, a legend was born. Crunchy and sugary on the outside, moist and slightly doughy in the middle. Who knows how many lives had been shortened by eating at Sid's Deli on a Monday morning.

Sid Jr. had burned out on BS Rolls when he was a kid. Funny how you only have to barf something up one time to make the magic go away. But he still loved the smell of the place on Mondays, and he even liked the way each week got off to a furious start. There were almost always four or five people waiting when he unlocked the doors at seven o'clock.

They'd been open for an hour now, and every seat in the place was taken. There was a to-go line waiting at the register, which is where Sid was stationed, collecting money and dropping BS Rolls in white paper bags as fast as he could. He thought, as he did each Monday, that he'd be rich if they made these things every day. A squatty guy with enormous sideburns and sunglasses ordered a half-dozen rolls and two coffees to go. Sid quickly filled the order as he decided that this was what Elvis would have looked like as a troll.

"That's five bucks exactly," said Sid.

The guy dropped a five on the counter and said, "Sorry to hear about your trouble."

"My trouble?"

"It's in the paper. Everybody knows what's goin' on." The guy took off the shades and gave Sid a stare that made him uncomfortable. "You're in deep doo-doo, pal. Really deep." He held the stare a moment longer, then stubby Elvis cut loose with a belly laugh like he'd said the funniest thing in the world, grabbed his bag and coffees and headed for the door, still amused with himself.

Sid immediately thought of Jackson Dexter and what he might have written about the shootings. What had that pinhead done to him? He grabbed an abandoned paper off the counter and opened it to the front page. Nothing. Not a word. In a curious way, he was almost disappointed. Surely implicating Sid in the Capital Shooter case should be front page news, right? Then it occurred to him that Dexter's column was in the Metro Section.

As he shuffled the paper to find the right page, he started getting heckled by the to-go line. "Hey, let's go...

114

What's goin' on, Sid?... Yo! Let's get moving…"

Sid held up a hand to shush them without even looking up from the paper. The smiling photo of Jackson Dexter made his stomach knot up. He scanned the article. There was something about a pirate-themed fundraiser for the Children's Home that was held at the home of Michael Bonaventi, a local developer. Apparently the sprinklers had gone off and most of the pirates and wenches had ended up soaked. And some nutty woman had managed to run completely naked onto the set of the five o'clock news on channel three and hug the anchorman. But there was nothing about Sid.

The noise from the to-go people had grown louder, and a couple of guys at the back of the line had given up and headed out the door. Sid gathered up the sections of the paper and headed back to his post. Over the next fifteen minutes Sid sold forty-seven BS Rolls, put on a new pot of coffee, collected money and made change, and slowly flipped through the pages of the Sacramento Bee. There was nothing about him that he could see in the front section, and no mention of the Capital Shooter case at all. He was about to give up on the Metro Section as he turned the last page, and there it was. B-14, left column, half-way down. A small article with the following headline: "Deli Owner Named in Fat Lawsuit." This is what the chunky Elvis guy thought was so funny. There was even a photo. Sid recognized it as one they took when he was interviewed for the Capital Shooter story.

"I see you've discovered the article."

Sid looked up from the paper to see the face of Vince Headley, lawyer of the now-famous fat guy. He wore a powder blue suit and a smile.

"You prick," spat Sid, quietly. "I can't believe you leaked this story to the newspaper."

"Oh, you must be wrong about that, Mr. Bigler. The lawsuit is a matter of public record. Anyone from the newspaper could have come across the information without my help. I'm sure that's what happened."

"Yeah, that must be it. You lying piece of…"

Sid stopped short. The words of his sister flashed through his mind. Gloria's only rule— *"Don't talk to anybody."* He stared at the lawyer, fuming.

"Hey, Sid!" It was the guy at the front of the line, who pointed at Headley. "This guy didn't wait in line."

"Well, there's a good reason for that, pal. He's an ass." Sid folded the paper and tried to get back to work. "And a lawyer."

The guy in line laughed. "I'll go for two Brown Sugar Rolls and a black coffee."

"Sure," said Sid, and he busied himself with the order.

"I spoke with your sister, you know." Herman Munster wasn't going away. In fact, he seemed to be enjoying himself, happily talking as Sid went about his work. "I know she's quite competent when it comes to contract and corporate law, but the matter with my client, Mr. Matheson, is not her area of expertise. Ours is a straightforward claim regarding product liability and negligence."

The words "Ambulance Chaser" came to Sid's mind repeatedly over the next several minutes as Headley went on and on about the merits of their lawsuit and their almost certain victory in court. Sid went about his business taking care of the line. Several times he was tempted to mouth off, but managed to keep Gloria's advice.

Next in line was an absolute mountain of a man, a regular named Pete who had been coming into the deli since Sid was a kid. Suspenders held up his pants that had to have a sixty-inch waist, a white t-shirt was stretched to its limit.

"Hey, Sid Jr.! Gimme the usual," said Pete as he leaned forward and rested his elbows on the counter.

Sid realized the timing for his visit was not good. "The, uh, the usual?"

Pete gave him an odd look. "C'mon, Sid, it's me. It's Monday. The usual."

Vince Headley's eyes twinkled as he watched the scene. Sid struggled to think of a way to avoid the inevitable.

"So, you'd like *one* Brown Sugar Roll?"

Now Pete laughed. "Yeah, Sid Jr., I'd like one Brown Sugar Roll. And three more to go with it, please. God, you're a funny kid."

Sid's shoulders slumped a little as he grabbed a white bag and began dropping the rolls in. Headley decided to strike up a conversation with Pete.

"I've seen a lot of people ordering those rolls. They must be good."

117

"Are you kidding me?" Pete could barely contain himself. "Best damn cinnamon roll on planet Earth. Dripping with butter, crusty outside all covered in brown sugar. You gotta try one, man!"

"Thanks, maybe next time," said the lawyer.

"Suit yourself. They make 'em every Monday. Hell, I've come in here and had four of 'em every week for... How long's it been, Joe? Twenty years?"

Joe looked over from the grill. "Gotta be, Pete."

By now Sid was desperate to stop the bleeding. He set the bag of rolls on the counter in front of Pete and said, "It's on us this week, Pete. See you later."

"Best damn cinnamon roll on planet Earth!" Pete said again with a grin as he snatched up the white paper bag in his giant hand and headed for the door.

"It would be wonderful if that man would testify at the trial," said a very satisfied Vince Headley. "If he lives long enough."

Sid had finally reached his limit. Gloria would simply have to forgive him. He was just opening his mouth to tell this jerk lawyer what he thought of him when the most wonderful thing happened. Headley had positioned himself on the stool closest to the register, one elbow on the counter, sitting sideways so he could watch Sid at work. His back was to most of the restaurant and he had no idea what was coming.

From Sid's vantage point, he could see Eddie making his way across the deli carrying the big plastic tub he used to clear the tables. He must have caught his foot on the leg of a chair or something, because he lost his balance and began to pitch forward. Sid watched in glorious slow motion as Eddie lost control of the load, his arms out in front of him. The tray full of dirty dishes hit Vince Headley squarely in the middle of the back, and a mixture of cold coffee, hash browns, oatmeal and other breakfast remnants sprayed over his neck and shoulders. It looked good on the blue suit.

Eddie got himself up off the floor, wearing that same, mysterious smile as always. The six people standing in the to-go line broke into applause.

Surprisingly, Headley kept his cool. He picked up a paper napkin from the counter and began casually dabbing the back of his neck. "You can settle with Mr. Matheson today for ten thousand dollars. No trial, no more articles in the paper."

"Get lost, Headley. You won't be able to squeeze the guy into the courtroom."

The lawyer thought for a moment, then smiled. "Good-bye, Mr. Bigler," he said, and stood to leave, still dripping here and there.

"You have some scrambled eggs on your shoulder," said Sid.

Headley turned and walked to the door as Eddie finished collecting most of the spilled food and dishes into his tub and made his way around the counter, heading toward the back. As he passed the grill, Joe raised a hand up and Eddie gave him a high five. Sid didn't seem to notice.

A little bell rang above the door as Sid entered Jock's

Pawn Shop. How had he not noticed that before? Didn't Floyd the barber have one of those on Andy of Mayberry? Or maybe it was Mr. Drucker's store on Petticoat Junction. Still savoring the morning incident with Headley and the flying breakfast, Sid had managed to get the deli closed and locked a little after 2 p.m. and was now on an errand he'd been looking forward to all day.

Jock Bell was nowhere to be seen, but a great big guy sitting behind the counter looked up from a Peter Benchley novel. He wore a mossy green three piece suit and the knot in his tie was as big as a softball. He was maybe thirty-five. Sid had never seen a hairline come down so low. There was, at most, an inch of skin visible between the prodigious eyebrows and the start of his thick, black hair. Sid had just seen a preview of "The Empire Strikes Back" at the movies last week, and now here he was, face to face with a Wookiee.

"Jock around?"

"Nope."

The voice was high. Really high. The guy could be the fourth Bee Gee. Sid fought back a laugh.

"My name's Sid Bigler. I was supposed to pick up some of my dad's stuff."

"Cardboard box?"

"Yeah."

"1800 dollars."

Well, Jock Bell ran a very efficient operation. Sid pulled out his wallet and fished around for his sister's check. He thought about humming "Stayin' Alive" but decided against it. The guy had the voice of girl but he was the size of Dick Butkus. Sid handed him the check. The guy held it in his thick fingers while he studied it, then reached beside his chair, picked up a box and set it on the counter. Keep Refrigerated.

Sid looked at the words and ran his hands along the side of the box. He'd been in a great mood ever since Headley the lawyer took his leftover shower, but now the day quickly turned sober. He looked inside and everything seemed to be there. He let out a long breath and looked up at the guy behind the counter.

"Thank you."

"You have a nice day," said the high voice, and it seemed sincere. Then the guy winked at him.

The bell rang again as Sid hurried out the door.

CHAPTER 16

Except for Amy's complete absence from his life, things felt pretty normal. Sid got in a good run in the early evening, then showered and had a late dinner in front of the TV with his mom. Objectively, Rose was not a great cook. But, good or not, there's something about the food you grow up with, and the familiarity of the chicken with cream of mushroom soup concoction was wonderful. Maybe it was the crushed Fritos on top.

Rose loved Mork & Mindy. At first Sid thought the show was ridiculous, but over the months since he'd moved back home he'd spent quite a few Monday nights next to his mom watching the dumb show and had to admit that it had grown on him. As often happened, after Mork they flipped over to One Day at a Time, then it was Alice, The Jeffersons, and then it was time for bed.

Tuesday morning Sid popped up and headed for work, and for the first time since the shooting at Fairytale Town, none of his recent troubles even crossed his mind. It was one of those occasional mornings when Joe and Eddie got to work before he did. Joe said Eddie had ridden his bike in and had been the first one there, so the place was lit up and already smelling like coffee when he arrived. Michael Jackson was singing "Don't Stop 'til

You Get Enough." All three busied themselves with their regular opening routines, and they were mostly ready when the first customers wandered in.

No one mentioned the Capital Shooter the first few hours they were open. Taking over the family business had never been Sid's plan, but he'd grown comfortable with the idea. There were certainly worse ways to make a living. Regulars and first-timers came and went, and while it didn't consciously occur to him, Sid was deeply enjoying the normalcy of the morning. Then the familiar police cruiser pulled up in front of the deli at nine—right on time.

"Sorry I missed out on the BS Rolls yesterday. You save me one?" The cop slid onto his favorite stool. Sid realized for the first time that Woody hadn't come in at all on Monday. He'd completely missed out on the excitement with the lawyer.

"I would've, but after a day the things turn into concrete," Sid replied, and he poured a cup of coffee.

If there was an uncomfortable moment, it passed quickly. At the grill, Joe went to work on a Breakfast Special without a word being said. Over the course of the next half an hour, Woody pounded down his breakfast as usual. Sid recounted the glorious incident with Mr. Headley, Eddie and the flying leftovers, and at least for a little while it felt like the good old days.

Sid was just finishing up with a customer at the cash register when Woody pushed the empty plate away and called out, "Best one ever, Joe," for probably the hundredth time. He picked up his hat as he dropped

123

three bucks on the counter. "Hey, Sid, will I see you at the gym?"

"Today? This afternoon?"

"Yeah. It's Tuesday."

Sid walked to the counter and gathered Woody's plate and coffee cup, then stuck the three dollars in his shirt pocket. "I thought the department wanted you to stay away from hardened criminals like me."

"Screw 'em."

" Eighteen... nineteen... twenty..." Sweat poured down Sid's face and a tremor went through his arms as he bench pressed the 150 pounds for the last time. Capital Gym was mostly empty at 3:30.

Woody put his hands on the bar and stopped it from resting in its cradle. Sid still felt the full weight, and his arms ached and shook. He clenched his teeth, determined to show no pain. Perhaps ten seconds went by, the two making full eye contact, but neither one speaking. Awkward. Then Woody leaned down closer and quietly said, "Give me the Lakers' starting five." The gym seemed to grow silent around them. Sid's lips were pressed together in a tight line, short breaths puffing in and out his nose and his nostrils flared. For just a moment, his chin quivered. He fought back a laugh.

Sid lowered the bar and pushed it back up as he said, "Jabbar". The bar went down and up again two more times. "Chones... Wilkes..." The fourth time the bar faltered badly on the way up. "Nixon," gasped Sid as he expelled a breath. He filled his lungs again as he brought the bar down and then pushed with all of his might as he yelled, "Johnsonnnnnn", and with a slight assist from Woody the bar returned to it's resting place an arm's length away. Sid's muscles screamed. He sat up.

"Bastard."

"You love it," Woody replied.

And he did. The thing with the list and the extra repetitions—like the Lakers starting five—began the very first day they went to the gym. Good workout partners find ways to make each other work harder. As Sid was struggling to finish his first set of curls, Woody had said, "C'mon, you candy-ass. You can do five more!" Breathing hard, Sid puffed out, "Okay, one for each of the Jackson 5." He ran out of gas between Marlon and Tito, but a tradition was born.

Over the months, Sid had discovered that running and weightlifting were not that different. If you wanted to be good at it, you had to push yourself to a place that not a lot of people were willing to go. Sid wasn't good at a lot of things, but he'd proven long ago he could handle the pain of training better than most. On their first trip to the gym, Sid couldn't have pressed half that weight twenty-five times. Now he was lifting more than his own body weight and it felt great. He didn't look any different, and he hadn't gained a pound. In fact, that had become a running joke between them. But there was no denying he'd gotten pretty damn strong.

They always finished with the bench press. Sid got up from the bench as Woody added fifty pounds to each end of the bar and then positioned himself gracefully underneath it. Without hesitation he lifted the bar, then lowered it to his chest and began. "One. Two. Three."

It just didn't seem fair. The weights glided up and down in Woody's powerful hands like he was lifting a broomstick. At moments like this Sid reminded himself that he could run this cop right into the ground. Sure, Woody could break him in half, but only if he could catch him, and that would never happen.

"Nineteen. Twenty." The pace had hardly slowed as Woody finished. Sid began pushing down on the bar.

"Give me the Brady Bunch kids!" shouted Sid.

Woody set his jaw and dug down deep. He began calling out names, slowing with each repetition. "Greg… Peter… Bobby… Marsha… Jan…"

Sid leaned harder on the bar with each name, and finally the bar stayed on Woody's chest and didn't move.

"What's the matter? That all you've got?"

Woody was breathing hard, but he looked totally calm. "No. Can't think of the name of the one with the pig tails."

Sid gave him a glare, now putting almost his full weight on the bar. "It was Cindy."

"Thank you," Woody flashed him a smile and with a yell he pushed Sid and the weights up one last time and then set them down. He wiped his brow with the sleeve of his shirt and sat up.

"Bastard."

"Yep."

It was at this point every week that both men would grab their gym bags and they'd head for the lockers. Sid began to gather his stuff, but Woody didn't move. Something was up. Sid's troubles with the police hadn't come up the entire time, and he was enjoying not talking about it. That was obviously about to change. Sid sat down on a nearby bench and waited. Maybe thirty seconds went by— Sid staring at Woody, Woody staring at his hands.

"Look, Sid, I'm a good cop and I do what I'm told. It's my job."

Sid had no idea where this was going. "Okay."

"When they asked me not to talk to you last week, that's what I did."

"So why are you talking to me now?"

"Because that's what I was told to do. Last night one of the Homicide Detectives called and asked me to hang out with you. See what I could find out."

"Is his name 'Stokes,' by chance?"

Woody didn't answer.

"Well, officer," said Sid, "Have I incriminated myself?"

"Shut up. I'm your friend. I'm not spying on you."

"You know I didn't do anything, right?"

Again, Woody didn't answer. Didn't move a muscle.

"My sister says that the gun by itself isn't enough evidence."

"It's not just the gun, Sid. Stokes has got more than just the gun."

Woody's words hit him like a two-by-four in the chest. What could he possibly be talking about? A lot of crap had happened. And, sure, Sid had screwed up plenty. But the bottom line was that he hadn't hurt anybody. Hadn't fired a gun in his life and hadn't had anything to do with the shootings.

"Woody, what're you talking about? What could he have? I haven't done anything wrong!"

Woody opened his mouth to speak, but nothing came out. Sid noticed that his friend hadn't stopped staring at his hands. Couldn't look at him in the eye. The cop stood, threw his towel and gloves in his gym bag, and left.

It had been days since Sid had taken a crack at Gloria's homework assignment. He'd almost forgotten about it, but his head was still spinning from what Woody had told him that afternoon. Now it was ten o'clock at night. He held the sheet of paper in his hands and was pacing around his room in his t-shirt and underwear.

There was Jock Bell's name, circled and underlined with the smiley face "O." Joe and Eddie's names had been written and crossed out, Joe's name written again, underlined. He didn't remember underlining that one, but there it was.

For several minutes he stared at the names, willing something new to pop into his head but getting nowhere. His mind wandered repeatedly. He hadn't spoken with Amy since the blow-up on the phone last Saturday. He should call her. What should he do about Lawyer Headley and the blooming news story about the lawsuit? Gloria said to ignore it. On the other hand, maybe he could get some mileage out of it. A little publicity for the deli. He could run a special on the meatloaf sandwiches. Change the name to "Death by Meatloaf." Sid's Deli— the home of Killer Sandwiches…

"C'mon, focus!" He said it out loud and surprised himself. He sounded a little mad. Sid sat down, grabbed a pen and wrote 'Eddie Davis' again below Joe's name and underlined it. He was sure Eddie had nothing to do with anything, but he had to get something else down on the paper and couldn't think of any other names.

Who else? Who else? *Think like Columbo.* Who stood to gain from Sid being in trouble? Or being in jail? Or just being frustrated and pissed off sitting in his room in his underwear staring at a piece of paper? Sid decided that he'd just write down any name that came to mind and sort it out later. *Yeah, that'll work.*

He wrote down the name 'Dominic Gamboa.' Dominic was a pretty fast kid from the high school cross country team. A total jerk who hated the fact that Sid beat him every race for four years. It was ridiculous, of course, but at least there was something new on the page.

Who else? There was the crazy guy who rear-ended him last year at a stop light on Watt Avenue. Completely that guy's fault, but he jumped out of the car screaming like Sid had done something wrong. He'd said he'd kill Sid if his insurance rates went up. What was that guy's name? Sid wrote down, 'Crazy Guy in Trans Am.'

Then he wrote 'Tommy Balfour.' Sid had stolen Tommy's Slinky when they were about six years old and spent an entire afternoon trying to straighten it out with a hammer on his garage floor. If anybody had a right to seek revenge against Sid Bigler, it was Tommy Balfour. But last he'd heard, Tommy was now a Lutheran minister. Still, it was a name and it felt like progress.

Sid's mind wandered briefly from his task. He thought about Stokes asking Woody to spy on him and he caught himself clenching his fist. And he thought about Stokes smugly asking him to check his runner's diary...

There was a thought! Who knew when and where he went running? That whole part of the story seemed like much more than just coincidence. Sid tapped his pen against the paper and squeezed his eyes shut. Who knew his running habits well? Only one name came to mind, and he immediately dismissed it. It was a ridiculous thought. Who else? Who else? But still, just one name fit. At the bottom of his list he wrote, "Amy Solomon."

"Dammit!" He surprised himself again. He dropped the pen, got up and paced the room for several minutes more, allowing a dozen unfocused thoughts to race through his mind. Gradually, his head cleared and his pacing slowed. He sat back down and looked over the list. It occurred to him how funny some of the names were, and he crossed off Tommy, Dominic and the Trans Am guy. That left four names.

Jock Bell. Yeah, lots of reasons he might have something to do with all this. Of the names on the list, that was the one Sid *hoped* was responsible. He had motive and opportunity. And he was creepy.

Joe Diaz. Could Big Sid's oldest and dearest friend be out to frame his son? What for? Maybe Joe felt slighted. Maybe he figured that, if Big Sid was gone, the deli should belong to him. Maybe he didn't like having to answer to a 27-year-old kid after all these years. Maybe he's bitter. Maybe. Maybe. Maybe.

Eddie Davis. This one was just plain silly. Eddie's a criminal mastermind, but has been pretending to not have all his marbles for the last ten years? *Right.* Then again, Yvonne the well-endowed social worker did say he "understands more than you think", or something like that.

And Amy Solomon. How could he leave Amy's name on the paper? Other than the running connection, what was there that justified keeping her name on the list? Maybe she was working in cahoots with Tommy Balfour or Crazy Trans Am guy. Sid grabbed the pen to scratch off Amy's name. But he didn't.

A few minutes later he flipped off the light and crawled in bed. The storm of names and faces that had been blowing through his head slowed to just a breeze, then faded altogether. Thank God he was a good sleeper. His last thought before he dozed off was a dreamy recollection of Woody's final words at the gym. *"They've got more than just the gun."*

CHAPTER 17

11:45 is a crucial time at Sid's Deli every day. The lunch crowd is just starting to pick up, and it's the last chance to make sure the place is stocked and ready for the looming, hungry mob. So it's a lousy time to get arrested.

Every Wednesday was "Chili Day" at Sid's. For an extra fifty cents, they'd put a ladle of chili over whatever you ordered. It was a hit when Big Sid thought of it in 1971, and had made its weekly appearance ever since. Customers generally showed good judgment, adding Joe's Chili to their hamburgers or hot dogs, a grilled cheese sandwich or maybe spread across an order of fries. But occasionally someone would order something disturbing-- Chili Cottage Cheese. Chili Pancakes. Chili Cherry Pie. Sid was in the back room at 11:45, getting a back-up batch of Joe's Chili started—just a giant can of Van de Kamp's Chili & Beans with some brown sugar and bacon added, but it seemed to put a smile on people's faces.

Joe leaned in the doorway and said, "Sid, better come out here."

Sid emerged from the back room to see a half-full deli and his favorite smiling blonde detective standing at the counter. There was another detective with him that Sid recognized from an earlier visit. *Kaminski, maybe?* A uniformed officer stood in the doorway holding the front door open. It took a moment for Sid to realize he wasn't the only one staring at this scene. Every customer in the place was looking up from their menus or plates, mouths slightly open, taking it all in. A police cruiser was parked on the street just outside the front window. The flash of its red lights gave the deli an odd, rhythmic pulse. There was a Snider Volkswagen commercial playing on the radio by the cash register. For some reason, Eddie walked over and turned it off. Silence.

Sid wiped his hands on a towel and made his way to the counter. "Donut, officers?" What the heck. It didn't work the first time. Why not try again?

Stokes gave a little laugh that had to be intentionally fake. "Donut. That's good. You ever heard that one before, Kenny?"

The other detective didn't react, and clearly wasn't enjoying the moment as much as Stokes was.

"Yes," continued Stokes, speaking loud enough for everyone in the place to hear him. "The donut joke is timeless. We cops never get tired of hearing it. And it's made even more enjoyable this morning by the fact that I've got you by the balls, Siddy."

Sid had forgotten how much he disliked being in the presence of Det. Stokes. Their last meeting at his mom's house had not gone well, and this one was starting out badly. The fact that there was an audience this time only made it worse. His pulse began to quicken, and he felt queasy. He remembered that Gloria had told him specifically to not talk to Stokes unless she was present, so he said nothing. Several seconds went by. Sid noticed a group of regulars approach the front door of the deli, see what was going on and walk away. A distant squawk came from the cop car's radio.

"Now this is interesting, Kenny." Stokes spoke to the other cop but his eyes never left Sid's. "I offer some indication that Mr. Bigler here is in trouble—as in, 'got him by the balls'—and he doesn't say a thing. Doesn't ask what I'm talking about, doesn't seem surprised. That seem odd to you, Kenny?"

Again, the second detective showed no reaction. Sid tried to look just as disinterested, but knew he was failing.

"No more funny comments, Mr. Bigler? Why so quiet all of a sudden?"

"My lawyer said I shouldn't speak to you unless she was present."

"Your lawyer. Oh, that's right…" Stokes turned now and looked around the deli, playing the crowd a little. "Mr. Bigler's sister is a hot shot attorney in town. I'm sure she's giving her baby brother very good advice."

Another few seconds passed in uncomfortable silence. Stokes turned back to Sid.

"Well, if you're not going to talk, I will. Sidney Bigler, I'm placing you under arrest. You have the right to remain silent. You have the right to an attorney. If your sister realizes you're a dumbass and won't do it for free, an attorney will be appointed for you. You have the right…"

"Oh, come on, Stokes! What am I charged with?"

"Reckless discharge of a firearm. Shooting at an

inhabited dwelling. Assault with a deadly weapon… "
Stokes paused slightly and gave him a little wink.
"Attempted murder."

As soon as the word "murder" was spoken, the place
started to come unglued. There was an immediate rumble
of conversation, and several people actually got up to
leave. Since the whole Capital Shooter thing started, Sid
had had the profound sensation on a number of
occasions that something terrible was going to happen.
Until this moment it always seemed nebulous. Now it
was crystal clear.

"Wait! No, stop!" Sid came around the counter and
approached the detective. "This is impossible! I really
haven't done anything! Where are you getting 'attempted
murder?'"

Stokes leaned into Sid, his face just inches away.
"You forgetting about the nice bum at Sutter's Fort, Sid?
You shot him in the big toe, but it just as easily could've
been between the eyes."

Sid opened his mouth and tried to say "No," but
hardly a sound came out. He tried harder. "No, it wasn't
me."

" Oh, are you talking now, Sid? I thought we had to
wait for your sister."

Sid glanced around the deli. Some people were still
staring, a few were trying with obvious effort to stop
eavesdropping and return to their food. More were
getting up to leave. He dropped his voice. "Do we have
to do this out here?"

"Oh, of course not, Sid." The mock courtesy was

sickening. "Shall we step into your back room where you keep the guns?"

Both detectives accompanied him into the storage room. On the way Sid made eye contact with Joe, whose expression, though serious, communicated nothing at all. Once inside, Kaminski closed the door. The second detective still hadn't spoken a word. Maybe he was just playing it that way for effect, but Sid had the sense that this guy didn't like being around Stokes any more than he did. For some reason he found the idea comforting.

"How can you arrest me? I thought the gun wasn't going to prove anything." Sid realized as he said it that this was a bad opening line.

"And who told you that?" asked Stokes. "Big sister?"

Sid waited.

"Here's what I'll do," Stokes continued, slightly warmer. "You answer a few questions for me, Sid, and then I'll tell you exactly what evidence I have that has led to your arrest. Will that be okay?"

"Sure."

"Alright, then. Where'd you get the gun?"

Sid paused, thought about Gloria's instructions. As long as he gave short answers, and only answered truthfully, how could he make a mistake?

"It's not my gun. I'd never seen it before you pulled it out of that drawer."

"Okay. If you'd never seen it before, then can I assume you are not the crazy son-of-a-bitch that shot up the State Capitol, City Hall, the Chevy dealer, Sutter's

Fort and Fairytale Town?"

"Of course not."

"You were there at the Capitol and the old fort when the shootings happened."

"Yes."

"But the last one—the one at the park—did you see that one?"

Sid didn't want to lie again, and he was clearly entering an area where he should talk with Gloria before answering. But then something occurred to him that he thought would've made his big sister proud. Stokes hadn't asked him if he was at the park when the last shooting happened. He had said, 'Did you *see* that one?' The fact was, it was dark and Sid hadn't *seen* a thing. Convinced he was making a good decision, he answered.

"No."

"Really? That surprises me, Sid." Stokes reached behind his coat somewhere and pulled out a pair of handcuffs. "That's all I need to hear for now. Let's go downtown, Sid. You can call your sister from there."

If anything about the last ten minutes had been surreal, it all became very real when Sid saw the handcuffs.

"But... wait! You said you had some kind of evidence. You said you..."

Sid's voice trailed off as the cuffs clicked into place, his wrists now bound in front of him.

"Had you by the balls," Stokes finished the thought. "Yeah, it took us a few days, but we managed to track down where the gun came from. It was purchased at a gun show in Reno. You've heard about those, right Sid? Gun shops and independent dealers take over the convention center. Hunters, gun collectors and various kooks all show up to look at the pretty guns. And it's a great way to sneak out of California and buy a cheap pistol in a hurry."

Sid stared at him like he was speaking Latin.

"The gun that I found in your filing cabinet—the one that was used to shoot up the city—it was bought in Reno three weeks ago. We got the bill of sale. You wanna know who bought that gun?"

Sid did what he should have done all along. He kept his mouth shut.

Stokes put a hand on Sid's back and began leading him to the door. Kaminski pushed the door open and stepped aside.

"The name on the paperwork is Sidney Bigler. You bought that gun."

There was no time to respond to Stokes' incredible statement. With the words 'you bought that gun' ringing in his ears, the next few minutes went by as a blur of images and sounds.

As they stepped back into the deli, there was a flash. Sid glanced up to see Jackson Dexter with a camera in his hand. It looked like the same Hawaiian shirt he'd been wearing last week.

At some point Joe Diaz stepped in front of Det. Stokes, turned to look Sid in the eye, and said, "I know you didn't do nothing wrong." Sid would remember that later and wonder about it.

Jackson Dexter's camera flashed again, and Stokes continued leading Sid to the door. Eddie flipped the radio back on and watched with his curious smile.

Outside the deli, the uniformed officer was waiting, and he put a hand on top of Sid's head as he guided him into the squad car. The door closed and Sid sat alone in the back seat. He couldn't make out what was being said, but just outside the door Stokes appeared to be giving some final instructions to Kaminski and the younger cop.

Sid looked through the wire mesh and out the windshield. Standing on the sidewalk in front of the car was Jock Bell. The collar was turned up on a tight yellow polo shirt that was tucked into a tight pair of white jeans. A sea captain's hat sat atop the pile of dark brown hair. Thurston Howell at the disco.

The uniformed officer opened the driver's door, slid in and started the car. He put it into gear and there was a flash outside Sid's window as Dexter got one more shot of the city's most famous felon.

Somebody tapped on the opposite window. Sid turned to see Stokes give him a wave and a phony smile.

Sid looked to his right once more as the cruiser pulled away. Jock Bell raised his right hand and gave him the finger.

CHAPTER 18

Nathan Bomke was born to do great things. The only child of two college professors, he was walking at eight months old, potty trained at a year and a half, and selling marijuana to his friends when he was just ten. Impressive. Nathan scored a combined 1540 on the S.A.T. even with a pretty serious hangover, and managed to get through UCSF in three years with a 4.0 grade point average. He was the youngest person to ever graduate from Boalt Law School, and was only 25 when he hit on *the great idea.*

Nathan always knew that he was special somehow, and that one day *the great idea* would come to him and it would be easy street after that. He was just too clever to have to work a normal job, do the normal things to get by in life. One day he'd hit it big. It was this confidence that allowed him to glide along through life, not applying what was certainly his extraordinary intellect and ability. It gave him permission to coast through high school, spend most of his college and law school days in a drunken fraternity stupor, and then to handle just enough accident and injury cases to live comfortably. Compared to Nathan Bomke, Vince Headley was a regular Oliver Wendell Holmes. What did it matter? Eventually *the great idea* would come along and after that he wouldn't have to work at all.

One day, in a rare moment when he was actually doing some research for a client, Nathan came across an interesting case— Mitchell v. Standeford. The Standefords were a wealthy family determined to spoil their kids, and so had hired a children's entertainer to come to little Kenneth's sixth birthday party. Jason Mitchell (a.k.a. Looby the Clown) was just about to pull something amusing out of his oversized clown pants when the railing on the back patio gave way. The kids cheered as Looby broke his leg in three places and bit off the end of his tongue. When all was said and done, the Standefords paid out four hundred thousand dollars and bought Looby a new Monte Carlo.

And so was born *the great idea*.

Within just a few days of reading the article, Nathan Bomke had recruited two trustworthy and unemployed fraternity brothers from college to be his clown assistants. Before a year had gone by, there had been eight very unfortunate accidents at the homes of eight very wealthy patrons in eight different counties in California. All eight had settled out of court, and Nathan Bomke's net worth was now approaching two million dollars.

Nathan was thinking it was just about time to call it quits and head off to Cabo San Lucas for a few years when something terrible happened. His buddy Carl (a.k.a. Jimmo the Clown) was doing a fairly crappy job of entertaining nine second-graders at the home of Robert and Gwen Merriweather in Carmel. The fake clown was looking around for a good opportunity to slip and fall as the caterer was bringing out a cake in the shape of a giant PacMan. The scammers had discovered that the arrival of a flaming birthday cake was an excellent distraction, and so an ideal time to take a spill. Unfortunately, the family's Dalmatian chose just that moment to jump up on Carl/Jimmo, pushing him face first into the cake. Thinking it was part of the act, kids and adults clapped and laughed until the clown's petroleum based make-up was ignited by the candles and the entire scene turned into something from a low-budget slasher movie. By the time the servants managed to extinguish Jimmo, the red nylon wig was melted into his scalp and a good portion of the skin on his face was missing. It was several days before Nathan's college friend was able to communicate with the police, but he managed to say a lot through the bandages.

And that's why Nathan Bomke found himself sitting in the Sacramento County Jail, facing fraud and extortion charges and waiting to make bail. He was sharing his temporary new home with a skinny, 27-year-old guy with red hair and a long face. The guy hadn't said a word since the cops had brought him in half an hour earlier.

"We know each other?" asked Nathan.

"No. No, I don't think so," answered Sid.

"Seems like I've seen you before."

"Yeah, I've got one of those faces."

Sid tried hard to make himself invisible, but his cellmate kept staring at him. Where was Gloria? He'd called her when they were booking him, and she said she'd be down right away. She'd said to not worry, and to not say anything. Not talking sounded good to him, but the fellow in the cell with him had other plans.

"I got it," Nathan Bomke said with a smile. "The paper. I've seen you in the paper."

Sid tried to change the subject. "Anybody ever tell you you look like Lee Majors?"

"I'm pretty good with faces," Nathan was undaunted. "You were in the paper just yesterday, right?"

Hmm. This is not what Sid was expecting. The Capital Shooter story was more than two weeks old, and there hadn't been a word about it in yesterday's paper. He'd looked for it.

"Yeah, I'm sure it's you. You're the one being sued by the fat guy. It is you!" And then Nathan laughed hard. "That's so awesome. God, fat boy's attorney had the great idea!"

"Yeah. Awesome." Sid clearly didn't share Nathan's enthusiasm.

"Oh, c'mon, man. Don't take it so personal. The guy's a lawyer. He's looking for work just like anybody else. You need customers in your restaurant, he needs customers, too."

Sid stared at the guy in disbelief. If he'd stopped to think about it, he probably would have been grateful that this jerk had gotten his mind on something else. He actually found himself getting a little mad.

"Are you kidding me?"

"Really, it's not that big of a deal. Trust me, I'm a lawyer, too. Nathan Bomke."

As he said his name, Nathan stuck out his hand and produced a fairly genuine smile. Sid didn't want to shake it, but couldn't think of a reason not to.

"Sid Bigler."

"Yeah, 'Sid's Deli,' right? I read that in the paper yesterday and I thought, 'Do I know any gigantic, fat people?' Really, the guy's got a great idea."

"No, it's not great. He wants ten thousand dollars!" Sid was raising his voice now.

"Is that all? It's worth a lot more." Nathan grinned and pulled his chair closer. "Oh, relax, Sid. It's not like it's your money. You got insurance, right?"

Sid was taken aback by the question for two reasons. First, it was just so absurd—the thought that taking money you didn't deserve was okay just because it came from some faceless insurance company. And secondly, Sid did not, in fact, know if he had insurance. His mom still paid all the deli's bills and handled all the paperwork. It never occurred to Sid to wonder about insurance until just now.

"Look," Nathan continued, "there's a certain amount of funds that every company allocates simply as the cost of doing business. It adds up to a big pile of money, and somebody's gonna end up with it. If I don't get some of it, the bastards at the insurance company get to keep it all, and that's not fair. C'mon, they expect to pay out some of it. It's in their business plan. What I do is just a part of the beautiful monetary food chain that is Capitalism."

"You are a parasite, and that is a load of crap." Sid was rarely glib, but he thought he got that one just right.

Nathan Bomke shrugged. "Tomato, *Tomahto*."

And with that last, clarifying thought by the crooked lawyer, the two of them sat quietly, each sure that the other's view of the world was simplistic and one-sided. Sid looked at his socks, wiggled his toes. They'd taken his shoes and his belt along with his wallet and watch when he was booked. Perhaps fifteen minutes elapsed in silence, and Sid was just beginning to wonder how much longer he could avoid using the sure-to-be-humiliating metal toilet in the corner of the cell when the door to the outer room opened and Gloria walked in followed by a uniformed officer.

"I'm really sorry, sis."

"And you're an idiot."

"Yes. I'm an idiot, and I'm really sorry."

After a splendid bathroom break, Sid found himself sitting across a table from Gloria in a small, private room. She reached over and took one of his hands.

"I'd love to dwell for a while on the fact that you're an idiot, but I'm already late for a meeting with a huge client. I'm going to ask you some questions and we're going to get out of here."

"I get to leave?"

"You made bail."

"Thank you."

Gloria gave his hand a good squeeze, then pulled a pen and a yellow legal pad from her leather brief case and dropped it on the table.

"Short answers, tell me the truth. Did you buy that

gun?"

"No! No, of course not. I told you the first day that cop came in…"

Gloria held up a finger and he stopped in mid-sentence. "Short answers."

"I didn't buy the gun. It's not my gun."

"Where were you on February 8th?"

"I don't know. What's February 8th?"

"It's the day somebody thinks you made a purchase at a gun show in Reno. They'll have to get us a copy of the Dealer Record of Sale. It'd be good if we could prove you were somewhere else. Check on that."

"Okay."

"Have you thought about who might want to make it look like you've done all these shootings?"

"Yeah, but I don't have much."

"Well try harder. Who could've put the gun there? Did Dad give a key to anybody in the past? Any disgruntled former employees we don't know about? Does the deli have any outstanding debts? Any competing restaurants nearby that stand to gain from you closing up the place? Anybody trying to blackmail you, maybe?"

About half-way through that list of questions, Sid's mind had started to wander. *How could Gloria just spit out so many smart and obvious questions off the top of her head? And why hadn't he asked them himself as he paced around his bedroom at night trying to figure this all out?* The two Bigler kids came from opposite ends of the gene pool…

"Sid. Sid, are you paying attention?"

"Yeah. Yeah, I'll work on that stuff some more."

"Okay, I really have to go. One more question. Besides me, who knows you were at Fairytale Town the night of the shooting?"

"Nobody."

Gloria set down her pen and crossed her arms. She gave him a familiar look. It was the one she first gave him in 1967 when he told her he had no idea who had painted the cat.

"Honest, I haven't told anybody else. You and I are the only ones who know."

"You're wrong about that, little brother." Gloria slid the pen and notepad into her briefcase and stood up. "Whoever bought that gun and put it in the filing cabinet—I bet they know you were there."

They came through the double doors and into the afternoon sunshine. Sid had never thought about what it'd be like to get sprung from prison, but it felt good.

"I've got to get to that meeting," Gloria said. "I won't be able to give you a lift back to the deli."

"No big deal. It's only about six blocks. I'll walk it."

"No, I arranged for somebody to give you a ride."

Sid looked up and saw a familiar red Karmann Ghia parked by the curb. Leaning against it with hands on her hips and a warm smile was Amy Solomon.

CHAPTER 19

Amy's first words when Sid got to the car were, "Dallas was really good on Saturday." Sid's first words were, "I love you." It was the first time either one had said it out loud, and the moment was not lost on them.

The drive to 11th & K took exactly three minutes. It had taken a few seconds for the two of them to get past Sid's profession of love—a moment that was both awkward and wonderful at the same time. Sid was at least as surprised as Amy that he'd said it. Maybe his time spent in The Big House had given him a new perspective. *Yes, two hours and fifteen minutes behind bars can change a man.* Sid Bigler—Ex-Con Philosopher.

As she drove, Amy appeared to be trying hard to avoid the subject of Sid's arrest. She did all of the talking, updating him on the lives of the Ewings of Southfork Ranch. She found a parking spot half a block from the deli, pulled in and turned off the car. Neither made a move to open their door. Sid spoke first.

"So, have you decided I'm not dangerous?"

"I never thought that. I was just scared. That creepy blonde cop scared me. He said things about you that I knew weren't true but…" Amy didn't know how to finish the sentence.

"It's okay."

"I was thinking of calling you when Gloria called me. Honest."

"Well, thanks for coming to get me out of the lock-up."

"I thought your sister didn't like me."

"Oh, no, she likes you a lot. Really."

Neither one was sure Sid was telling the truth, but neither one wanted to press the issue.

"I've got some stuff to do tonight," Amy said, "but how about dinner tomorrow?"

"And Dallas on Saturday."

"Done." The corners of Amy's mouth turned up slightly, then she leaned over and planted a very convincing kiss on Sid Bigler. He ran the tip of his tongue along the edge of her big front teeth and his right hand slid up her ribs. Both of them said "Mmmm."

Sid hopped out of the Ghia feeling better than he had in days and decided to walk past the deli before heading to his car. It was 4 p.m., and it occurred to him that he was the only person to have locked up the deli each day since they reopened. As he approached it, he could see that the lights were off and the 'Sorry, Closed' sign was facing out. *Looks like Joe and Eddie did fine without me*, he thought. Just for kicks he gave the doorknob a twist as he passed by and he stopped in his tracks when the door swung open.

Sid stepped into the deli. People passed back and forth on the sidewalk behind him, and a city bus rumbled by. The place was dark and quiet. Sid closed the door, and was just going to make sure the register was empty when a voice nearly made him jump out of his skin.

"You okay?"

It took Sid a long moment to realize that Joe Diaz had been sitting still as a statue at the counter. He hadn't even turned his head when he spoke. Sid had let out a yelp at first as his heart rate tripled. "Oh, jeez, Joe. I didn't see you there."

Joe lifted a Budweiser and took a long drink, then turned to Sid. "You okay?"

Sid stood still and felt his heart pounding hard. Slowing down, but still a good, steady thump, thump, thump. "Yeah. Yeah, I'm good."

Joe held the tall Bud bottle between his huge hands on the counter. "Your sister told me she'd get you out before the day was over. I thought you might come back by."

Joe took another pull from the beer and said no more. Sid had no idea what to do with the information. Didn't know if he should respond or not. So he waited. After what seemed like a long time, Joe spoke again.

"We should talk."

"Yeah. Sure."

Sid went behind the counter, filled a glass with Coke—no ice—then circled back around and sat two stools down from Joe. Taking the one right next to him would've felt too close. He drank down half the soda all at once, stopping when he felt a good burn in his throat. He set the glass down and let out a satisfying, "Ahhhh." Then it was quiet again.

"So…" Sid started to speak but realized he really

had nothing to say, so the word just hung there. It was Joe who had said they should talk, but Joe showed no signs of initiating a conversation. Each stared at his respective beverage. Sid racked his brain trying to come up with a good conversation starter.

It occurred to him that maybe he should ask the question Gloria asked the day Stokes first visited the deli. What the hell. Might as well get it out of the way.

"Did that gun the cops found in the storage room belong to you?"

"No."

Joe Diaz said it without hesitation, and without expression. And something about his reply didn't invite further discussion. So the deli returned to silence. Sid took another sip of Coke. Joe drained his Bud.

In the afternoon light, Sid studied the photos on the wall behind the counter. There were a few pictures that were clearly from sometime before he was born. A boxer and a couple of movie star head shots. Sid recognized Sam Yorty and the guy who played Jethro from the Beverly Hillbillies. And Walt Disney, too. Sid remembered the day he got home from school and his dad handed him a drawing of Mickey Mouse that Walt had done on a paper napkin. "To Sid & Gloria with Best Wishes, Walt Disney." Where was that napkin now? Gloria probably had it.

"Your dad wasn't perfect, but he was the best man I ever knew."

Joe's words brought Sid back to the deli, and they were spoken like it was the last line of some great oratory.

Sid considered for the first time that this awkward attempt at conversation might be harder for Joe than it was for him. For all he knew, Joe had been sitting there for hours, struggling to put together the right words, searching for a way to tell his dead friend's son something important. And that sentence—*Your dad wasn't perfect, but he was the best man I ever knew*—that was the conclusion, the result of his struggling. Sid noticed that there were three empty Buds in addition to the one Joe still clutched.

"First time I saw Big Sid he was gettin' the shit beat out of him by a couple of Marines near the port in New York."

Joe was still looking at his empty beer. Or maybe his hands. Or maybe nothing at all. There were long pauses between sentences, but this was apparently how Joe spoke, when he finally got around to talking. Sid had never seen it before. He kept quiet.

"Your dad was full of piss and vinegar, and he was shootin' off his mouth and puttin' up a pretty good fight. But there was two of them, and he was gettin' beat pretty bad. I just watched for a minute. Then I saw a little Puerto Rican gal kinda crouched down nearby, real scared."

This time Joe's pause lasted longer. Maybe a minute. Sid couldn't wait.

"What happened?"

"I stepped in and the jarheads backed off. Turns out Big Sid came up on these guys as they were gettin' rough with the girl, and he told 'em to knock it off. So they started beatin' on him. Most guys wouldn't have said

152

nothin.'"

Another long pause, like Joe was all done. But then he spoke again.

"Big Sid looked like hell. But he put on his cap, walked over to check on that Puerto Rican gal. She didn't speak a lot of English, but she spoke enough. Them two went off together arm in arm."

A grin crept across Joe's face. He turned for the first time and looked at Sid. Sid grinned, too.

"I won't tell mom."

"He was the best man I ever knew."

This time it really felt like he'd said all he had to say. Joe began to pick at the label on the beer bottle. Sid studied him for a few moments. He thought about Joe and his dad, maybe nineteen or twenty, thrown together by chance and saving the world together almost forty years ago. Was there anybody he knew at that moment that would still be in his life forty years from now? Amy? Maybe.

"Why'd you tell me that story, Joe?"

Joe continued to pick at the label. At first it seemed like a thoughtful pause, but after a while Sid decided that either Joe didn't know or didn't want to answer.

"You know anything about what's been happening?" Sid asked. "The shootings?"

Sid was surprised to see Joe's smile return briefly as he worked intently on the Budweiser label. But it only lasted a moment. Joe slid the bottle away on the counter, forcing himself to stop picking at it. He turned and looked Sid squarely in the eyes.

"I can't say nothin'."

"What's that mean?"

"Means I can't say nothin'."

Joe slid off the stool and headed for the door, and Sid watched him go. He sat alone in silence for a minute or more, then spoke again.

"What's that mean?"

CHAPTER 20

Sid probably should've turned back already, but it just felt too good.

"Chili Day" had been quite eventful: handcuffed and hauled away in front of his customers, his time in jail with Nate Bomke, and the very odd conversation with Joe Diaz. And he had told Amy that he loved her. Maybe he should've had her name tattooed on his arm while he was in the slammer.

By the time he'd gotten home, his mom was heading out the door for an early dinner before going to her Eastern Star meeting. Sid gave her a kiss and decided not to tell Rose that her only son was now an ex-con. He made himself a salad and a big glass of Ovaltine, and by seven o'clock he was out the door wearing just a pair of shorts and some old Adidas. The first couple of miles felt lousy, but then came that familiar moment when the fog cleared and it became almost effortless. It's like he had been running through oatmeal, and now he was on roller skates. He was probably eight miles from home, cruising down Fair Oaks Boulevard with the sun setting behind him and no thoughts of turning back for home. Traffic was fairly light, His breathing was steady and comfortable, and the Beatles' *Octopus's Garden* had found its way into his brain a few miles back. *Who sang that one? Ringo?*

Yeah, it was probably Ringo…

The light at Watt Avenue turned green just as he approached. Sid grinned and took it as a sign to keep going. He was just clearing the intersection when a sharp, familiar noise made him stop and sent his heart racing.

Bang-Bang!

Sid whirled around to see a rusty Plymouth Valiant spewing smoke as it pulled out behind him. Bang! The car made the noise again and died. The guy behind the wheel cursed loudly and threw a lit cigarette out the window. He looked like Archie's son-in-law from *All in the Family*. Sid watched the guy struggle to re-start the car and pull away as the light turned yellow. Sid was shiny with sweat, and his heart was pounding. Ringo had stopped singing in his head.

"Crap," he said. Sometimes the good thing about a great run—about being in the zone—is that everything else in the world goes away. For a little while, there's only running and rhythm. And sometimes Octopus's Garden. But all of it was gone in a moment, and the events of the last two weeks began to press in around him. There was no specific thought, just the general realization that life had gone wrong and now his run was ruined, too. He turned toward home and said it again. "Crap."

After a mile or so of making a conscious effort to put one foot in front of the other, he started to get his stride back. It wasn't the magic of six or seven minutes earlier, but it felt pretty good. Only now his mind wasn't wandering. The sky ahead of him was turning a deep orange as Sid Bigler ran toward home. He found himself focusing on the Capital Shooter— whoever the hell he was— and the questions that Gloria had asked him that afternoon played in his mind. It had just been a few hours earlier. What were her questions?

"Who could've put the gun there?" The more he thought about it, the more he was certain that just about anyone could have done it. It's not like Sid's Deli had any kind of security plan. His father had built the success of the place on the perception that customers were treated like friends and everybody treated the deli like it was their own. Regulars still wandered to the back room to make a phone call or use the bathroom without anyone giving it a thought. Off the top of his head he could easily name twenty or more people who would just walk behind the counter to refill their own coffee or grab some ketchup.

There was a new thought. If a stranger was wandering around in the back, surely he would have noticed. So was it someone familiar that planted the gun in the cabinet? Roy and Matt were there all the time, usually just having coffee and playing a game of cribbage for an hour in the morning. What about Denise, the big-haired life insurance lady who met a different client for lunch at the deli probably twice a week? Or Sudhir the urologist or Marvin the cab driver or that guy who worked at Macy's who looked just like Richard Pryor? For a couple of miles the names and faces of various regulars popped into Sid's mind. State workers and RT bus drivers, lobbyists and commercial real estate agents. There was that bald guy who got pretty upset when they took the pot roast sandwich off the menu. And Jerry

157

Brown had stopped in for some Navy Bean Soup last week. Maybe he had one of his security goons drop a gun in the filing cabinet when he was securing the place before the Governor entered. Hmm. Perhaps Sid had taken this line of thought about as far as it was going to go for now.

What were Gloria's other questions? *"Does the deli have any outstanding debts?"* How was he supposed to know? He only worked at the place. Until all this trouble started, Sid hadn't given a thought to the fact that he wasn't really running the deli. His mom still did the books and wrote the checks. Joe ordered the supplies and did all the cooking. What was Sid's role there? It occurred to him that Eddie was more indispensable to the place than he was. He resolved to take on more of the day to day responsibilities of Sid's Deli. He'd get on that right away. Unless he ended up in jail.

"Any competing restaurants nearby that stand to gain from you closing up the place?" This one sounded like a good question, but as he thought about it, it felt like a dead end. The closest place to the deli where somebody could get a bite to eat was a little coffee and donut shop that was even closer to the Capitol, but they weren't really competitors. That was just a stand-up place—just a counter and a cash register. Didn't even have any tables. Within a couple of blocks of the deli there had to be six or seven places that you could get breakfast or lunch—it was the heart of downtown. But Sid couldn't remember there ever being a problem with any of them. There was a lunch counter at the Woolworth's at the other end of

the block. Surely the Woolworth's people had better things to do than frame Sid Bigler. And the more prestigious political hang-outs—Frank Fat's Restaurant and The Senator Hotel—what did they care about Sid's Deli? Nope, nothing there made sense.

"Anybody trying to blackmail you, maybe?" Sid thought as he had several times in the last week or so that it just wasn't worth some bad guy's time to trouble with someone like him. He simply wasn't significant enough to have acquired any enemies. Certainly not enemies that would have gone to all the trouble to make it appear as though Sid was the Capital Shooter. That was the kind of thing that happens in movies, and his life seemed entirely too unremarkable.

Sid struggled to think if there was anything else that Gloria had asked him. It seemed like he was missing something.

"Did Dad give a key to anybody in the past? Any disgruntled former employees we don't know about?" That one was anybody's guess. He couldn't think of any other employees, but Big Sid trusted everybody. Would he have given someone a key? Why would they need it? About a year ago an old Navy buddy of his dad's had shown up—Cliff? Cliffy. The guy hung out at the deli all the time, even came home with his dad sometimes. Young Sid had his own life at the time and hadn't paid much attention, but he remembered now that his mom was very vocal in her dislike for Cliffy. Dad was letting the guy eat for free, claiming that he helped out at the deli. Mom said he was just a freeloader. Apparently,

Rose finally really put her foot down, which rarely happened but when it did it was significant. Big Sid told Cliffy he couldn't hang around so much and he couldn't eat without paying, and Cliffy didn't take it well. There was a big scene after lunch one day at the deli, and Dad's old Navy buddy hadn't been back since. So did Cliffy have a key?

The problem was that the best person to talk to about all this would be Joe Diaz, and talking to Joe was, to put it generously, difficult. Sid had always known that to be true, but it was made especially clear earlier that afternoon when they had their first real conversation, if you could call it that.

What had that been about anyway? Joe had clearly hung around the deli to have a talk with him, then he'd hardly said anything. He'd said that Big Sid was the best man he ever knew and he told the story of how they met. Was there some genuine significance to what he'd said, or was that just four Budweisers talking?

Sid didn't realize it, but his pace had quickened. This line of thought felt like it was getting him closer to some kind of answer. But whatever it was, it was still hidden and he had no idea what he might be getting closer to. He strained to remember exactly what had been said just a couple of hours ago as they sat together in the closed deli. He'd asked Joe if he knew anything about what was going on, and Joe said that he didn't. No. No, that wasn't right. He hadn't said that he didn't *know* anything, just that he couldn't *say* anything. And he'd smiled right before that, right?

For the third time that day he asked aloud, "What's that mean?" This time he said it between steady, deep breaths as he cruised past the entrance to the university on J Street. With a mixture of suspicion and frustration, Sid's thoughts focused more intently on Joe Diaz. That cryptic ending to their conversation really began to weigh on him. If Joe knew something about the events of the last two weeks, why wouldn't he talk? Unless he had something to do with them. And if he didn't, at least he could help answer some of those questions that Gloria had posed earlier today. Dammit. Joe could be a lot of help right now, but for some reason he wasn't.

Thoughts like these ran through Sid's mind the rest of the way home. And his questions gradually became broader. Bigger and more important. Questions from six months ago. Joe was Big Sid's closest friend in the world. What about his father's gambling debts? And what else might have been going on in Big Sid's life that would lead him to put a gun to his head? Joe had never talked about any of that. Could he answer those questions? And if he could, would he?

CHAPTER 21

It was just a few minutes before 6 a.m. and Sid was making his way along the empty sidewalk toward the deli. Once he got used to the early hours, this had become a time that he really enjoyed every day. It was dark and quiet, and the five or six block walk from his favorite free parking spaces let him stretch his legs from the previous night's run. Given the events of yesterday, it had been a surprisingly normal morning so far. Up just before five, shower, shave and blow-dry, out the door in forty minutes.

He recalled with a smile his conversation with his mom after he got home last night. Knowing that it was unavoidable, he had started to tell her everything that had been happening in recent weeks, but it quickly became clear that Gloria had been keeping her informed all along. Rose O'Brien Bigler could keep a secret. He didn't bring up the subject of whether or not he had actually witnessed that last shooting at Fairytale Town, and his mom didn't ask. He realized now as he walked through the cool morning air that her words to him last Saturday morning were more serious and precious than he could appreciate at the time. *"Siddy, you know you can talk to me about anything."* She was a great mom. Surely she'd come visit him in jail...

In the moonlight he noticed a homeless guy curled up asleep at the base of a tree by the sidewalk in Capitol Park. He had a blanket bunched up around his shoulders and about four inches of butt crack showed above some jeans that were way too big for him. Sid walked over and straightened out the blanket, pulling it down in the interest of modesty and warmth. A steady, droning snore assured him that the guy was alive. If he had time before the deli opened he'd run some coffee and a sandwich out to him.

Sid did his usual jaywalk in the dark across L Street and then stopped in his tracks as he rounded the corner at 11th. At this hour of the day it should've just been him and the bums downtown. But up ahead, at the entrance to Sid's Deli, there was a small crowd waiting outside the door. It looked like eight or ten people. Some of them carried notebooks and some carried TV cameras. Sid Bigler was back in the news.

He was still half a block away when someone must have recognized him, because bright lights snapped on above the video cameras and a din of voices began shouting questions as he approached. He actually recognized a couple of the reporters from the local TV stations, and it struck him as so odd that these famous people would be bothering with someone like him.

"Mr. Bigler, are you the Capital Shooter?" "Sid, why were you arrested yesterday?" "Sid, the police say they found a gun here at the deli. Is that the gun you used?" "Mr. Bigler…" "Sid…" "Mr. Bigler…"

He must have said "No comment" twenty-five times

before he managed to get into the store and lock the door behind him. Good news travels fast. The blinds in the front windows were only partially closed, and shafts of light squeezed between them as the TV guys tried to get a shot of the suspect inside the deli. Sid closed each of the blinds tightly and took a deep breath.

From the time he'd been arrested yesterday until the time he turned the corner at 11th this morning, countless thoughts had run through his head. But for some reason it never crossed his mind that the Media Circus was about to set up its tent again, only this time it would be much, much worse. Before, he was just a witness—someone who had seen the star, but not the star himself. Now he really was the Main Attraction. He was the Bearded Lady and the Two-Headed Snake. The Tightrope Walker, the Lion Tamer and the Human Cannonball, all rolled into one.

Lacking a better idea, Sid resolved to go about his life. He flipped on the lights and began setting up the deli for the day's business. As he took chairs down from the tables and wiped down counters, he found himself increasingly resolved to not be victimized by whatever storms were on their way. He hadn't done anything wrong, unless you count lying to the cops, and at the moment that didn't seem to count. He certainly hadn't done the things that the rabid crowd of reporters outside the front door suspected. Sid plugged in the radio. Dusty Morgan said the temp would be jumping up near a hundred over the weekend, and then Joni Mitchell began singing about paving Paradise and putting up a parking lot.

Most mornings Joe and Eddie were there by a little after six, but it was almost 6:30 when Sid heard a commotion outside the front door and his co-workers pushed their way through the crowd and into the deli. Once again bright light from the TV cameras filled the room, and then it was gone as the door closed behind them. Joe's jaw was set in a way that said, 'Don't screw with me.' Eddie looked like he always did, his smile unfazed by the crowd and noise.

As if nothing were out of the ordinary, Joe mumbled "Sorry we're running late" as he picked up his soiled apron from the place he'd dropped it yesterday and got to work behind the counter. Eddie grabbed the clean silverware tub and a stack of napkins and began setting tables. Sid hadn't expected any reaction from Eddie, but it was kind of weird how the two of them just got busy with their work like it was any other morning.

"Crazy out there, huh?" Sid said.

"Yeah. Gotta expect that, I guess." Joe genuinely seemed unconcerned by the commotion and unchanged by the events of yesterday. It was just another Thursday at the deli.

Sid walked to the cash register to be nearer to Joe and lowered his voice. "I need to talk to you about some stuff." Then it occurred to him that there was probably no need to lower his voice, since the only other person in the room was Eddie. But it still felt right.

"I'm late getting set up. Maybe later."

"How about after we close?"

"No. I gotta get Theresa to a doctor's appointment."

And that was it. Joe was all done talking. Sid had spent the final fifteen minutes of last night's run convincing himself that Joe somehow held the key to all the mysteries in his life, and now the conversation was over. In his frustration, he vented a little sarcasm towards someone who didn't deserve it.

"Well that's fine, Joe. Then maybe I'll have a nice talk with Eddie." He said it loudly and regretted it immediately.

At the sound of his name, Eddie looked up from his silverware task. Sid saw the smile, and even a look of anticipation. Eddie left his job and started walking towards Sid, expecting some new instructions.

"No, Eddie. I was just… It's nothing."

Eddie stopped and stood in the middle of the deli. From Sid's experience, the man was incapable of looking confused, but he clearly didn't know what was expected of him. Eddie just stood and looked at Sid. In his clear eyes, there was, unquestionably, no capacity for malice or deceit. He looked completely at peace, waiting to be told what to do.

"You're doing a great job, Eddie. Finish up with the silverware."

Eddie turned and went back to setting the tables, and Sid felt lower at that moment than at any time in recent memory. Worse than the break-up call with Amy. Worse than sitting in the back of the squad car. In his mind, he scratched Eddie off of his list of suspects. For now, at least.

At two minutes after seven o'clock, Sid unlocked the door and swung it wide open. The sun was up now, but still the bright lights clicked on above the cameras. He loudly announced: "Welcome to Sid's Deli. We reserve the right to refuse service to anyone. No cameras allowed. And if you're not eating, don't come in." With that, he pulled the door closed and headed behind the counter. Eddie was in the back helping Joe with some restocking. He was alone out front and he felt remarkably calm.

A couple of minutes went by in silence. There were still people milling around outside, but the camera lights were off and nobody was coming in. Were they just going to hang around the front door all day?

Eventually the door opened and Sid again recognized a couple of local TV reporters. Chet Somebody and Don Somebody. Channel 3 and Channel 13.

"Can we come in?" It was Don Somebody who spoke.

"We're open," Sid spread his arms indicating that the place was all theirs.

The two exchanged glances and walked over to the counter as the door closed behind them. Sid set out a couple of coffee cups.

"Coffee?"

"Yeah. Sure."

"You guys got fifty cents apiece?"

The reporters smiled and Sid poured. Here he was, schmoozing away like it was any other day and these were any other customers.

"Can we ask you a few questions?" Chet Somebody took the lead.

"Nope."

"No?"

"Nope. No comment."

Sid had seen these guys plenty of times on the news. He was struck by the fact that they looked so much better on TV. Chet had on a brown sport coat with navy blue slacks and a tie that matched neither. Up close he could see that the guy was not gifted with a razor, and had missed several spots shaving. Don's suit looked like it hadn't seen a coat hanger since the day he bought it, and there were some food stains on his shirt.

"What can I get you fellas?" Sid asked as he clicked his pen and grabbed an order pad off the counter.

"Just the coffee is fine."

"Well, today and today only, Sid's Deli has a two dollar minimum order." If media clowns were going to ruin Sid's day, he might as well make some money.

"Can you do that?" Chet asked.

"Probably," Sid smiled. "You wanna stay, you gotta pay." It sounded pretty good.

The TV stooges both ordered bacon and eggs, then talked in hushed tones over the next forty-five minutes as they ate. Their only conversation with Sid had to do with coffee refills and asking for Tabasco. They didn't try to ask any more questions, but they appeared determined to hang around. *Working their beat*, Sid thought.

On a normal morning, there would be a dozen or

more customers having breakfast and chatting by 7:30, but on this morning more than forty minutes had gone by and it was still just the two reporters. What was up? Probably the cameras out front keeping people away.

At a quarter to eight the first regular came through the door. It was Pete, the big guy who loved the Brown Sugar Rolls, and he had a newspaper in his hand. Joe looked up from the grill.

"Hey, Pete!" Sid was genuinely happy to see a customer.

But Pete was not his normal, jovial self. He headed straight for the counter and dropped the paper down facing Sid. Sid looked at the headline and swallowed hard.

"What's going on, Sid Jr.?"

Pete had been coming into the deli for as long as Sid could remember. He'd been close to his father. He was as regular and reliable a customer as the deli had. And Sid could tell by the tone of his voice that the deli might be in trouble.

"Is this true?"

What was that look on Pete's face? He wasn't upset. He was scared. He was afraid that something he loved—something that had been a part of his life for twenty five years—might be taken away from him.

Sid realized that Chet Somebody and Don Somebody were watching the scene, licking their chops.

"Pete, how about Joe makes you some ham and eggs, on me? You go grab a table and I'll run it out to you."

Pete looked uncertain, but free food was his Achilles

Heel. He headed for a table near the window while Sid picked up the paper and went into the storage room.

"Deli Owner Arrested in Capital Case"

He stared at the words. The letters seemed larger than usual, but maybe Sid was imagining that. The article was written by Jackson Dexter and began with the line, "Is Sid the Shooter?" *Damn.*

Sid read the entire article. It took up a decent chunk of the front page, then concluded on the back of the front section. A sidebar showed a timeline of the shootings, from the Capitol Building on May 1st to Fairytale Town nearly two weeks later. Sid found himself increasingly angry as he read the article. Not angry at that turd, Jackson Dexter. Not angry at Detective Stokes. He was angry because he read every word, and every word was true. He was angry at himself.

He folded the paper back up and looked at the headline again. Then he stared at his photo, studying his mug shot for the first time. The face on the paper looked surprised and clueless and, well, guilty. There were just two words below the photograph: "Did Sid?"

CHAPTER 22

Thursday, May 22nd ended up being the slowest day at Sid's Deli since 1948. They had a total of nine paying customers for breakfast, and thirteen for lunch. For a while Sid blamed it on the reporters and cameras hanging around the front door, but they were mostly gone by nine o'clock. And still the customers didn't come.

Maybe people didn't want to be served their food by a deranged public menace.

The phone rang more than usual, and each time Sid hoped that it'd be a nice, big "To Go" order. Not even close. There were twenty or more calls from the media— some local but quite a few from San Francisco, LA, even New York. He told them all that Sid wasn't there and he didn't expect him anytime soon. There were six prank calls that sounded like kids and four calls from lawyers hoping to make a name for themselves by representing California's most famous new felon. And there was only one call that Sid was happy to get. Gloria called about one o'clock and said she'd be there in half an hour. Sid assured her they'd have the place all to themselves.

When his sister arrived at 1:40, the blinds were drawn once again and the "Sorry, We're Closed" sign was facing the street. No sense staying open if nobody was coming in.

"You doing okay, little brother?" Gloria asked the question as she set her briefcase down on a table and kicked off her shoes.

"Yeah. Okay."

She gave him a very genuine hug and then kissed him on the cheek. This was not Gloria's standard greeting, and he couldn't figure if that was good or bad.

"Can I get you a soda or something?" Sid asked.

"Got a beer?"

Sid raised an eyebrow.

"It's hot out," said Gloria.

She flopped into a chair and rubbed her bare feet as Sid popped the cap off a Budweiser, poured himself a Coke, then pulled up a chair next to his sister. She clinked her bottle against his glass and said, "Cheers."

"So how much trouble am I in?" Sid asked.

Gloria took a pretty good drink of her beer and then dabbed her mouth with a paper napkin. It came back with a lipstick smudge.

"Well, I'm not exactly a criminal defense attorney…"

"No, but you work for free," he interrupted.

"Only for family." She smiled at him. "You're not going to jail, Sid. I'm almost positive."

"Well, that's *almost* good news. Why 'almost'?"

"I'll get to that in a minute. Here's what's going on. First of all, you're not going to jail soon. It'll be at least thirty days before your first court appearance. We can get that extended if we want, but I don't think we'll need to."

"Why's that?"

"In a minute. By the way, your buddy Det. Stokes wanted to see how long he could keep you locked up yesterday. He was pulling for a much higher bail, but it was a lame effort. You're not a flight risk and the stuff they've got is thin. Judge wouldn't even look at it."

"So, why was I arrested?"

"Okay," said Gloria, then she took another drink and began rummaging around in her briefcase. "I'm a little surprised they brought you in when they did, because once they do that, of course, they're obliged to give us whatever they have on you." Gloria found the folder she was looking for and laid it on the table.

"So far they're basing their entire case on only three things." She flipped the folder open, and Sid saw that the top page was just some notes scrawled on a lined yellow page. He recognized her handwriting. "First of all, they did get a tip—a phone call—saying that you were the shooter and telling them where to look for the gun. The call was obviously made sometime before Stokes showed up and found the pistol. They haven't given us any more information about that call, but they'll have to."

"Do they know who called them?"

"They say it was anonymous, and that makes sense. If someone's trying to frame you for a major crime, they're not going to give their name and address."

"Uh-huh." *Yep, Gloria was smart.*

"But it'd be nice to know what time the call came in, and they'll have that information. They're just not making it too easy. It's part of the game. No big deal. Second thing they have, of course, is the gun itself and the ballistics report."

Gloria slid the yellow page of notes out of the way to reveal an official looking document—several photocopied pages stapled together.

"Just like we thought, this confirms that the bullets fired by the Capital Shooter could have come from your gun. But they can't say definitively that the bullets did come from your gun. Too much damage to the recovered slugs."

"It's not my gun."

"Sure," Gloria dismissed his objection.

"I just think it sounds bad when my lawyer keeps calling it 'my gun.'"

"I'll try to be careful."

"It's like the third time you've done it."

"Shut up, Sid."

"Okay."

Gloria placed the ballistics report on top of the yellow note page and picked up the next document. It was a single sheet of paper with print that was hard to read. It looked like some type of form that had been faxed and then copied. She set it on the table in front of her brother.

"Here's the good stuff. This is called a D.R.O.S.—a Dealer Record of Sale. Ever seen one?"

"No, never."

"That's because you've never purchased a gun, Sid. And that's why you're not going to jail."

Gloria smiled again, but this time it was different. Triumphant. He was reminded of the time she won the spelling bee in junior high. He tried to look as happy and satisfied as she did, but came up a little short.

"Sid, every time a gun dealer sells a gun, they have to fill out one of these. It reports the sale of a firearm to the government. The gun that Stokes found in your filing cabinet—the gun that's not yours—" Gloria gave him a reassuring wink. "This is the D.R.O.S. for that gun. It says it was purchased by Sidney Bigler at a Gun Show in Reno on February 8th. It's a little hard to read the date, but you can see it there."

Gloria indicated the space on the form. The date prompted Sid's memory.

"Oh, hey! I checked my runner's log when I got home yesterday. Remember? You asked me to check on it when you bailed me out. February 8th was a Saturday. No way I was in Reno. I ran a 10K in the Bay Area that day."

"Can you prove you were there?"

"I won it."

"Great. Although I don't think we'll need that."

"Because?"

"Sid, take a look at the signature." Gloria indicated a space at the bottom of the page.

Sid looked at the signature and then he actually laughed out loud. "That's supposed to be my signature? Really?"

"Yeah, I knew it wasn't yours right away. It's nothing like that squiggle thing you do. I can actually read it."

Sid now took a moment to look over the document

more closely. He'd definitely never seen it before. Most of the boxes were nearly impossible to read, but it looked like whoever filled it out got his name and address right. Then he looked at the signature again. Not even close.

"Here's the deal," Gloria pressed on. "The gun was purchased from a reputable dealer in Reno. It's somebody who owns a local shop there. If the person who bought that gun was smart and they wanted to, they could have been much more sneaky. If you're willing to snoop around at a gun show and spend a little extra money, you can get a gun from someone who pays very little attention to the paperwork. Or loses it altogether."

"But whoever set me up would've wanted the cops to find this thing, right? It ties me to the gun."

Gloria looked at Sid with a slight look of surprise. Maybe surprise mixed with pride. Her little brother was famous for using his feet, not his brains.

"Right. Good, Sid. But it was a lousy job. Somehow they got your name and address to put on the form, but had no idea how to forge your signature. Whoever's out to get you, they don't do this for a living."

This conversation was something entirely new to Sid Bigler. He had never been into reading mysteries or detective stories, and he favored sit-coms over cop shows. But this was real life—his life—and it was exhilarating.

"So why would Stokes arrest me if this is all he's got?"

"Because he's an idiot that doesn't always do his homework. Because this is the most high profile crime this town has seen in years, and he's got a big boner to be the cop who solves it."

Pause. Sid was shocked by her choice of words and a grin crossed his face.

"Boner?"

"It's lawyer talk. Don't read too much into it." Gloria looked serious. Another few seconds passed in silence.

"You said *Boner*?"

They sat and looked at each other—a brief staring contest reminiscent of the ones they had as kids. Sid's grin began to expand as he sensed victory approaching. His sister started to crack. Then Sid gave her the eyebrow again and Gloria lost it. They both ended up laughing hard.

Now it was Sid who clinked his glass to Gloria's bottle. "To my sister, who had a beer and said 'Boner.' What a great day."

Gloria drained her Bud and said, "Don't tell mom." She reached down and started putting on her shoes.

Sid savored the moment. He couldn't remember a time, even when they were kids, that the two of them had a conversation like this. A conversation where he felt like they were equals. He'd spent much of the past couple of weeks feeling helpless. But in the last two minutes something had changed. He couldn't exactly put his finger on it, but for some reason he no longer thought of himself as a victim, a part of someone else's story. This was his own story, and for the first time it looked like it might have a happy ending. It felt great.

"Any questions?" Gloria finished with her shoes and stood, then began gathering up the papers and putting them back in the folder. Sid stood with her.

"Yeah, two. First, we can prove I didn't buy that gun, so why don't I just come clean now about where I was the night of the last shooting?"

"I thought about that," Gloria replied. "Remember I said I was *almost* positive you weren't going to jail?"

"Yeah."

"I can pretty much guarantee that they're not going to get you for shooting up the city. You didn't do it, and their evidence is weak. But lying to a police officer in the course of an investigation—you've done that, Sid. Generally it's not that big of a deal. Guys lie to the cops all the time and rarely get charged with anything if that's all they've done. But you never know with Stokes."

"Well, yeah. He's got that boner and stuff."

"Right. So keep your mouth shut for now. The information you're keeping won't help solve the Capital Shooter case. And whenever this thing is all over, it won't matter where you were on that night."

"Okay."

Gloria finished putting the papers away and picked up the leather briefcase, then ran the strap over her shoulder. "What's your other question?"

"Who's trying to set me up?"

Gloria looked at him and took a deep breath, then let it out slowly through her nose. He'd seen it many times. That was Gloria getting serious. Gloria thinking hard. Gloria searching for the right answer.

"I don't know, little brother. And I don't think I'm the person who's going to figure that one out."

"How come?"

"Because you're going to do it, Sid. I think you're going to figure it out. You've got one big advantage over anyone else."

Sid didn't say anything, but the look on his face was a question mark. What could Gloria mean? She let him wonder for a moment, then answered the question that he hadn't asked.

"It's gotta be somebody you know, Sid."

CHAPTER 23

Sid and Gloria walked out of the deli and into the hot afternoon. He took her briefcase for her and asked, "Where are you parked?"

"Couple of blocks that way."

"I'll walk you."

Along the way, he gave her a very short version of his conversation with Joe from the night before, ending with that curious last line—*"I can't say nothin'."* Sid found it a little satisfying when his sister asked the same question he had.

"What's that mean?"

"Beats me. That's all he'd say. The whole thing was weird."

"Funny that he and daddy were so close," Gloria said, and then they walked in silence for a minute, each trying to figure out Joe's cryptic answer.

When they reached Gloria's yellow BMW, she unlocked the passenger door, took her briefcase from Sid and threw it onto the front seat. She gave him a quick, final hug.

"I might see you later tonight," she said. "I'm thinking about stopping by the house and just chatting with mom for a while."

"Well, you'll miss me. I'm having dinner with Amy

tonight."

Gloria circled the car and unlocked the driver's door.

"That reminds me," she said. "I've got something to tell you about Amy…"

It had not been a typical Sid and Amy date night. First of all, Amy had insisted on paying. That had happened exactly once before, and it had been on Sid's birthday. Secondly, they'd come to a very nice place for dinner. As Sid thought about it, he realized the only other time they'd gone to a classy, expensive restaurant was also the only other time Amy had paid. *Hmm, was there a pattern here?*

The Firehouse Restaurant in Old Sacramento was an institution. If Sacramento had a tourist destination—a debatable proposition— Old Sac was it. Overlooking the Sacramento River, its wooden walkways and cobblestone streets had suckered countless tourists into thinking it might be a genuine, historic attraction. From Sid's non-scientific survey, the area was primarily comprised of just three kinds of stores: places where you could buy caramel corn and Slurpees, places where you could buy cowboy hats and ash trays in the shape of California, and places where you could get a black & white photo taken of yourself dressed up in hokey old-time costumes that had been worn by God-knows-how-many-people before you. But the Firehouse was an exception to the tacky rule. Built in 1853, it really had been the local firehouse back in the good ol' days. Now it was one of the best places in town to eat and everybody knew it.

On a few occasions during the meal it was pretty obvious that someone from another table had recognized Sid from the news. There was whispering and pointing, and then the averting of eyes when Sid glanced in their direction. But the two of them could not be distracted from what had been a wonderful evening and a splendid dinner. Sid had never heard of *demi glace*, but drizzled over a filet mignon it was spectacular. Amy was full after eating only about half of her pasta, and Sid managed to polish off the rest. Now they were awaiting dessert.

"Thank you," Sid said.

"For what?"

"Dinner. And driving me home from jail yesterday. And believing me."

"My pleasure." Amy's eyes sparkled. Her foot tapped against his ankle as she took a sip of coffee.

"It's hard to get into this place. How'd you get us a table?"

Now Amy smiled. She glanced briefly down to the table, then looked deeply into his eyes. Sid was struck again by how beautiful she was.

"I made reservations three days ago." She laughed softly, and Sid thought she might have blushed just a little, too.

It took a moment for the math to sink in. The two of them had blown up on the phone last Saturday morning—five days ago—and hadn't spoken a word to each other until she picked him up from jail yesterday. For the past five days, Sid had been vaguely aware that he was carrying around a weight inside him—something that nagged at his subconscious, burdened him. It was as if some part of him had been holding its breath. He realized now that Amy had come back to him three days ago. He just hadn't known it until this moment."

"So you're sure I'm not some crazy gunman?"

"I told you, I never thought that."

Sid moved the candle from the center of the table, then reached across and took both of Amy's hands in his. They were quiet for a minute, and there was nothing awkward about the silence.

"I made the reservations and I kept meaning to call you and ask you to dinner," Amy broke the moment, "but I didn't know what to say exactly. I felt so stupid. And then I heard you'd gotten arrested yesterday."

She squeezed his hand, and now there was something different about her eyes. Tears were welling at the corners.

"Who told you?"

"Your sister."

With a slight sniffle, Amy pulled her hands away, retrieved her napkin from her lap and dabbed at her eyes. "She called and told me you'd been arrested and said that she wanted to talk to me."

"What'd you two talk about?"

"You. She didn't really say much. Just wanted me to talk about you. She asked me what you were like. I thought it was kinda funny, since she's known you your whole life."

Sid thought about what Gloria had once said to him. *"Good lawyers listen more than they talk."*

"I guess she thought you'd know me better. How long did you two talk?"

"Maybe half an hour."

"And what did you tell her about me."

Amy set her napkin down and took his hands again. "The truth."

It was clear that was all Amy was going to tell him about her conversation with his sister, but that was enough. The nebulous weight that had been pressing on him since last weekend was gone. Completely gone. Sid wondered for a moment if his sister really did have an appointment to get to yesterday, or if she'd just made that up.

His mind wandered to the last thing Gloria had said to him earlier that afternoon. She was just about to climb into the BMW when she'd said, *"I've got something to tell you about Amy."* She'd seemed to search for the right words for a moment, and then she said, *"Take Amy off your list."*

"What list?" he'd asked her.

"Your list of suspects. She's got nothing to do with the shootings. She's on your side. She's okay."

"How do you know?"

"I know," had been her reply. *"Sisters know."*

A deep voice said, "Cherries Jubilee," and Sid was suddenly back in the restaurant with Amy. A fellow in a tuxedo had rolled a cart up next to their table and set to work making the dessert they'd ordered. The two exchanged an occasional lovers glance as they watched the butter sizzle in a pan followed by sugar and fresh cherries and then some cognac that made flames leap in the air. Amy laughed and clapped. The man rolled the cart away and left them with the most delicious thing either had ever tasted. They savored the moment and the exquisite food.

"You said you love me yesterday," said Amy.

"Yes."

"Was that just a desperate prisoner talking, or did you really mean it?"

"I mean it."

"Thank you."

Amy wouldn't have any more to say about it for the rest of the night, and neither would Sid. And that was fine.

Here's a curious thing about The Firehouse. Its front entrance is rather cold and austere, but the rear of the place opens onto a back alley that is warm and inviting. They have outdoor seating and beautiful landscaping and when the weather's right, there's no lovelier place to be. And so, once dinner was over, Sid and Amy went out the back of the restaurant and found themselves walking arm in arm alone down one of Old Sac's nicest alleys. It was just after nine o'clock on a Thursday evening and it was wonderfully quiet. Some live music could faintly be heard spilling from a bar a block or two away, but not loud enough to break the spell.

Ahead of them, a figure stepped casually out of the shadows and began walking in their direction. No surprise. In fact, Sid would've expected there to be more people out on a beautiful night like this. It was probably still eighty degrees outside.

As they walked, Sid and Amy subconsciously crossed from the right side of the alley to the left. The shadow guy was still maybe thirty yards ahead. Neither one gave it much thought when the stranger also crossed the alley to be on the same side as they were. With a little more purpose, they crossed from left to right as they walked. And both began to feel quite uncomfortable when the man ahead crossed also, staying directly ahead of them. Amy's arm stiffened and she pulled herself closer to Sid.

All three continued to walk until they were only perhaps ten feet from each other. Sid and Amy stopped, and so did the stranger. Definitely a weird moment.

"Can I help you?" Sid asked. He tried for a little bravado, but his voice sounded thin in the dim light.

He could just begin to make out the person ahead of them. A guy, maybe thirty, who had yet to move beyond the look he probably had in the sixties. Long hair parted down the middle. Where there should've been a mouth there was an enormous moustache that must have made it completely impossible to eat without making a mess. He was close to six feet tall, and it looked like he'd spent a lot of time in the gym. *David Crosby turned weight lifter*, Sid thought.

"Maybe we could help each other," the guy replied.

"Okay." Sid didn't know what else to say.

Moustache Guy slowly walked toward them. Sid wished, as he had many times as a kid, that he were taller. He didn't glance at Amy, but he could hear her breathing, shallow and quick. The man stopped only a couple of feet away. He was wearing blue jeans and work boots, with a jeans jacket over a t-shirt, and the guy's hands were plunged into the pockets of the jacket. Sid thought he was dressed a little too warmly for the weather.

"Your father owed a lot of money."

Sid didn't know what he had expected the guy to say, but it certainly wasn't that.

"Whose father?"

"Your father, Sid." Whoever Moustache Guy was, he clearly had the advantage.

"Who are you?" It was Amy who spoke up, and Sid was surprised at how she sounded. Mad and not the least bit intimidated.

The guy wasn't impressed. In the dim light he smiled at Amy, then looked at Sid.

"I'm just somebody who's looking out for your boyfriend. Somebody who wouldn't want to see him get hurt."

Sid noted quietly to himself that he was remarkably calm. He liked that. For a guy who hadn't been in a fight since the third grade, he was keeping his cool pretty well. And he felt some of the same energy that he'd felt while talking with Gloria in the deli that afternoon. It was now perfectly clear that getting sprung from jail was not the end of his troubles, and that Gloria might be right about who would figure out this whole mess. For some reason, he was the magnet to which trouble was attracted. So it was time to see what he could find out.

"Who did my father owe money to?"

"People."

"If your goal is to not be very helpful, you're doing an excellent job."

"Here's my goal." Moustache Guy lowered his voice and took half a step closer, staring at Sid and ignoring Amy. "To deliver the message that there's a $60,000 debt, and it don't matter if your old man is dead. Somebody's gotta pay it."

"Assuming I believe you and I want to pay, where am I supposed to get that kind of money?"

The guy probably smiled behind the moustache, but it was hard to be sure. "I hear that your deli building is all paid for. Maybe you could sell it or something."

Sid let that sink in. It was the answer he expected to hear. A few of the pieces were starting to come together.

Standing there in the dimly lit alley, he didn't really feel threatened. It had recently occurred to him that, in all of the craziness since the shootings began, nobody had been hurt intentionally. Sure, a bum had gotten shot in the toe, but that was probably an accident. The whole Capital Shooter crime spree seemed to have been designed for maximum drama but minimum actual violence to people. There was no reason to think that whoever was behind all this really wanted Sid or anybody else to be seriously injured.

"You know where I might find somebody interested in buying my building?" Sid asked. Gloria would be proud of him. He kept his head. He was thinking. And he was using this opportunity to dig around for some useful information. He was pretty confident he knew what the guy would say, but he had to ask just to be sure. Sadly, the guy never got a chance to answer.

Sid felt Amy's arm move abruptly, and then the world went into slow motion. Out of the corner of his eye, he saw Amy's right foot coming up off the ground. She cut loose with what can only be described as a loud growl—not a scream, and certainly not something that sounded like fear. Sid saw Moustache Guy's eyes grow wide, and he tried to pull his hands from his coat pockets, but there was no chance. Amy's foot connected with the guy's crotch, and over the sound that was coming from her throat, Sid was sure he could hear a crunching noise. Moustache Guy began falling to his knees, and his hands were finally free enough to reach for his privates. But they were too late to protect them, only to try to bring comfort. For a fraction of a moment, Sid felt sorry for the guy. He was like Godzilla, pierced by the Army's artillery and not fully understanding where the pain was coming from.

Then life jumped back to regular speed, or perhaps even faster. Amy was pulling on his arm and yelling, "Let's go! Let's go!" And Sid remembered that there was one thing that he and Amy could do better than almost anybody else. They ran. Even if the guy behind them had two good nuts, there was no way he could've caught them.

CHAPTER 24

Friday morning there were fewer reporters waiting at the deli door when Sid arrived in the dark to open up. Maybe that made up for how his day had started.

Twenty minutes earlier—just as he was walking out his front door—he had been hit with a painfully bright light and some goober from Channel 40 sticking a microphone in his face. Even as Sid squinted and raised his hands to block the light, he thought *"Oh, this'll look great on TV. Very innocent…"* The guy and his cameraman followed him down the driveway, peppering him with questions along the way.

"Mr. Bigler, any comment?"

"No."

"Mr. Bigler, wasn't it your gun that was used in the shootings?"

"No."

"Were you involved with the Capital Shootings in any way?"

"No."

Sid had finally arrived at his car and was unlocking the door when the reporter asked a new question. One that no other reporter had asked.

"Well, if you're not the Capital Shooter, any idea who

is?"

Sid turned the key and the door lock thingy made a clunk as it popped up. He stood up straight, then turned toward the reporter. In the glare of the bright light, he could just see that the guy's jacket was a very loud plaid. Classy.

"Do I know who the Capital Shooter is?"

"Yes, Mr. Bigler. Do you?"

Sid searched to find the camera lens, then looked straight into it. It might have been a mistake to say anything, but he figured it was worth the risk. His last conversation with Gloria had given him a welcome shot of confidence, and he decided it was time to let somebody know he might be onto them.

"Yeah. Yeah, I might know who it is."

There was no response for a second, and Sid gave the camera a wink. Then he slid into the front seat and ignored the follow-up questions that came as he buckled up and closed the door.

Once the deli was open for business, the day turned out to be a great improvement over the one before. Not as busy as a usual Friday, but almost. The phone rang a couple of times each hour, always some newspaper or TV station somewhere. But the ol' "He's not here" line continued to work beautifully. Several of the regulars went out of their way to tell him they were sure he was innocent, but most avoided eye contact and ate quietly. Sure, Sid might be a homicidal maniac, but good food is good food and the people couldn't stay away for long.

And there were some customers—maybe five or six over the course of the morning—who Sid had never seen before. People who came and had breakfast, but there was more to it than that. They came in alone and they stared at Sid while they ate. Maybe he was reading more into it than he should have, but it really felt like they'd come in to get a look at the freak—the guy who had shot up the city. It was as though he was on display, like the lizard he'd kept in a glass terrarium when he was a kid.

"Got some strange ones in today," Joe had said once as Sid was picking up an order. He had noticed it, too.

As one of those odd guys was paying his bill at the register, he said to Sid, "What was it like?"

"Hmm?" was Sid's response.

"Was it cool?" the guy asked.

"Don't know what you're talking about."

"Okay," said the guy with a smile, and he left.

A shiver ran down Sid's spine.

At 11:15 things were fairly quiet. No sign of reporters and just a few customers. Eddie was getting the tables re-set for lunch and Joe was filling square metal pans with pickles and lettuce and whatever else he needed. Sid had once offered to help in this pre-lunch routine, but Joe made it very clear that this was a personal, intimate ritual. Like a gunfighter checking and loading his pistols before high noon. So Sid was sitting at the counter, sipping a Coke and working a crossword puzzle with a stubby little golf pencil when Vince Headley came into the deli.

"Mr. Bigler, how are you?"

The lawyer wore a burgundy polyester three-piece suit with unnaturally shiny leather shoes that were the exact same color. Or maybe they were plastic. Sid glanced up and down, alternatingly admiring the amazing shoes and the Herman Munster forehead.

"Oh, I'm sorry Mr. Headley. I almost didn't recognize you without some pancake syrup running down your neck, or maybe an english muffin on your head."

Headley ignored what Sid thought was quite a clever opening remark, though he did cast a glance in Eddie's direction. Then he plunged into what sounded like a rehearsed presentation.

"Mr. Bigler, I know that these are difficult times for you. Regardless of what you think of me, I have no desire to add to your considerable troubles right now. After a lengthy discussion with my client, he has agreed to drop the settlement price for our claim to $7,000."

Well this was interesting. Masquerading as an attorney with a heart, Headley was offering to drop the blackmail price by thirty percent. Surely a gesture borne of his desire to comfort a fellow human being. Sid looked back down at his crossword.

"What's a six-letter word for sausage? The last letter is an 'R'."

"Mr. Bigler, this is a very reasonable offer that could quickly put an end to at least one of your problems right away." The guy was unflappable. Unwavering. Uninteresting.

"So tell me," Sid spun on the stool to face the

lawyer. "How much does your fat boy client weigh now?"

"850 pounds."

"No, that's what he weighed a couple of weeks ago. What's he weigh now?"

"I... I don't have any idea."

"Because if it was my meatloaf sandwiches making him fat, I figure that after a couple of weeks without 'em, he's gotta be down twenty or thirty pounds. Wouldn't you think? A guy that size, suddenly cut off from his sole source of fatness?"

"As I told you before, Mr. Bigler, the 850 pound figure is an estimate."

"So you don't know exactly what he weighed before, and you don't know what he weighs now that he's stopped eating our food."

Not bad. Not bad at all. Maybe a little of Gloria was rubbing off on him.

Vince Headly, Esq., moved slightly closer to Sid and lowered his voice, like a guy trying to scalp some tickets to a ballgame.

"Perhaps my client can be persuaded to lower his settlement fee. Perhaps $6,000?"

Sid took a few seconds to enjoy the moment before responding.

"Wiener."

"Hmm?" It was as though the attorney hadn't heard him correctly.

"Wie-ner." Sid said it slowly and clearly, pronouncing each syllable.

"I'm sorry, I don't understand."

"It's the six letter word for sausage. Wiener."

Sid returned to his crossword, and didn't look up when Headley dropped a fresh business card on the counter next to him.

"I'm sorry you won't listen to reason, Mr. Bigler. I came here in your interest."

Sid heard the burgundy shoes squeak across the linoleum floor as the attorney left, and didn't turn to look until he heard the door close. The look of satisfaction on his face didn't last long.

Outside the deli window, Headley the lawyer was stopped on the sidewalk engaged in an animated conversation. He glanced into the deli a couple of times as he chatted with someone whose back was to the glass. Sid couldn't see the other guy's face, but he didn't need to. He recognized the Hawaiian shirt.

Sid made himself turn back to his crossword puzzle. He stared at the words, but didn't see them. His mind began to race as he tried to make sense of what was going on just outside his front door. Headley and Jackson Dexter knew each other? What could a lawyer he hated and a reporter he hated have in common? And what could they be saying out there? And why would they be talking right in front of the store where he could see them? Maybe they were just casual acquaintances. Maybe they just happened to run into each other there. Maybe it had nothing to do with him. Maybe. Maybe. Maybe. Sid wasn't exactly sure why, but something about all this was pissing him off. The lead on his pencil snapped against the paper and he didn't notice.

Sid continued to wrestle with this new information and quietly fume until he heard the door open behind him. He turned, ready for a confrontation, but Headley and Dexter were nowhere to be seen. Instead, two of his favorite regulars were headed his way.

Thankfully, business picked up, and thoughts of lawyers and reporters gave way to more practical matters. By a little before noon the place was just about full. The "To Go" line at the register was shorter than usual, but not bad. Somebody from some State office had called in an order for nineteen sandwiches, so they were temporarily swamped.

Sid enjoyed it when the deli was busy. He, Joe and Eddie got into a kind of groove—Sid taking orders, dropping checks and working the register, Joe producing food at an amazing speed, and Eddie clearing tables and delivering the food. The tables were numbered and Eddie had no problem getting an order to the right place.

The three were in a pretty good rhythm when the last seat at the counter was taken by Jackson Dexter.

"Hey, Sid, how's it goin'?" Dexter said it like they were pals. Like he wasn't the person primarily responsible for most of Sacramento thinking Sid was the Capital Shooter. What was he up to? Did he know Sid had seen him talking to the weasley Vince Headley less than an hour ago?

"I'm good, Dexter." Sid answered. "What can I get you for lunch?" Sid played it cool, and it felt right.

"Whatever I had last time I was here. It was great."

"You want blueberry pancakes for lunch?"

"Oh. Well, give me a cheeseburger and fries and a Coke."

"You got it."

Sid scribbled the order on a pad, tore out the page and laid it on the back counter next to the grill. Joe snatched it with his right hand as he flipped a couple of patty melts with his left, gave it a quick glance, then slid it in next to the others on the ticket order rack. The entire process took maybe a second.

Sid grabbed a glass and began filling up Dexter's Coke. It was good that he'd had some time to cool down. Maybe Dexter had wanted to be seen earlier, and maybe not. Didn't matter. Either way, it was time to go fishing for some information, and it only added to Sid's conviction that his sister was right. The mystery of the Capital Shooter was his to solve. Hell, it wouldn't leave him alone. As he delivered the reporter's drink, he decided it was time to blow off Gloria's advice about not talking to anybody. It was time to get some answers.

"Mind if I ask you a few questions?" Dexter asked. Friendly and non-threatening.

"Not if I can ask a few, too."

"Okay by me." If the reporter was surprised by the request, he didn't show it. "We can take turns. Who goes first?"

"Well, technically, that would be your first question. But I'm not a stickler for rules. You can start." Sid took the white towel from his shoulder, wiped his hands off and dropped it on the bar.

Jackson Dexter pulled a pen and a small notebook with a spiral wire binding from his shirt pocket. "Okay. Can I assume you're officially denying that you had anything to do with the shootings?"

"Officially. Yes."

Dexter just looked at him. He didn't make a note of Sid's answer, and he didn't look away. He just stared. What was *this* all about? Was the reporter trying to get into his head? Looking for some cue that Sid might be lying? As the seconds ticked by, it started to feel a little weird.

"I guess that answer wasn't worth writing down, huh?"

No response.

"Okay, my turn. How'd you know to be here two days ago when I was being arrested? That wasn't just a coincidence, right?"

"Of course not. I got a call. The paper's just a few blocks away."

"Who called you?"

"Well, that's two questions in a row Sid. No fair. And I won't answer that one, anyway." Dexter made about a third of his Coke disappear in two gulps. "What does Stokes have on you?"

"Not much. Not enough to put me away."

"You seem pretty sure."

"Yep."

The customer next to Jackson Dexter—a guy named Curtis who worked at the bank on 9th Street—dropped a five dollar bill on the counter and got up. Sid picked up the money and stuck it in his pocket.

"When you showed up here two days ago, was that the first time somebody had called you about me? Connecting me to the shootings?"

"No." The reporter didn't hesitate. "Somebody called pointing to you the morning after the last one. Fairytale Town."

Now it was Sid's turn to not show any surprise, but it was tough. Dexter's last comment made his pulse quicken.

"My turn, Sid. Ever owned a gun?"

"No. Never."

For the first time the reporter looked down at his notepad and scribbled something. His handwriting was appalling. It made a doctor's prescription look like an illuminated manuscript. When he finished writing, he looked back at Sid.

"Your turn."

"Okay," Said Sid. "How do you know Vince Headley?"

"The lawyer?"

"How many Vince Headleys can there be?"

"Good one." Dexter grinned. "I've been around town for a long time, and so has he. I think I mentioned him in an article a few years ago when he was suing Campbell's Soup."

"What for?"

"Somebody said they found boogers in the Chicken Noodle."

Without saying a word, Joe reached across Sid and set a beautiful, greasy cheeseburger and fries down in front of Jackson Dexter. A little steam was rising up from it, and the top of the bun had a buttery shine.

"A work of art," said the reporter. "Lemme ask one more question, and then I'm gonna shut up and eat." Dexter took a moment to tuck his paper napkin into the neck of his Hawaiian shirt. "I talked to Stokes and he says he's got you nailed. Tell me why he's wrong. Is somebody setting you up?"

Jackson took a huge bite of the burger, but kept his eyes on Sid. It was a good question. It was the same question Gloria had asked him over a week ago. It was the question he'd asked himself every time he sat down with that stupid list of names.

"Yeah," said Sid. "Yeah, that's the only thing that makes sense."

As he said it, a new thought flickered at the edge of his mind. It was fuzzy for a second, and then it came into focus. Crystal clear and obvious.

"I don't know who it is, Dexter. But maybe you do. I think it's the same person who called you. It's gotta be. Here's my last question. I've asked it before, but I'm asking again. Who is it? Who called you and said I was the shooter?"

Jackson Dexter rearranged the food in his mouth so it looked like he had a golf ball in his cheek. He drained the Coke and set the empty glass on the counter. Then he looked at Sid and said, "Sorry. If I don't protect my sources, I'm out of a job." He chewed a few more times and swallowed. "Besides," Dexter continued, "It wasn't just one person."

From the look on Sid's face, it was obvious he hadn't seen that coming. He struggled to process what he'd just heard. Dexter watched as confusion slowly gave way to realization. Dexter saw it, and he liked the reaction.

"Yeah," said the reporter. "Two calls, two different people."

"You're sure?"

"Trust me."

Jackson Dexter took another big bite, and a drop of grease rolled off his chin and onto the napkin at his neck.

CHAPTER 25

When Sid got home in the afternoon he was restless. The last two days had been a ride on a self-image roller coaster: He'd been a frightened and confused suspect in the back of a squad car, a clown in the reporters' media circus, a sleuth encouraged by his big sister, a love-struck dope at dinner with Amy, a tough guy in the alley afterwards. And what had he been during that odd conversation with Joe that afternoon in the deli? Shrink? Confessor?

Despite the heat, he decided to blow off a little steam and go for a short run at about 5 p.m. It was in the mid-nineties and the heat made him miserable right away. But it felt good to be working up a sweat, and the discomfort took his mind off some of his troubles. Unfortunately, the reprieve didn't last long.

Sid had planned to just do a lap or two around the park and head home. He was less than a mile from his house when he realized that he had company. A couple of guys in a dark sedan had passed him several times, and now they were driving slowly next to him as he trotted down Land Park Drive. As a rule, cars go much faster than people on foot, so when they slow down to a jogger's pace, it's painfully obvious. Sid could see the golf course through the trees off to his left, and the entrance to the zoo up ahead. And out of the corner of his eye, the brown Chrysler.

It was a weekday and it was hot, so there weren't a lot of people in the park. Still, it was a public place and Sid wasn't exactly scared. More frustrated. Frazzled. He didn't need any more drama in his life right now. He wanted to convey some confidence to whoever these guys were, so he made the decision to simply turn his head and look straight at them as he jogged along.

Neither one looked familiar. The driver was about his own age—looked a little like Bruce Springsteen. The guy in the passenger seat was older. Maybe sixty. Wavy gray hair. Captain Kangaroo with an overbite. Neither one seemed particularly threatening. It was odd, the way the two parties traveled down the road at the same speed, looking each other over for maybe twenty seconds. Then Sid simply stopped in his tracks and the car continued on.

Sid stood, hands on hips, and watched them drive away. For lack of any evidence to the contrary, he assumed that the guys in the car were just a couple of schmucks who recognized him from his pictures on the TV or in the newspaper. Lord knows, his face had been all over the place since this whole mess started.

Sid rolled back into a comfortable pace as he headed toward the intersection at Sutterville Road. He was just nearing the entrance to the zoo when he saw the Chrysler up ahead, coming back again. For some reason, it seemed much more ominous now. Sid didn't break his stride, didn't do anything to show fear or concern. But he watched closely as the sedan drew closer. It slowed dramatically as it got very near. And as Sid passed the car, the older guy lifted up a camera and snapped his picture.

Whatever was going on, Sid decided that he'd had enough. He hopped the curb and took off across the wide, grassy lawn of William Land Park. He was calm and controlled, but he was certainly running faster than before. He stayed on the grass until he crossed Eighth Avenue, then stuck with smaller neighborhood streets until he got back home. It took seven or eight minutes to get there, and he never saw Bruce or the Captain in their crappy Chrysler again.

Sid grabbed a quick shower and showed up in the kitchen right on time. Friday nights had been Spaghetti Night for as far back as he could remember. His mom had made it the same way since Hoover was president—a thin sauce with crumbly chunks of hamburger—and he loved it. Rose had never learned to make a smaller batch of the stuff, so the big cast iron pot was full and bubbling and the smell of canned tomato sauce and McCormick Schilling Italian Seasoning filled the house. In recent years she'd started taking the substantial leftover portion to the family across the street every week. They always thanked her profusely, but Sid wondered if it really got eaten.

"How was business today? Better?"

"Yeah, mom. Not bad. And not so many reporters."

They had an oddly comfortable mother-son chat about life as a famous suspect while he put together a couple of salads on small plates and his mom scooped spaghetti into bowls. You always ate Rose's spaghetti out of a bowl so you got lots of the soupy sauce. It required both fork and spoon to consume it properly.

The sun was low in the sky, and filtered light gave the dining room a pleasant glow. Mother and son were settled at the table and talking about the TV reporter that had been waiting for him in front of their house that morning when the doorbell rang. Rose and Sid looked at each other, appreciating the curious timing of the 'ding-dong.' Sid headed for the door.

"Mr. Bigler, I hope I'm not interrupting dinner."

On the front porch stood Yvonne Wilcox, the blonde social worker. All five feet of her. Once again, what she lacked in height she made up for in contour. Sid struggled to recall her name.

"Uh, no. No, it's fine."

The woman glanced at the napkin he was still holding in his hand.

"Really," said Sid, "It's fine. Please come in."

She wore dark blue slacks with a matching, form-fitted jacket buttoned over a white blouse. As they walked to the living room, Sid wondered where she had to go to get clothes that fit her figure. There was nothing remotely lustful about the thought. Just curious.

They stopped in the living room, and Rose could plainly be seen enjoying her spaghetti in the room next door. She looked up and said, "Everything okay, Siddy?"

"Yeah, mom. I'll be back in a couple minutes. You go ahead." Sid's mom had always been very careful not to hang around and eavesdrop whenever he had a girlfriend stop by in high school, and this felt exactly the same. Funny.

"I really am sorry, Mr. Bigler. We could speak another time."

"Honestly, it's okay. Is this about Eddie? Is there a problem?"

"Well, that's the thing. Some people in my office are worried about him. Worried that maybe it's not safe for him to be at the deli anymore. Not safe to be around..." She hesitated, but she finished it. "...around you."

The roller coaster ride continued. It was crazy, but understandable. Sid sat on the couch and Yvonne did the same. He wasn't sure what to say.

"Your father was always wonderful to Eddie, and you seem very nice. But my job is to keep him safe, and given what I've read in the paper and seen on television, I just don't know if your restaurant is the best place for him."

What's the most polite way to tell someone you're concerned that they may be a psycho? Yvonne Wilcox was certainly taking a very professional stab at it.

As they sat together on the living room sofa, Sid could see that she was trying very hard to stave off the advance of years. The slightly excessive make-up was doing an admirable job disguising the lines around her eyes and the corners of her mouth. She was probably close to his mother's age, but what a contrast. Rose sat in the other room, happily embracing her housecoat and slippers and her increasing resemblance to Edith Bunker.

And Yvonne sat beside him, strategically packaged and arranged in an effort to retain the appearance of youth in the face of small but convincing clues to the contrary.

"What am I supposed to say, Miss...?" Sid searched for her name and she filled in the blank.

"Wilcox."

"Thank you. Miss Wilcox. What am I supposed to say in my defense? When Nixon said 'I'm not a crook,' it wasn't very believable, was it?"

Yvonne smiled. "Tell me something you've learned about Eddie."

She was good at her job. The question was a nice detour around a conversational roadblock.

"Well, let's see," Sid said, stalling while he tried to think of something. "I've decided he looks a little like a young Sidney Poitier."

Yvonne Wilcox laughed, and it completely transformed her. Sid got a glimpse of what she might have been like if he could have seen her twenty-five years earlier at a college party. Stunning.

"You're right," she said. "I hadn't thought about it, but I can see it now. That's very good." The laugh had given way to a smile, and now the smile gave way to concern. "But that's not exactly what I was looking for. Tell me how he's doing at work."

"Oh, Eddie's fine. He's a hard worker. As far as I can tell, he's always happy."

Yvonne nodded, but didn't reply. What more did she want to hear? Eddie wasn't exactly a deep character. He showed up, he worked his butt off, and Joe took him home. That was all there was, right?

Or was it? How many times had there been something about Eddie—some clue—that made you think he was more complicated than what was on the surface? Why had Eddie's name appeared repeatedly on that list that was sitting on his desk in the bedroom down the hallway? Sid had a mental image of flying breakfast remnants heading towards the back of Vince Headley's noggin, and it filled him with a curious mixture of fondness and suspicion. Again he asked himself the question that he'd asked countless times before. How much did Eddie Davis really understand? Sid's father had told him of a time a few years ago when some guy tried to dash without paying his bill. Eddie ran out the door after the guy, chased him down and brought him back to pay, always with the smile. How'd he know to do that? For a little while in the early seventies Big Sid had let him work the cash register. Then they discovered that he did fine with coins because they were different sizes, but he couldn't always tell the difference between the bills. A couple of unscrupulous customers walked away with tens and twenties they didn't deserve, and that was the end of Eddie's cashier days. He couldn't read, but when things were slow at the deli he'd stare at the newspaper for long periods of time.

"Eddie can't read, right?" Sid thought he'd just double check.

"Not much. Not really," Yvonne replied.

"Look, Miss Wilcox, I don't know what to tell you. Eddie's been at the deli for so long. As far as I can tell, he loves it there. And the fact is, I need him there. I didn't do the things I'm accused of, and I can assure you I'm not going to jail for it. I'd hate to see Eddie leave the deli because of something that never happened."

"I do want to believe you, Mr. Bigler."

"Then believe me. And like I told you the first time we met, it's Joe that really looks out for him. Please let him stay."

Yvonne Wilcox studied Sid's face for several seconds, and then apparently decided she was satisfied. "You're right that he loves being at the deli. Your father and Joe Diaz made that place a second home for him. He stays for now."

"Thank you."

The two stood, and Yvonne reached out her hand as she had done the day of their first meeting at the deli. Sid took it.

"I'm sorry to have interrupted your dinner, Mr. Bigler."

"Call me Sid."

Yvonne smiled again. "I called your father 'Sid.'"

She let go of his hand, and as the two headed back toward the front door the phone rang.

"I'll get it!" Rose called out, and Sid could hear her pushing her chair away from the table behind him. He and Yvonne exchanged goodbyes and he got back to the dining room as his mother returned from the kitchen.

"Your sister's on the phone for you," said his mom.

Sid went into the kitchen and picked up the phone that had been in his parents' kitchen for at least thirty years—black and clunky, with a cloth cord instead of one of those curly-cue plastic ones. He looked through the window into the back yard and noted that it was starting to get darker.

"Hey, sis."

"Sid, I've found something," he heard Gloria say over the phone. "Just as I was leaving work I got a packet from the D.A.'s office. Stuff related to their case against you. I had a courier pick it up for me."

"Yeah, so?"

"So I didn't look at it 'til I got home. Mostly required paperwork— the official complaint and the charges against you, some police records. But there was a clean copy of the D.R.O.S. You remember what that was?"

"Sure, it was the thing that said I bought the gun in Reno. The 'Dealer Record' something."

"Right. But this one is a much better copy."

Gloria paused, and he could hear his nieces hollering in the background, then Marty's voice shushing them.

"Okay," Sid prodded his sister. "What's the news?"

"There's a space on the form for your drivers license number. I couldn't make it out on the first copy we had. But this one's easy to read. Sid, it's not your number."

Sid's first reaction was underwhelming. *So what? Whoever bought the gun had done a lousy job of filling out the form. Didn't even make an effort to forge the signature.* Then a question occurred to him.

"How do you know what my drivers license number is?"

"I don't, Sid. But I recognize the one that's on this form."

Gloria paused, probably just for a second or two. But it was enough time for Sid's heart to jump up into his throat. Enough time for his breathing to grow shallow and to press the phone tighter against his ear.

"Sid, it's dad's. It's our father's drivers license number."

CHAPTER 26

It had been nearly two miles since he'd seen the other runner, and Sid was no closer to catching him. The guy was fast.

There are those who will tell you that the American River Parkway is Sacramento's greatest asset. More than twenty miles of bike paths and trails run along the American River from Folsom to Discovery Park where the river joins the Sacramento, then continues off to the delta. No cars allowed. Just bicycles, runners and walkers, which meant there would be no Chrysler sedans or TV vans. So that's where Sid chose to spend his Saturday morning. It had been a couple of weeks since he'd gotten in a twenty-miler and he was looking forward to the solitude.

It was a thirty minute run to the university and the J Street Bridge over the American, where he could drop down to the bike trail. As soon as he hit the path along the river, he saw another runner ahead of him, maybe 200 yards. The guy was wearing a racing singlet, and even from a distance it was obvious his stride was superb. Sid felt a welcome, familiar surge of competitiveness, and he picked up his pace.

He ran hard. Not at his limit, but hard. A mile went by, and the figure ahead of him was just as distant. He pushed harder and his breathing grew heavy. At seven in the morning it was still cool out, but his Humboldt Cross Country t-shirt was already beginning to cling to him. Two miles, and the gap wasn't closing. The casual observer might not have seen it, but Sid smiled as he pushed air in and out of his lungs.

As he had done many times before, he dug down and found another gear—the fire that had helped him to beat plenty of better runners through the years—and after a couple more miles, the man ahead was beginning to draw closer. There aren't a lot of guys who can click off five and a half minute miles one after another. It's a small community, and Sid was pretty sure he knew everybody in Northern California who was capable of the pace. Who was the runner ahead of him? It had to be somebody he knew...

"It's gotta be somebody you know, Sid." In his mind he heard his sister's voice from their conversation in the deli two days before. *"It's gotta be somebody you know..."*

Over the last couple of days, Sid had learned several new things about whoever was behind the Capital shootings. He'd tried to go over it all last night, after he got off the phone with Gloria. But an hour of pacing around his room and staring at his pitiful list of suspects left him frustrated and sleepy. This morning's run was, in part, an effort to clear his head and think through what he knew about the case.

Case. In his mind, that's what it had become. *The Case.* He was Columbo. And if he tried hard enough, he could catch the guy.

The runner ahead of him was unaware that there was someone behind him. Unaware that Sid had closed the gap by half. Occasionally the bike trail would bend and Sid would lose sight of him, then he'd come back into view. Sid was beginning to hurt, but he had decided long ago that was no reason to slow down.

The events and circumstances of the last few weeks, and especially the last two days, played in Sid's mind as he ran. He knew there was a thread that connected them. Knew he had collected puzzle pieces that, when assembled, would be a picture of whoever was behind the Capital shootings.

If Jackson Dexter could be believed, there was more than one person who was setting him up. He'd said that two different people had called him with information. Well, whoever the second caller was—the one that tipped him that Sid was being arrested—they had to know when the police were making their move. Somebody who knew a cop? Somebody who was a cop? Hmmm. That was an interesting thought.

Sid had been presuming that one of Jackson Dexter's two callers had also called the cops to tell them where they'd find the gun. But what if one of the callers *was* a cop? That made some sense—simplified what was a confusing collection of clues. Certainly Det. Stokes was a creep and he made no secret of the fact that he didn't like Sid. But Sid had never even heard of the guy before that first day he walked into the deli. What would motivate Stokes to go to all the trouble to set up someone he didn't even know? That didn't make sense. In fact, the only cop that Sid knew was… Woody. When Woody's name occurred to him, Sid subconsciously slowed his pace a little. It was like he'd been punched in the chest. The thought was crazy. Sure, it connected a couple of dots, but there was zero motivation for it. Zero.

The runner ahead of him had been getting steadily closer, but was now starting to pull away again. Sid grunted loudly a few times in rhythm with his footsteps and began closing on the guy.

What about Jock Bell? Surely one of the callers was Jock Bell, right? He'd been about as subtle as a foghorn. Moustache Guy in the alley all but admitted he was working for Bell. He was just about to say Bell's name when Amy planted her foot in his Happy Place. Yeah, weird old Jock Bell wanted to buy the building that the deli was in. He was somebody who always got what he wanted and he couldn't stand being told 'no.' Jock Bell had to be one of the callers. That one's a slam dunk.

Sid was making some progress. He had the odd feeling that the answer was already somewhere in his head, but he couldn't find a way to get to it. It was simultaneously encouraging and frustrating.

The runner ahead was now less than twenty-five yards away. His stride was smooth and his steps were silent. His straight black hair dripped with sweat, but didn't bounce at all as he glided down the bike trail. There was something familiar about him, but Sid couldn't get a look at his face. It was definitely someone he knew—someone he'd run against in the past. But he couldn't place him.

As he continued his pursuit, Sid's phone conversation with Gloria from the night before popped into his head. It was twelve hours later and he was still trying to grasp the meaning and significance of what she'd told him. Whoever bought the gun that was used to shoot up Sacramento had used his dad's personal information. It was Sid Bigler, Sr.—Big Sid—that, according to the official form, purchased that pistol. Six months after he died. What the hell was that?

The death of his father was the saddest and surest thing in the world. Big Sid couldn't have bought the gun that the Capital Shooter used, but somebody made it look as though he had. What was the point of that? At least Sid now knew why the signature on the dealer's form looked nothing like his own. It was probably supposed to look like his father's signature, and Sid couldn't recall what that would've looked like. Big Sid always used the darned typewriter, and the only thing he ever wrote by hand to his son was what he always signed at the bottom of birthday cards. "Love, Dad".

That last thought was painful. Sid clenched his jaw, and with the front of his shirt he wiped something from his eyes that was either sweat or tears. Breathing hard through his nose for a moment, he struggled to keep the pace he'd been running at for over seven miles now. He'd stopped gaining on the runner ahead of him. He was close. But not close enough to see who it was.

Who knew his father well enough to have personal information like a driver's license number? Sid thought about the list on the desk in his room. In his mind he could see Joe Diaz's name circled. If Joe had anything to do with all this, then maybe their strange conversation in the deli the other afternoon made a little more sense. What was Joe's point in all that? He was half drunk and lost in reminiscing about his best friend of forty years. If Joe had some hand in Sid's current trouble, maybe that rambling confession was his way of saying he was sorry. What else could it have been?

And then Sid thought of Eddie Davis. Yvonne the social worker once told him that Eddie was good with numbers. Maybe Eddie knew Big Sid's driver's license number. If Sid hadn't been so exhausted he might have laughed at the idea of Eddie masterminding the Capital Shooter conspiracy.

The trail splits at Goethe Park, with one part making a big, sweeping turn to the left toward the river. Sid realized that he'd lost sight of the runner ahead of him. He was already aware that he'd been losing ground for the last half mile or so. His legs ached. His breathing was faster. Sid went left and ran hard through the turn. When the trail straightened, there was no runner ahead of him. A slight sense of panic made him push hard one last time. He clinched his teeth, searching for that extra gear. But the trail ended after another hundred yards at a parking lot overlooking the river. And the runner was nowhere to be seen. He jogged along the row of cars, looking in each one, and felt a sadness and frustration creeping over him. He even called out, "Hey! Hello!" But no one answered. There was nobody there. Damn. Sid had gotten close, just never close enough. It had to have been someone he knew.

The rest of Sid's run proved to be uneventful. He was mentally and physically exhausted from the pursuit. The trip home took twice as long as the first part of his run, with Sid taking a break to walk on several occasions.

He wasn't far from home, jogging down Broadway when he accidentally discovered what the two guys in the Chrysler had been up to the day before. He was passing a coffee shop named "Pancake Circus" when he happened to glance at the newspaper boxes facing the street. The Sacramento Union featured a bold headline that read, "Shooter Returns to Scene of Crime!" And there was a nice big picture of himself staring into the camera, jogging along with Fairytale Town right behind him.

CHAPTER 27

So the morning run hadn't quite gone the way he'd planned. At about 9:45, Sid finally made it back to his mom's house to discover Gloria's BMW parked in the driveway. Playing in the front yard were Niece Nicky and Niece Nelly, who ran to him with arms outstretched shouting "Uncle Sid! Uncle Sid!" He raised his hands in protest and called out, "Stop! Sweaty, smelly uncle here!" And to Sid's great delight, the girls ignored the warning and hugged him anyway.

Once inside the house, he found Gloria at the dining room table, surrounded by stacks of paper and a few cardboard boxes.

"Hey, sis, what's up?"

"Oh, I'm just double checking myself." She hardly glanced up when she heard his voice. "This is all the stuff from dad's estate that I went through six months ago. Seeing his drivers license number on that form last night… I don't know. I just got to thinking that maybe there was something in here that I missed back then."

"Like what?"

Now Gloria paused and turned her attention to her brother. Big Sister Look #17. The one that says, *Do you enjoy being stupid?* Sid managed to stand still and endure it for several seconds before making a move towards the kitchen.

"Where's mom?" Sid called as he opened the refrigerator and grabbed the orange juice.

"Somebody started a Saturday morning Bingo somewhere. A blue-haired woman in an Oldsmobile picked her up about half an hour ago."

"Yeah, I'm starting to get worried about the crowd she's hanging around with. They seem a little wild." Sid returned to the dining room as he took a drink straight from the carton. "So... found anything interesting?"

"Probably not. I found that written offer Jock Bell made dad for the building." Gloria quickly located a piece of paper and pushed it in Sid's direction. He picked it up and studied it.

"Two-hundred fifty thousand dollars."

"Uh-huh." Gloria sounded unimpressed as she continued to shuffle through other papers. "Daddy told us about that, remember? He said it's worth more."

Sid remembered the conversation from last year, but not the number. Two-hundred fifty grand. Standing there in his shorts and t-shirt with an orange juice carton in his hand, it sounded like a lot.

"Couple other things that might be interesting..." Gloria picked up some more papers. "This is a police report about a break-in at the deli last October. Do you remember anything about that?"

"Nope."

"Me neither. I don't think dad ever mentioned it." Gloria scanned the front of the form, then flipped it over. "It happened on a weekend. Looks like nothing was taken, but the front door lock was clearly broken. Weird, huh?"

Neither one had to say out loud that the break-in was just a few weeks before their father killed himself. And neither one could figure how this information played into the current circumstances.

"Oh, and I found this." Gloria dropped an envelope on the table in front of her brother. It was addressed to "Mr. Bigler, 1028 K Street"—the deli's address. The envelope had been cancelled by the post office and opened, but whatever had once been inside was gone. The postmark was August, 1965. Almost fifteen years ago.

"It's an empty envelope." Now it was Sid's turn to be unimpressed.

"Yeah. When I saw it, I remembered that I found it in dad's safe. That's why I hadn't thrown it away. The only other things in there were important papers like his mortgage, life insurance policies, the deed to the deli building. Seemed funny that there was an old, empty envelope in there with that stuff."

"Huh." Sid would've said something more clever, but nothing came to mind.

"How long are you planning to stink up this room?" Gloria had always been subtle.

Sid drained the O.J. and left the carton on the table as he walked down the hallway. He ducked into his room to grab some clean clothes before heading for the shower. He paused when he saw his list of suspects on the desk, then walked over to look at it. It was a mess, with cross-outs and scribbles and circles. Still standing, he leaned over the desk, grabbed a pen, and next to Jock Bell's name he wrote, *'Yes! And somebody else!'* Then, at the bottom of his list, he added *'Maybe a cop.'* Below that he wrote, *'Who called Jackson Dexter?'* Sid shook his head. For a while when he was running, he really thought he was figuring something out. But that was all he could add to his list. Pitiful. Colombo made it look so easy.

Sid showered and shaved, then put on his best jeans and a shirt that actually had buttons. He was going to Amy's later to watch the Dallas rerun courtesy of her VCR and figured he might as well get properly cleaned up now. He gave the shoes he'd been running in that morning a sniff, then put them back on before returning to the dining room to check on Gloria.

Most of the papers had been returned to the cardboard boxes. Jock Bell's offer still sat on the table, along with the police report Gloria had found, and that empty envelope he'd seen earlier.

"All done, Sis?"

"Yeah. Hey look at this before I go."

Sid saw now that his sister had Big Sid's wallet in her hand. After his father died, there was some conversation about what to do with it, and they'd decided to just put it in a box with the business and personal records. Sometimes it's funny and surprising to discover what things carry sentimental value. Sid's glimpse of the wallet filled him with myriad fond memories of Big Sid. It was ancient and worn, and Sid couldn't remember his old man carrying any other one.

Gloria flipped it open to show its contents. They'd left his driver's license, Kaiser card, and other personal stuff where they'd found them. *What else are you supposed to do with it?* Sid thought. Also in the wallet was a stack of about ten "Sid's Deli" business cards. Big Sid always carried a supply of them. He loved the cards, and would schmooze and leave them with everyone he met wherever he went. He was always hustling for new customers.

"Look here," Gloria said, as she flipped over one of the cards and laid it on the table. "There's an address written on the back of this one. That's daddy's handwriting. I never saw him write much, but that's it. I'm sure."

Sid struggled to read what was written there. "384 Revere Street." It didn't ring a bell.

"Is that supposed to be familiar?" he asked.

"It wasn't to me. Not at first. But take a look at the envelope."

Gloria picked up the odd, empty envelope from the table and laid it next to the business card. Sid stared at them for a moment. And then he saw it. The address on the back of the card was the same as the return address on the envelope. Sid reached down and tapped the upper left hand corner.

"384 Revere Street. What is this place?"

"No idea. Probably nothing, but it's worth looking into." Gloria folded Big Sid's wallet and put it in one of the boxes. "Can you get this stuff back into the attic for me?"

"Sure."

"Thanks. I gotta get Nicky to a Daisies thing. One of the other moms is teaching the girls how to make sock puppets." Gloria stood and picked up her purse and car keys. "Oh, hey, I was supposed to bring socks. Do you have any extras?"

"You really want Nicky sticking her hands in Uncle Sid's socks?"

"Maybe we'll just buy some on the way."

"Good call."

Dallas was nearly over—it was the episode where Miss Ellie gets a mastectomy—and Sid wasn't remotely interested. It was not for lack of compassion for Miss Ellie, but this was a rerun of a TV show and he had non-fictional things on his mind. Amy was leaning up against him while she finished off a dish of Neapolitan ice cream.

He'd spent much of the afternoon helping his mom with some chores. There were boxes and boxes of Big Sid's stuff in the garage and Rose had decided it was time to get it all organized. Which meant that young Sid had spent four hours in nearly hundred degree heat trying to find places for tools and sports equipment and old Navy uniforms and at least 500 magazines of various sorts. When he was done, he took his second shower of the day, put on his second best jeans, a t-shirt and the same old running shoes and jumped in his car.

Before heading over to Amy's, he had stopped by a gas station on Broadway to look at a street map. He glanced back and forth, from the map to the business card in his hand until he located Revere Street and was surprised to see that it was only about a mile from his mom's house. Off the top of his head he couldn't picture the street or the neighborhood, so he decided to drive by.

The Old City Cemetery occupies a unique place in Sacramento, both historically and geographically. It opened for business in 1849, and thanks to a cholera epidemic the following year, business was good. Over time it became a very desirable place to find one's final repose. A walk among the tombstones reveals a veritable 'Who's Who' of deceased Sacramentans. John Sutter himself—the guy with the Fort and the Mill—is buried there. Look closely and you'll find governors and debutantes, mayors and moguls, even a couple of survivors of the famous Donner Party.

Over time, the Old City Cemetery became a dividing line of sorts. On its east side, across Riverside Boulevard, lies one of the city's more quaint and desirable neighborhoods. The tree-lined avenues of Land Park are home to post card perfect bungalows and brick tudor houses, and people walk the streets without fear. It's where Sid and Rose Bigler raised their young family. But to the west it's another story altogether. On the other side of the cemetery—behind the cemetery—lies New Helvetia. It's a collection of small homes and apartments that were built following World War II as military housing, but over time had become what most people would call "The Projects." Hundreds of publicly subsidized units and thousands of people living in close proximity, it's an assortment of culture and color that is more often a cause for conflict rather than a celebration of diversity.

Sid drove down Broadway, turned left after he passed the cemetery, and found himself looking at a neighborhood he always knew existed, but that he'd never taken the time to really see. It was late on a hot Saturday afternoon, and a few small plastic wading pools dotted the patchy brown and green lawn areas. Little kids, some just in their underwear, splashed in the shallow water or ran squealing through sprinklers. Older kids, who had somehow lost the ability to recklessly enjoy life like their younger siblings, stood sullenly in groups, watching cars drive by or watching the other groups of similarly sullen teens.

Some of the apartments appeared to be clean and well cared for, with potted plants and folding chairs outside of front doors, and perhaps smoke coming from a lit barbecue. Others were downright depressing. Garbage and empty gas cans, weeds and broken furniture. They communicated not just neglect, but disdain.

It took Sid several minutes to find 384 Revere Street. It was in the middle of a long, low building that probably contained eight or ten apartments, mostly brick and stucco. There was nothing remarkable about it. The entrance was neither tidy nor trashy, and Sid thought that, had it not been for the address written on the back of one of his father's business cards, he would have driven right by. But he didn't. He stopped the car in the street in front of the place and he stared at it. *What was the date of the cancellation on that envelope this morning? 1965? Could the person who addressed the envelope back then still be living here?*

What could this place have to do with Big Sid? And what about the Capital Shooter? And why were there so damned many questions with so few answers?

Out of the corner of his eye, Sid caught some movement in his rear view mirror. He glanced up to see a group of six or seven kids—teenagers—walking down the middle of the street coming up behind his car. They were probably harmless, but he played it safe and pulled slowly away from 384 Revere Street.

Larry Hagman was smiling his phony smile and expressing some phony concern for Miss Ellie. Amy said, "I'm glad somebody shot him." Sid realized that he hadn't really been watching the TV for quite a while. Images from that neighborhood behind the Old City Cemetery had kept coming to him, and he had allowed his mind to wander.

"I've changed my mind about who shot J.R.," Amy said as the closing credits started to roll. "I say it was Sue Ellen."

"Nah. Had to be Bobby. If he was my brother, I'd have shot him, too."

"Maybe under the circumstances…" Amy paused, then tilted her head and gave Sid a quick kiss. "…you shouldn't talk about shooting people."

She flashed him a smile that made him forget about Revere Street, and he pulled her closer.

CHAPTER 28

Sid loved waking up to an empty house on Sunday mornings. His mom and sister had tried on numerous occasions to make him feel guilty that he had stopped going to church with them, but without much effect. Like father like son. On a scale of one to ten, his no-church guilt was about a two. But this Sunday morning he was restless. He'd slept fitfully, then laid in bed later than usual hoping to get back to sleep. Instead, he dozed in and out. And somewhere between asleep and awake, faces and voices from the past few days came back to him.

Jackson Dexter made a dreamy appearance to remind him that two different people had called him with information. The guy with the moustache in the alley shouted that Big Sid owed sixty grand and somebody had to pay. Yvonne the blonde hinted that it might not be safe for Eddie at the deli. He heard Joe Diaz confess, *"I can't say nothin'."* His sister, in her best lawyer suit, displayed ballistics reports and forged gun registration forms, and an envelope with an address on Revere Street. In this sleepy, Sunday morning state, Sid heard the reporter that had been in his driveway in the dark on Friday ask him, *"Well, if you're not the Capital Shooter, any idea who is?"* And he heard Gloria say, *"It's gotta be somebody you know."*

Before Rose and Gloria got home, Sid dragged himself out of bed and made himself some pancakes. Coach Armbruster at McClatchy High School had encouraged him to pound down pancakes, especially on the days before cross-country meets, and he must have eaten a million of them since. At 27, he was just beginning to have his first suspicions that he might not be able to eat an unlimited number of the things anymore. The waistband on his pants had been feeling a little snug lately, and yesterday morning's run had left him with the strong suspicion that he was slowing down. Nevertheless, he stacked the pancakes high and parked himself in front of the television to get caught up on the news. The death toll from last week's eruption of Mt. Saint Helens was up over fifty. The Pope was about to make his first trip to France. Inflation was running at over fourteen percent.

The affairs of the world seemed small compared to his own problems. Now that he was out of bed and having something to eat, his mind was no longer playing the "Capital Shooter Slide Show." But the pieces of the puzzle were never far from his thoughts, and at some level he was always aware that he didn't know how it all fit together. One piece in particular kept coming back to him—that apartment on the other side of the cemetery. The TV and the pancakes couldn't make it go away.

Woody answered the phone on the third ring.

"What are you doing today?"

"Sid?"

"Yeah, it's me. What are you doing today?"

"Uhhh…" Woody thought for a moment. "Some buddies and I are going to a sports bar to watch the Giants get their butts kicked by the Pirates. Wanna come?"

"What are you doing after that?"

"Sid, what is it you want?"

It took Sid several minutes to catch Woody up on the events of the past few days. He just hit the highlights, and finished up with the story of the envelope and the business card and the plain looking apartment in the projects.

"Okay," Woody prompted him again. "So what is it you want?"

"I want to go case the place."

"Did you say *'case'* the place?"

"Or *'stake it out'* or *'do surveillance'* or whatever you cops say. Yeah."

"And why is it that you're calling me?"

"Well, because it's…" Sid was hesitant to admit it, but there was no turning back. "Because it's scary. It's a scary neighborhood."

Sid was pretty sure he could hear Woody suppressing a laugh. Since that afternoon at the gym when Woody had told him that Stokes had more evidence than just the gun, the two of them had managed to go for a run together and have a cup of coffee, and their relationship appeared to be back on track.

"I'm going no matter what, Woody."

"Yeah. Yeah, I can tell that you are. Look, I'm gonna watch the ballgame, and I've got some other stuff to do. Can this wait 'til tonight?"

"You'll come with me tonight?"

"Yeah, Sid. I'll be your *backup*." Woody said the word in a way that made it clear he thought the whole business was funny. "Besides," he added, "stakeouts are always better in the dark."

It was a challenge for Sid to fill the hours until he set out on his spy mission. Not long after he got off the phone with Woody, Gloria dropped their mother off at home. He made his mom some pancakes while she recapped the morning sermon, and by the time Rose was eating he had a pretty good grasp on the idea that the meek would be inheriting the earth.

The early afternoon found Sid and Rose in the living room in front of the television. His friend Woody's interest in the Giants game was probably just a social one, heightened by the certainty that he and his buddies would be eating and drinking their way through all nine innings. Who won and who lost was not crucial to Woody's enjoyment of the event. Rose, on the other hand, was a true believer. She sat wearing a Giants ballcap, sitting in her favorite chair with pencil and paper, keeping the box score and yelling at any umpire or manager that dared to cross her. She cheered loudly when San Francisco went up three to nothing in the first.

Rose dozed off between the fifth and sixth innings,

and Sid took the opportunity to head to his room to re-work his list of suspects. He transferred the few names that remained onto a clean sheet of paper. He included the additions he'd made yesterday—'*A cop?*' and '*Who called Jackson Dexter?*' It was during this process that it first occurred to him that Dexter might belong on the list himself. Maybe he was lying about the two callers. Why couldn't a reporter, desperate for a good story, simply create one? It'd be easy to scoop the rest of the media if you were the person behind the whole thing. *Interesting.* He circled Jackson Dexter's name.

Then, in a separate column, Sid wrote down all of the things he could think of that might be clues pointing toward who the real Capital Shooter might be: "*Gambling. Gold. Phony Gun Record. Access to Deli…*"

That last item prompted Sid's memory. Something he'd forgotten. It was more than a week ago that he walked into the back room at the deli to find Joe having an angry conversation with someone on the payphone. What had he said? "*He doesn't know anything, so stay the hell away.*" Something like that. Who was he talking about, and who was he talking to? And how could Sid have forgotten about that?

Before he put down his pen, Sid added a few more things to the page. "*Dad's Drivers License. Runner's Log. 384 Revere Street.*"

It was nine o'clock, and they had only recently arrived. The sun had been down for less than an hour. It was still hot, the windows were rolled down, and Sid was grumpy.

"We're probably too late."

"Sid, you keep saying that. What's it mean? We're too late for what?"

"I don't know, Woody. That's the point. I don't know why this place is important, so I wanted to come out here to watch and see what happens. I want to see who lives here, or who comes and goes. And I sat around waiting and waiting for you to call, and now we're probably too late to see anything."

Streetlamps cast circles of yellow light here and there, and the moon was about two-thirds full. They were parked in Woody's dark '76 Impala about twenty-five yards away from the front of 384 Revere Street. Some lights were on inside the apartment, but it was all shadows outside the front door. Hard to tell if anybody was home or not.

"I wish you were taking this a little more seriously," Sid said.

"And I wish you could see how funny this is. We're sitting here in the dark outside a house in a very questionable part of town based on a hunch and a scrap of paper. And you were going to drive us here in *your* car."

"What's the matter with my car?"

"Well, as a general rule, private eyes like us don't like to do covert operations in a bright green Dodge Duster with a hula girl on the dash."

Sid might have seen the humor in it, but there wasn't time. There was a loud bang and the car shuddered, followed by the sounds of laughter. Woody was out the driver's door before Sid could even react. Sid took a moment to make sure he hadn't been shot, then opened his door and stepped out, too.

In the moonlight, it took a moment for Sid to grasp the situation. A group of Asian teenage boys in shorts and t-shirts stood in the street behind the car, and Woody was in front of them with jaw and fists clenched. Whoever had been laughing wasn't laughing now. The boys were silent and terrified, staring at the off-duty cop like he was The Incredible Hulk.

"What did you guys do to my car?"

The kids were still as statues. Sid counted six of them. Not a one was over five foot three, and he'd never felt so tall in his life. It was clear from the looks on their faces that Woody's power to intimidate had nothing to do with his uniform. Standing there in jeans and a tight t-shirt, he had them paralyzed.

"Somebody better start talking to me. What happened to my car?"

One of the boys in the back pointed to one of the boys in the front and said, "He hit you car." English was not his first language. "On the back of car with his hand. He hit you car."

Woody turned his most potent stare on the kid in the front. Then he pointed to his trunk. "Show me where you hit the car."

It was too dark to see if the kid had peed his pants, but no one would have blamed him. He took a step forward and pointed to the middle of the trunk lid.

Woody reached over and ran his hand over the trunk.

"Okay. It looks like there's no damage. If you'd hurt my car, I would've hurt you. Understand?"

The kid in front swallowed hard and his eyes grew wider. He nodded.

"Why did you do that?" It was Sid who spoke, and all six kids turned their heads, realizing for the first time that he even existed. "Why'd you hit the car?"

The kid in front—the trunk whacker—mustered some courage as he looked Sid over. "You guys don't belong here." His English was better. "We were just screwing around."

Out of the mouths of punks. The kid was right. They didn't belong, and they couldn't imagine what it must be like to grow up there.

"I think we're all done here." Woody spoke and all the boys turned to him again. "Gentlemen, please. Rest your sphincters."

If the kids understood what he'd said, you couldn't tell. They just stared back at him blankly. Sid, however, was shocked.

"That's from Blazing Saddles." Sid said it like an accusation.

Woody looked at him and shrugged—a look that said *"So what?"*

"I can't believe you're ripping off Harvey Korman at a time like this."

"You kids get out of here," Woody said. "And don't let me see you again."

Before he was even done saying the words, the six

boys had taken off running. As they disappeared down the street some of them began laughing again.

"Let's get in the car and get outta here," Woody said, and he slid back into the driver's seat.

"We've only been here ten minutes," Sid protested as he got in on the passenger side. "You have to give me at least half an hour."

Woody scowled in the dark, and tried to angle his wristwatch so he could see the time in the moonlight.

"Half an hour, then we leave."

The thirty minutes proved to be disappointing. It turned out that, once the sun goes down, not much happens in New Helvetia. At least, not on this night. A few cars came and went. They saw a group of eight or nine black kids walk by at about 9:20, and a couple of white kids went by on bicycles a few minutes after that. But nobody entered or exited 384 Revere Street and they hadn't seen any movement inside.

Woody made one, final exaggerated effort to read the dial of his watch, then he reached down and started the car without saying a word. He put it in drive, and was reaching to turn on the lights when Sid reached out and put a hand on his arm. Then Sid pointed.

Someone was approaching the door at 384. It was a man, but that was all they could tell in the shadows. He knocked at the door.

"Either he doesn't live there, or he forgot his keys," Sid whispered. Woody remained silent.

After a moment, the door opened, and the guy went in. From their angle, Sid and Woody couldn't see anyone or anything inside. The door closed.

Woody turned to his friend and spoke very quietly. "Your half hour is up, you know."

"Oh, c'mon. We can't leave now!" Sid whispered, but it was urgent.

Woody reached and turned off the car. He checked the rear view mirror, then he slid down a little lower in his seat. Sid did the same. Neither spoke.

They didn't have to wait long. Less than five minutes after he entered the apartment, the guy came out the front door alone and closed the door loudly behind him. He headed toward the street, then turned right onto the sidewalk. He was on the opposite side of the road from Woody's car, but he'd be walking right past them.

The guy was big, easily over six feet. He walked with his hands stuffed into his pockets and his shoulders hunched forward. His body language said "angry." Sid sat up a little and leaned forward to keep the guy in view. The pool of light beneath the lamppost across the street was only a few feet wide, but it was wide enough. As the guy passed underneath the streetlight, he turned his head and looked right at Sid and Woody. It was Joe Diaz.

CHAPTER 29

It was a strange, strange Monday morning at Sid's Deli for a couple of reasons.

First of all, it was Memorial Day. The deli was usually closed on holidays, because when state workers have the day off, downtown Sacramento is a ghost town. But Memorial Day was an exception. The Sacramento Dixieland Jazz Jubilee had become the largest gathering of Dixieland musicians and enthusiasts in the world, and every Memorial Day Old Sacramento is packed to overflowing. Everywhere you look, guys in straw hats and suspenders are escorting ladies in tank tops and feather boas, and the happy sound of Dixieland Jazz is so ubiquitous and relentless that it makes you want to puke. Add to that the fact that Memorial Day always falls on a Monday—which means it was Brown Sugar Cinnamon Roll day—and you end up with the absolute busiest day of the year at Sid's Deli. Locals would fill the place in the morning, drawn by the promise of the world's greatest cinnamon rolls, and all through the afternoon the place would be a madhouse with a line out the door thanks to the music festival. In the last few minutes before opening, it felt a little like the calm before the storm.

The other reason it was a strange day is that Joe Diaz showed up for work like it was any other Monday, and didn't act like it was strange at all.

Sid didn't exactly know what to expect that morning at work. He wasn't even sure that Joe would show up. Joe had looked right at them the night before as he walked down Revere Street. But it had been dark, and Sid couldn't be sure that Joe had really seen them at all. He might have just been looking in their direction. There was no way to know.

At seven o'clock Sid unlocked the front door. Four customers were waiting outside and came in immediately, filling their noses with the fantastic smell of the BS Rolls. They were all to-go orders. One guy still had pajama bottoms and slippers on under his t-shirt. Sid had them taken care of and out the door in just a couple of minutes.

For a moment, it was quiet again and there were no customers in the store. More would soon be arriving. Sid saw his opportunity and seized it.

"So, how's everything going?"

There was a long pause, and then Joe turned and said, "You talking to me?"

It was a very reasonable question. Sid and Joe had been following the same routine every morning for the last six months, and this was the first time either of them had attempted anything that resembled small talk.

"Yeah. How's everything going?"

"Good." For Joe, that was a long answer. He turned back to the grill.

"You do anything special last night?" *Subtle, huh?*

"Nope."

Sid let it rest for a minute. Joe simply wasn't a

talkative person, so there was no telling if he was being evasive, or just being Joe. He tried another angle.

"Woody and I went for a ride last night."

Joe said "uh-huh" as he turned and headed for the back room, wiping his hands on his apron. The front door opened and two more customers entered, and that was the end of their small talk.

Just before ten o'clock, the BS Rolls sold out. It was a good thing Joe had made extras. There was a very slight lull in business after that, but by 11:30 the place was really jumping. The deli was packed with Dixieland revelers and the door was blocked open so the line could snake out onto the sidewalk. One of the guys in line had a banjo and was under the assumption that everyone would like to hear him play. Sid was busy clearing tables when he wasn't making change and taking care of to-go orders. And the orders were large ones, as some people were obviously picking up lunch for friends or band members that must have been elsewhere.

A thin woman with bird-like features in her late fifties approached the register when her turn came, and something about her was familiar. Maybe it was because they'd met before, or maybe it was because she looked a little like a red-headed Gladys Kravitz from Bewitched. Sid wasn't sure.

"What can I get you?"

"Four meatloaf sandwiches and four orders of gravy fries, please."

Time stood still. The earth stopped spinning. Sid

heard a choir sing. How could he not have recognized Meatloaf Lady right away?

"I'm sorry, could you... Could you repeat that order?"

Up until this point, the woman had managed a very casual yet businesslike front. She was any other customer in any other restaurant. But when Sid asked the question, small cracks in her veneer started to form.

"Four meatloaf sandwiches and four orders of gravy fries, please." This time, when she said it, her chin quivered ever so slightly.

"Is your name *Matheson*?"

"Yes." She had been clutching a baggy purse in front of her with both hands. Now she drew it up closer to her chest, willing herself to hide behind it.

Sid lowered his voice a little, and leaned towards the woman. "Do you have a son named *Roger*?"

"Yes." She lowered her voice to match his, as though they had a secret.

"And is he a little bit overweight?"

"Yes."

Now Sid put most of his weight on his arms as he leaned even further over the counter, which, in turn, drew the woman even closer to him.

"Oh, no he's not..." It was barely more than a whisper. Their eyes were locked. Then Sid smiled just a little, and he practically shouted, "HE'S FAT!"

The woman was startled. She tried to take a deep breath but it caught in her throat. Her mouth opened slightly and her eyes began to fill with tears. Surprisingly,

241

she didn't back away. Their faces were just inches apart as he continued, speaking very slowly, and loud enough for everyone in the deli to hear. "YOUR SON... IS FAT! SUPER... DUPER... FAT!

Sid's first clue that he'd made a huge mistake was the deafening silence. He allowed himself a brief glance around to discover that his short but impressive tirade had gotten everyone's attention. Every single person in the place was staring at him. The banjo guy had stopped playing, but Sid could just detect the lingering "twoing" of his last note. The silence lasted for eight or ten seconds, and wasn't broken until Connie Matheson completely and loudly burst into tears.

The eyes of the spectators glanced back and forth between the pitiful woman and the creep that had just humiliated her. Sid hadn't thought it possible, but time seemed to slow down even more. Mrs. Matheson continued to bellow and wail, then stooped and buried her face in her purse, muting her sobs. People in the deli began to murmur, and some who were waiting actually stepped out of line and left the deli, their faces showing undisguised contempt.

And Sid felt bad. He really did. The feeling was made even worse when Mrs. Matheson lifted her head and sobbed out the words, "I'm so sorry! I'm so, so sorry!"

She started to look a little wobbly, and Sid hurried from behind the counter to steady her. He put an arm around her and said, "No. No, I'm the one who's sorry. I'm really sorry, Mrs. Matheson..."

For some reason, the remaining spectators found this moment even more uncomfortable than the one that immediately preceded it. Most of the people who were waiting to order or waiting for a table now took the opportunity to get out of Sid's Deli and away from one of the most awkward moments in recorded history. Sid guided the woman to a recently evacuated seat at the counter.

"Can I get you a glass of water or something?"

"No, I'm fine." The woman fished a handkerchief out of her bag and wiped her eyes. "I shouldn't have come here."

The statement was hard to argue with, so Sid said nothing. Connie Matheson blew her nose loudly.

"Please," she said, "don't be mad at Roger. He didn't even know at first. The lawsuit was my idea. I saw an ad for the lawyer in the yellow pages and I called him. Roger doesn't have any way to provide for himself. I thought that if I could get him a big settlement, I wouldn't have to… to worry about…"

She choked up and began sobbing again. Sid patted her on the back as he glanced around the deli, wishing that he was almost any other human on the planet. A guy with a black case that had to contain a trombone walked up to the cash register, and Sid was happy for the opportunity to step away from Mrs. Matheson and do his job. By the time the transaction was completed, the woman had regained her composure.

"You can see why I was upset, right?" Sid walked back over to Roger Matheson's mom. "I mean, you're suing me."

"Yes, and I'm sorry. I've told Mr. Headley we're dropping the lawsuit. You won't have any more trouble from us." The woman reached up and grabbed a hold of his arm. Sid had never seen anyone look more remorseful in his life.

"You're dropping the lawsuit?"

"Yes. Yes, it's already done."

Hmmm. No wonder Vince Headley had been in such a hurry to cut a deal last Friday.

"Well, thank you, Mrs. Matheson. Thank you."

The woman tightened the grip on his arm. There was an urgency about her, and Sid couldn't figure it out. Around them, the deli was trying to return to normal. Conversations had resumed. A guy had just walked up to the register wearing a t-shirt that said, "If it ain't Dixieland, it ain't Jazz!"

"I have to get back to work," Sid said, in the hopes that she might release her grip. Instead, the woman pulled him closer, and fixed her red, puffy eyes on his.

"Please, Mr. Bigler," she said. "Roger is so hungry."

The Dixieland Jazz Jubilee crowd was showing no signs of letting up. It had been almost three hours since Connie Matheson had left clutching the precious brown paper bag full of meatloaf sandwiches and gravy fries, and a line still spilled out the door. Roger's mom had tried to talk him into a couple of pies, too, but Sid had said no. Maybe Vince Headley had made a little bit of sense.

Sid grabbed his ticket book and started walking

down the line taking orders in an effort to speed things up. Four guys in lederhosen with German accents all ordered reubens and potato salad. The manager of a band called The Dixie Damsels ("They're the only all-female, all-brass band at the festival!") ordered enough food for a small army. A middle aged couple in matching Hawaiian shirt and muumuu ordered two Bleubirds and two chocolate shakes.

Sid had almost reached the door, thinking he'd just take one or two more orders when he glanced out the window and across the street. A little flash of reflected sunlight lit up the door of Jock Bell's Pawn Shop as it swung open. Jock himself emerged into the afternoon sun. He wore a black suit with a shiny yellow shirt underneath. The collars on the shirt spread across the lapels of the jacket and nearly came to the ends of his shoulders. If a breeze came up and caught one, it could flip up and put his eye out. He was followed by the man Sid had met the day he'd stopped by to pick up his dad's stuff—the Wookiee-looking guy with the thick black hair and the high voice. And one more person came out before the door closed behind them. A good-sized guy with long hair parted down the middle and an enormous moustache. *David Crosby turned weight lifter.*

Sid Bigler was not impetuous by nature. He was, in fact, so cautious that a callous observer might call him cowardly at times. And he had a life-long track record of avoiding conflict whenever it was possible. So it was a surprise even to himself when he dropped his pencil and ticket book, shoved his way past some customers at the door, and took off running across the street.

At his first glimpse—at the instant he had recognized the third guy—Sid had involuntarily shouted out, "Hey!" Jock and his boys apparently hadn't heard him. But when he shouted again half-way across the street, all three snapped their heads in his direction. Maybe he got their attention this time because he was closer to them. Or maybe it was because this time he yelled, "Hey! Assholes!"

Call it the element of surprise. None of the three made any kind of aggressive move, or even tried to protect themselves. Sid had only slowed a little when he jumped onto the sidewalk and shoved Jock Bell in the chest. Jock stumbled backwards and might have fallen if he hadn't been steadied by his two flunkies.

The short dash and the shot of adrenaline had Sid already breathing hard. Bell, on the other hand, was remarkably cool. Both the Wookiee and Moustache Guy took a step toward Sid once they had their boss safely back on his feet, but the old guy put his arms out to keep them in check.

"No, boys. No, it's fine."

He took a moment to reach up and make sure his big yellow collars still laid flat, then ran a hand through the magnificent chestnut crown of hair-like material that sat atop his head.

"Watsa matter, Little Sid? You seem upset."

Sid pointed at Moustache Guy. "You sent your thug here to threaten me."

"Help me understand this, Little Sid. Your girlfriend

kicks my nephew in the nuts, and *I'm* the bad guy?"

"Your *nephew*?"

"Sure. I run a nice, family-owned business. I like the thought of having the next generation waiting in the wings to keep the place going. Like you did at the deli, Little Sid. Charlie here can take over the business if I should ever, oh, I don't know…" Jock's eyes had a little twinkle. "Maybe shoot myself in the head."

Had Jock Bell actually said that? It was so unexpected—so completely out of bounds—that Sid questioned what he'd heard. He stared at Jock, narrowed his eyes, and tried not to look confused. Then Jock eliminated any doubt. He winked at Sid, raised his hand to his own head with index finger pointing and thumb sticking up, touched his temple and said, "Pow."

That was it. The same, involuntary reflex that made Sid dash across the street and shove Jock Bell took over once again. This time, it caused him to make his right hand into a fist, rare back, and take a full, hard swing at the old man's face. Bell was surprisingly quick, pulling away from the incoming fist so that Sid's knuckles barely grazed his chin. After failing to make solid contact, Sid's follow-through left him spun half-way around and off balance.

Before he could turn back and appraise the situation, Sid felt strong arms grab him from behind. It must have been the Wookiee doing the grabbing, because he found himself face to face with Moustache Guy, and he didn't look happy. Jock stood behind his nephew, gently rubbing his own jaw. Sid had the presence of mind to note that Bell's hair still retained its perfect shape.

Moustache Guy reached up with both hands and grabbed Sid's ears. He squeezed them tightly, and Sid was surprised how much it hurt. Then Sid had the terrible realization that the initial pain was only the appetizer. The guy began to slowly pull hard on his ears, down and away. It was like Moustache Guy thought they could just be yanked off, like a Mr. Potato Head. And as he pulled harder and harder, Sid began to suspect that maybe the guy was right. The pain was searing.

In the future, Sid would recall that it was in the middle of this encounter with Jock and his boys that he discovered something about himself. Yes, Moustache Guy trying to pull his ears off hurt like hell. But it was just pain. Since junior high school, Sid had been dealing with pain five or six days a week. He'd made it his passion, his goal in life, to overcome pain. If Jock Bell thought this was torture, he should try picking up the pace the last two laps of a 10K. He oughta run intervals at three in the afternoon on a summer day. Sid knew pain, and knew how to use it. As he'd done countless times before in a completely different situation, he used the pain to make himself calm—to make himself focus—to make himself think of a way he could win, even if his opponent was better than him.

It was at that moment that Sid heard a sound he'd never heard before. Maybe one that *nobody* had ever heard. From across the street came something like a scream, but there was an almost other-worldly quality to it. It was louder than any noise Sid thought a human was capable of making. High-pitched, but raspy. And it somehow communicated both fear and rage simultaneously. Everyone within earshot was startled. Moustache Guy let go of Sid's ears and turned to look. The Wookiee relaxed his grip a little. Sid noticed Jock Bell beginning to glance across the street just as he himself turned his head.

It was a sight Sid Bigler would never, ever forget. At least eight members of some Dixieland band were on the sidewalk waiting to get into the deli. They wore matching outfits—navy blue pants, white shirts with red garters on the sleeves, and straw hats. And standing in front of them, looking across the street with his mouth wide open, Eddie Davis was screaming his eerie scream.

CHAPTER 30

The competitor in Sid knew that you take advantage of every opportunity. Tempting as it was to keep staring at Eddie, it was time to act. His first thought was, *'If it ain't broke, don't fix it,'* and he kicked Moustache Guy hard in the groin. There was that crunching sound again, and down he went. Sid twisted one arm loose from the big guy behind him, spun and began poking at his face with the now free hand. Not the kind of thing Clint Eastwood would've done, but what the heck. Sid must have managed to get a finger in his eye, because the guy screamed "Ow!" in his high voice and suddenly let go completely, bringing both palms up to his own face. Then he hopped up and down a few times and said "Ow-wow-wow!" Too bad there wasn't time to laugh.

It registered in the back of Sid's mind that Eddie's screaming had stopped, but he wasn't looking toward the deli now. He was looking at Jock Bell, who was standing five or six feet away from him—relaxed, arms down by his sides.

"That's not a nice way to fight, Little Sid."

"Sorry. I'll give 'em free sandwiches sometime."

Sid took a couple of menacing steps toward Jock Bell. Then stopped and decided maybe it wasn't so menacing. Given his recent and unexpected success in the scuffle with the two thugs, he made the mistake of assuming he knew how to fight. Which meant that Bell should've recoiled a bit—taken a step back and showed a little fear. But Bell didn't move, and now Sid was only three feet away. And he realized he had no idea what he was going to do next.

Moustache Guy managed to get up on his feet and, bent over with his hands on his knees, blew air out in repeated puffs, waiting for the nausea to pass and willing himself to recover. The other guy had stopped hopping, but continued to hold one palm pressed against his left eye.

"This is quite a moment, isn't it Little Sid? You're thinking about taking another swing at me, aren't you?"

Sid didn't really have an answer, and said nothing. He consciously thought about the fact that he didn't know what to do with his hands. Should he make them into fists and raise them up? Let them hang loosely at his sides? Put them in his pockets? *How ridiculous! What a stupid thing to be thinking of at a time like this!* Sid crossed his arms, knew it looked dumb, but was now committed to the position.

"I have a housekeeper." Jock Bell said it as he casually unbuttoned his black jacket and took it off.

Sid couldn't make sense of what the guy had said, and it showed on his face.

"At my house," Jock explained, "I have a housekeeper. I could take care of the place myself— probably do a better job of it than she does—but I prefer to have someone else do menial jobs like that."

By now, Bell had folded his jacket nicely, and he took a couple of steps to his right to drape it over the back of Moustache Guy, who still had his hands on his knees. Jock unbuttoned his cuffs and began rolling up the sleeves on the shiny yellow shirt.

"It's the same with my guys here," Jock gestured towards the two wounded stooges. "I'd just as soon have them do some jobs for me, but I can probably do it better myself."

"And that's how it'll be." A new voice joined the conversation. It was Joe Diaz. Neither Sid nor Jock Bell had seen him cross the street from the deli, but there he was—big enough and strong enough to put an end to this, but that wasn't his plan. He pointed the spatula that was still in his hand at Bell's henchmen.

"You two ain't gonna move. You understand?"

The one with his hand over his eye nodded like a little kid. The one that was still doubled over grunted something that sounded like "Uh-huh", but he didn't look up.

"And you two…" now Joe pointed at Jock and Sid. "You're gonna do what you gotta do."

Sid shot a look at Joe. One that said, *What are you doing?* Joe answered with a small shrug that said, *What the hell.*

Sid was still looking in Joe's direction when Jock Bell tackled him. Jock had gotten up a pretty good head of steam and led with his shoulder, knocking the wind out of Sid. They flew horizontally off the sidewalk, through the air and came down in the street with Sid flat on his back.

He was stunned long enough for Jock Bell to get up to his knees and punch him hard in the face. Way harder than Gloria had socked him nearly two weeks ago. Broken nose. No doubt about it.

Sid had another one of those clarifying, pain-is-my-friend moments, and this time he had it in a hurry. Jock reared back and brought his fist down again, but now Sid quickly rolled out of the way, Jock's hand struck the pavement, and Sid was surprised to hear a loud cheer. He glanced up to discover that the Dixieland band guys in the blue pants and straw hats had come out into the street to enjoy the fight, and it looked like they were rooting for him. It's good to be the home team.

Sid tried to get to his feet, but Jock was too quick, wrapping his arms around him. They rolled over repeatedly until the gutter stopped them, this time with Jock on the bottom. They were face to face, Sid's arms pinned to his sides. He got a fresh whiff of the breath that first caught his attention the day Jock Bell came into the deli. Not good.

"I'm kicking your ass, Little Sid." The voice was low. Powerful.

Sid knew it was true. He had thought that his youth would be his advantage, but Jock Bell had proven to be amazingly fast and clearly much stronger than he.

"I don't know, Jock." Sid tried to say it with a smile. "I'm on top."

Now, looking down for the first time, Sid felt a hot ooze spreading through his nose. It would hurt later, but now it was numb except for the almost pleasant sensation of warmth. He looked down at Jock. Jock looked up at him. And an enormous drop of bright red blood rushed to the tip of Sid's nose and dangled there.

Jock Bell had a lifelong phobia about blood. Sid couldn't have known that, but it was a fact that, in the next few moments, would work greatly to his advantage. Bell traced it back to catechism when he was a child. The nuns told young Jock about The Blood and its miraculous power to save his soul, but the boy found the whole thing frightening and gross and deeply disturbing. It all seemed so vampire-ish to him. And when finally asked to drink the blood for the first time at the age of eight, he was horrified. The first few opportunities to take Holy Communion, he actually faked being sick. When his parents caught on and he was finally forced to do the deed, faking was no longer necessary. He vomited right back into the beautiful silver cup and was permanently excused from communion thereafter. Jock was, of course, relieved, but always felt bad about the incident. In later years, he gave large sums of money to the parish to pay for one project or another, and believed that in so doing, he'd made up for his lack of communal consumption. But his deep, deep fear of blood never left. Never waned.

So now, lying face up in the gutter in front of his own pawn shop, Jock Bell was focused on the drop of blood that dangled from Sid Bigler's nose, and he was in a complete panic. His eyes grew wide in fear, and, paralyzed, he watched the red glob as it broke free, then grew larger and larger until it landed with a splat right between his wiry, manicured eyebrows.

Sid's view of the event was wonderful. From above, he saw Jock's eyes slowly cross as the drop grew closer and closer, and he felt the instant reaction as Bell let him go to bring his hands to his face and began furiously rubbing the blood away.

The whole thing struck Sid as funny, and when he laughed, he snorted a spray of blood that covered Jock Bell from the neck up.

The guys in the Dixieland band let out a collective "ewwww."

And Jock Bell freaked out. The first drop was bad, but now he was reliving the worst nightmares of his ecclesiastical childhood. He screamed, and in one powerful, involuntary movement, Bell rolled away and onto his stomach to escape the continuing drip that was now coming from Sid's nose. He began wiping his face wildly on his sleeves.

Sid saw the smears of red on the yellow fabric, and for just an instant he flashed back to that moment when he saw his father's body slumped over the old typewriter—Rose's yellow dress and his father's red blood.

Before the opportunity was lost, Sid put the image from his mind and leapt onto Jock, straddling his back. And then he reached up with both hands, grabbed hold of Jock Bell's trademark—his pride and joy—his magnificent head of hair, and he pulled very hard. Sid half expected it to come off in one big piece, but it didn't. *'Son-of-a-gun'* he thought. *'It's real.'*

The result of Jock's hair being firmly attached to his scalp was that his head snapped back dramatically. From where Sid sat atop Jock Bell, he couldn't see the blood-smeared face. But he could hear the old guy, and what he heard surprised him. Like Eddie Davis' scream, it was another sound he would long remember.

For the second time that day, Sid Bigler had made someone cry.

"Please," the man managed to say between sobs, almost strangling. "Please."

Sitting astride his back, pulling on his hair like Jock was a runaway horse, Sid realized he might be doing some serious damage. Bell's head and neck were at an unnatural angle. Sid backed off the pressure, still holding tight with his right hand while he reached up with his left to pinch his nose and stop the bleeding. Jock had a chance to breathe and gather himself. Slowly, the crying and sniffing sounds grew quieter. Sid didn't notice that the crowd around them had pressed in closer. It was just him and Jock Bell.

"Did you plant the gun in my place? Did you call the police?"

"No."

Sid gave the hair a little extra tug. Jock made a strained, grunting sound, then hurriedly added, "No! I swear to you. I never saw the gun, I never called the cops." He was still breathing pretty hard, more from his panic attack than from the fight. But he sounded like he was clear-headed. Sid backed off again on the hair.

"Did you call Jackson Dexter?"

"Yes." No hesitation

"How many times?"

"Just once. The day you were arrested."

"You never called him before that?"

"Not about you. Dexter and I have some history. Sometimes I help him, sometimes he helps me. When I saw the cops pull up right in front of your place the day they came to arrest you, I called him. I knew he'd be interested. And I figured any bad press for you was good for me."

"Why?"

Up until this point, all of Jock Bell's answers were accompanied by an occasional sniffle, and sometimes a grunt that indicated that it was hard to talk while being held in such an uncomfortable position. Now he let out a long, slow sigh.

"I'll tell you what you want to know, Little Sid. Would you let go of my damn hair?"

Sid complied, and Jock Bell allowed his head to drop and rest on his forearms that were crossed in front of him. He was face down, his nose only a fraction of an inch from the pavement. He lay there for what seemed like a long time, not talking.

"Why is bad press for me good for you?"

When Jock Bell began to speak, he did so quietly. But Sid could hear him clearly, and he could feel the rumble of the man's low voice in his legs as he sat on top of him.

"I'm not a complicated person. I spend my time and money trying to get what I want, that's all. Sometimes I play rough. I've wanted to buy the building your family owns for the last few years. It wasn't a secret. I made several offers to your father. He always said no. I don't like to hear no. Last year he came to the shop a few times to pawn some stuff—the stuff you bought back."

"You said it was to pay gambling debts," Sid interrupted. "When I was in your pawn shop, that's what you said."

"Yeah, okay. Maybe it was gambling. There was talk about that. I might've read something about it in the paper. But I don't know for sure."

"What about what your nephew said? About owing $60,000?"

Jock Bell let out a small, low chuckle. "I told you I play rough. I'm not a nice person. I made that up— trying to put some pressure on you, Little Sid. I don't know who your father owed or how much. I just knew he needed money because he kept coming to me with stuff."

Jock paused, maybe to rest. It gave Sid a chance to process what he was hearing. He didn't like the guy, but what he said made sense. He could feel the truth of it like he could feel the vibration of his deep voice.

"Then Big Sid was gone, and you took over the place. And I figured that was my opportunity. Your generation doesn't understand hard work—can't appreciate what it takes to do what your father did. So I waited a while, but you didn't quit and business started picking up again. I was starting to think things weren't going to go my way, and then the shootings started. Bad press for you, good for me."

"But you say you had nothing to do with the shootings."

Another chuckle. "I'm not a criminal. I'm an opportunist. The cops thought it was you doing the shooting, and I figured this was my chance to get the building, that's all."

For the first time, Sid noticed how hot it was. Really hot. It beat down on his neck from above and radiated up from the street below. How could he not have noticed before? His shirt was soaked through, front and back. He suddenly and desperately wanted to get up and get out of the street, but he had to be sure he was done with Jock Bell. This was a situation that would never be repeated, mostly because he was certain it was only a stroke of wild, bloody-nose luck that allowed him to prevail this time. Had he asked every question? Learned everything he needed to know from Jock Bell? Maybe not.

"Why do you want to buy the deli building so badly?

"It's a gold mine."

"I think that's crap," Sid said, and he poked a finger in Jock's back for emphasis. "There's no gold under the building. I've been down there a hundred times."

"Not real gold, Little Sid. Opportunity."

"What?"

"God, you're stupid." Sid couldn't see his face, but he heard something change in the man's voice. "All you Biglers, huh? Your old man didn't get it either."

Jock now turned his head to the right, straining to

catch a glimpse of Sid out of the corner of his eye. In return, Sid got his first look at Bell's face since he'd flipped out. It was a curious sight. Most of the blood had been wiped away, but it left red lines in the myriad of deep wrinkles—a spider web of crusty crimson. He looked weary, and far older than ever before. But there was a small look of satisfaction, too. Of superiority.

"It's not the damn building or what's underneath it. It's what could stand in its place. The whole block is going to be redeveloped. I already own the rest of it."

A few more seconds ticked by. Sid finally looked up—not at anyone or anything in particular. Just up. Maybe he was giving his eyes a rest. He'd seen enough of the old bastard to last him a lifetime. The heat seemed to reach a crescendo. Sid felt a strong hand come to rest on his shoulder, and he heard the voice of Joe Diaz.

"Sid. The dude's old. Better get off him."

CHAPTER 31

It was just after four o'clock when Sid finally managed to lock the door to the deli and walk to his car—way later than he would be closing up on a normal Monday, but it was fairly typical for a Memorial Day. He would've been there even later if he hadn't turned the "Sorry, Closed" sign around when he got back to the restaurant following his adventure with Jock Bell.

After receiving numerous congratulatory pats on the back from the guys in the straw hats (who, it turned out, as members of "The Iceland Dixie Band," didn't speak a word of English), Sid had headed directly to the back room to clean himself up. There was a shirt on top of the filing cabinet that, while not technically clean, was a great improvement over the sweaty, bloody one he was wearing. He'd washed his face, arms and hands, put on a fresh apron, and used the first aid kit to doctor himself up as best he could.

Now, as he walked toward his car, he reached up and touched the piece of white tape across his nose. He could tell it was swollen, but on the whole didn't think it was too bad. He'd broken it once before, in college at a track meet. The memory made him smile. Sid had been goofing around before his race, trying to stay loose, and he challenged a buddy to jump a few hurdles. They'd gotten tangled up and he went face first into the track. Looking back, that had been at least as damaging to both his nose and his ego.

He was dying to see Amy, but she had a class after work. Maybe they could grab a late cup of coffee. In the meantime, Woody was probably already waiting for him at the gym. He reached his green Duster, unlocked it and climbed in. The A/C wouldn't have a chance to cool the car during the short drive, so Sid rolled down the front windows and put it in gear.

He was still, for the most part, believing the things that Jock Bell had said. The problem was, if that was the case, then he had to scratch Bell's name from his official list of suspects, and there were hardly any other names left. The only remaining one that didn't seem just plain silly was Joe Diaz. Sid could think of a number of suspicious things that pointed Joe's way—the abruptly ended phone call, the almost incoherent conversation at the deli, his visit to 384 Revere Street—but Sid just wasn't ready to go there.

He made the decision to think about it later. For the moment, he was in an inexplicably good mood. Yes, it was miserably hot and sweaty. No, he couldn't breathe through his nose. But Sid decided he was happy with who he was. It seemed like not very long ago that his life was beyond his control—that someone else was calling all the shots and he had nothing to say about how it all would end. In a number of ways, that had changed over the last few days.

He had been the one to take the next step in his

relationship with Amy. He'd told her he loved her, and even if everything else was going wrong in his life, that was right.

A lot of the change could be traced back to Gloria. She not only expected him to take care of his own problems, she believed that he could. *"I think you're going to figure it out,"* she had told him that afternoon at the deli. The pieces hadn't yet come together, but something in the back of Sid's mind told him it was going to happen.

Increasingly, each new problem or encounter wasn't something to be avoided or just patiently endured, but an opportunity to move forward. A chance to get one step closer to taking control of his life. To figuring it out. No, Sid hadn't solved any great mystery. Not yet, anyway. But he was not the same person he was before. The old Sid was a runner in more ways than one. He ran from his problems. He certainly would have never run *toward* Jock Bell and his men. But the Sid Bigler that was now driving his '71 Dodge down H Street was somebody different, and Sid had to admit it was an improvement.

Woody was, indeed, already at the gym. He'd apparently spent the time waiting for Sid to arrive running on a treadmill, as that's where Sid found him, puffing away with the thing set at a seven minute mile pace. Woody had shown surprising improvement as a runner, and was getting remarkably fast for a guy that was built like Popeye's big brother. Sid reached up and pushed the red button, causing the conveyor belt to slow quickly and come to a stop. Woody stood with his hands on his hips, breathing hard.

"I promised myself I'd run on this thing 'til you got here. If I'd known you were gonna be this late, I'd have gotten a pizza instead."

"Sorry. I was busy beating the hell out of Jock Bell."

"I bet. Looks like you hit him with your nose."

Over the course of their standard workout, Sid gave Woody a longer and slightly more accurate version of what had happened that day. As always, they finished up at the bench press. Woody volunteered to go first, and had just gotten comfortable under the weights when he paused with his hands on the bar. His eyebrows knitted, and he obviously had a question.

"Jock Bell admitted to calling the reporter, Dexter, tipping him that you were being arrested last week."

"Yeah, that's right."

"So who made the first call to Dexter? The one after the last shooting at Fairytale Town?"

"That's the million dollar question, buddy. Because I'm saying the person who did that is the same person who called the police. It's the same person who shot up the town. It's the same person who bought the gun in the first place and planted it at the deli to set me up. All the same guy."

"Huh," was Woody's only response. He easily lifted the massive weight from its cradle and pressed it twenty times, breathing calmly and steadily through his nose. As Woody finished the set, Sid put a hand on the bar.

"Give me five breakfast cereals with cartoon characters on the box."

"Too easy," said Woody, and he pumped the weights up and down five more times rapidly. "Fruit Loops, Sugar Smacks, Cap'n Crunch, Lucky Charms, Frankenberry."

"Impressive," said Sid, and he pulled a couple of big weights from each end of the bar, lightening it by a hundred pounds. He laid down on the bench and found a comfortable position.

"Don't drop it on your nose."

"Thanks."

Sid got through his twenty reps, slowing some at the end but still looking fairly strong. As expected, Woody stopped the bar from resting in its cradle, but he didn't say anything at first. He left Sid straining under the weight, and his arms began to shake a little. Sid had been focused on the bar above him, but now he glanced at his friend, waiting.

"Give me your top five suspects," Woody said, and he raised his eyebrows a couple of times like Groucho.

Sid clenched his teeth. His pulse pounded at his temple. His cheeks puffed out with each breath as he slowly lowered the bar, then pushed it back up.

"Joe Diaz."

"Maybe," Woody said as the bar went down and back up.

"Jock Bell."

"Not if he was telling the truth today when you had him pinned in the gutter, but okay." The bar came up again, noticeably slower.

"Eddie Davis."

"I say 'no chance.'"

Sid was running out of strength and running out of names. He brought the bar back down, and struggled badly with it on the way up again. It was touch and go for a moment, but then his arms finally extended and he heard himself grunt out the name, "Detective Stokes."

"Stokes?" Woody sounded surprised and rather delighted. "Didn't see that one coming, but I like it."

Sid knew he wouldn't be able to press the weights a fifth time, but it wasn't in him to quit. He lowered the bar one last time, let it rest against his chest for a moment, then pushed hard. It rose just a few inches and stalled.

"I can't… I can't…"

Drained, he started to let it come back down just before Woody snatched the weights and returned them to their resting place. Sid spread his arms and allowed gravity to take them.

"So who's the fifth suspect, Sid?"

"I was trying to say…." Sid closed his eyes and felt his shoulders ache, his heart pounding. "I can't think of one."

The two of them walked toward their cars, gym bags in hand. Woody stopped to watch Sid delicately jiggle the key back and forth until his trunk popped open. It was an art. Sid's bag disappeared into the trunk and he slammed it shut.

"One day that thing's not going to open."

"And that's when I'll stop lifting weights," Sid

grinned. But then he looked at Woody and sensed something was up.

"Listen, Sid, I'm going to tell you something I shouldn't. Really. The department finds out I told you this, it's my ass."

"Okay."

A look Sid couldn't read passed across Woody's face. He seemed to stop and then start again. "You're a suspect in a high profile investigation. I'm not supposed to be telling you anything."

"Okay."

Woody set his bag on the roof of Sid's car and stuck his hands in his pockets. He turned and leaned against the fender. "I went out for a couple of drinks last night with Kaminski. He was the detective who…"

"Who came with Stokes to haul me away," Sid finished for him. "I know who he is."

"Yeah, well, Kaminski's a good guy. Not like Stokes. Anyway, a couple of weeks ago I put in for detective, and Ken's been good to talk to."

"*Detective* Woody Carver. I like how it sounds."

"Yeah. Shut up. So I'm talking to Kaminski about the job, and he's telling me about the department and what they're doing. And he mentions that there's this new technology. We're testing it here in Sacramento, and some other department in Florida is doing it, too. *'Caller Identification.'*"

"What is it, like tracing phone calls? I see it on TV and in the movies all the time."

"Yeah, this is kinda like that, but different. With call

tracing, we have to initiate the trace, and it can be between any two phones. And, of course, we need a judge's permission to trace a call or tap a phone. Caller Identification is a lot simpler, and it's automatic. Whenever somebody calls the police station, the phone number automatically pops up on a screen. It's amazing. And because the other party voluntarily chooses to call us, we don't need their permission to look at their number, see?"

Sid saw where this might be going, and decided to keep his mouth shut.

"It's gonna be a great tool for a lot of reasons. The thing is, it's brand new. It works great, but it's never been tested in a court. For now it's just a big experiment. We can't use any information it provides as evidence at a trial, okay?"

"I get it."

"So Kaminski gives me an example of how Caller Identification can provide clues for investigations. He starts talking about the Capital Shooter case. And before he remembers that you and I are friends, he tells me about the call that pointed them to you. The first call."

They'd been out of the gym for a couple of minutes now. Sid had gotten a fresh, cool shower before they left, but now he could feel a trickle of sweat making its way down the small of his back.

"I swear to God, Sid, I'm not supposed to be telling you this."

"Yeah, I understand. It's a secret." Sid was growing impatient.

"Okay," Woody said, and he turned to grab his gym bag from the top of the car. He let it swing down by his side, and looked as though he was taking one more moment to decide for sure he was going to say it.

"Sid, the call came in at 4:30 a.m. on the morning of Wednesday, May 14th. That's just five hours or so after the shooting at Fairytale Town. The call came from inside the deli, Sid. From the payphone in the back of the deli."

CHAPTER 32

Sid's head was spinning. For the seven or eight minutes it took him to get to his mom's house, he was probably the most dangerous driver on the road. Like a Friday night drunk, he wouldn't remember how he got home.

'The call came from inside the deli, Sid.' Woody's words rang in his mind. *'From the payphone in the back of the deli.'* The plain meaning of the words was easy enough to understand, but for some reason Sid couldn't focus on the big picture. Maybe it's the same feeling when a doctor says, "the X-ray shows a large, dark mass on your right lung." You know what it means. You know it's life-changing. But you can't take it in all at once. It's too much.

Sid parked the car across the street from the house. There was a note on the kitchen counter in Rose's familiar handwriting. She was off to Sambo's to get a bite to eat with her friend Aliene, then going to the movies to see "The Shining" with Jack Nicholson. "Don't wait up. Love, Mom"

Sid stepped on the pedal that lifted the lid on the little chrome garbage can, crumpled the note, and dropped it in. It would've been good to talk to his mom—to talk to anybody that he knew loved him.

Because whatever else this latest revelation meant, it meant that somebody Sid thought he could trust was trying to hurt him.

He dialed his sister's number. It picked up on the fourth ring and a voice said, "Hello, the Farrell residence." Sid recognized the babysitter's voice right away. Jenny? Julie? Something like that. Gloria and Marty were out to dinner with one of her clients. Sid said there was no need to leave a message.

He glanced at his watch. 6:15. Amy's class went 'til nine. Sid slapped the kitchen counter with his hand, frustrated. At the moment, he could think of a grand total of three people in his life he was sure he could count on—all women—and none of them were around when he needed them.

Sid realized he was starving. Between the busy day and the extracurricular brawling and the workout, he hadn't had time to eat. He walked to his room, grabbed a pen and his list of suspects, jumped back in the car and headed for the Squeeze Inn. It's an aptly named, tiny dive of a burger joint on Fruitridge Road, about ten minutes from the house. One step inside the front door you bump into a wooden bar that runs from one side of the place to the other. There's room enough for exactly eleven stools across the bar, and that's all the place will hold. One overmatched air conditioning unit hummed as it hung on the back wall, losing the battle against the heat of the day and the heat from the fryer. But sweaty or not, Sid thought they had the only hamburgers in town that were better than the ones he served at the deli. He snagged the one open stool and drained two Cokes with no ice while he waited for his food. Nothing clears the head and focuses the mind like carbonated water, sugar, caffeine and artificial coloring.

Sid took a deep breath, blew it out. He closed his eyes for a moment and asked himself what he now knew about the case.

Somebody had called the cops really early in the morning after the Fairytale Town shooting. Really early. 4:30 a.m. It was probably safe to assume it was the same person who called Jackson Dexter to tip him off, too. And it was someone who had a key to the deli, right? It had to be. The call came from inside the deli, and there had been no signs of a break-in. Sid could feel himself being pulled quickly toward an obvious conclusion, like a raft floating through some rapids on the American River. But he didn't want to go fast, and he didn't want to miss anything.

Sid took the folded piece of paper from his back pocket, opened it up and laid it on the bar in front of him. He had to find a way to think this through, and his only idea was to evaluate his list of suspects in the light of the new information Woody had given him.

He stared at the list, both familiar and unimpressive. The same name was still at the top, but the Capital Shooter wasn't Jock Bell. What he'd said that afternoon had made sense. Add to that Woody's news that the informant was someone with access to the deli, and Sid was sure. He grabbed the pen from behind his ear and crossed off the first name he'd written down two weeks earlier. Jock Bell was off the list, and Sid was sorry to see him go. That's who Sid had always hoped it would be.

The next name on the list was Joe Diaz. *Damn.* Sid didn't want it to be Joe. But other than a total lack of motive, Joe was the perfect fit. He had access and he'd been acting very strangely. Sid remembered Joe's half-drunk story about Big Sid and the Marines and the girl from Puerto Rico. What had been the point of that? What was Joe really saying? Plus, he'd seen Joe last night on Revere Street. Sid didn't know for sure if that apartment was connected to all this, but something told him it was important. And then there was that mysterious call he'd walked in on—Joe on the payphone in the back of the deli.

Joe on the payphone. Damn again.

Sid wracked his brain trying to remember the details of that day. When did that phone call happen in relation to everything else? Before the last shooting? After? Sid couldn't remember. He drummed his fingers on the table. How could he not have been writing down stuff like that?

Sid told himself to slow down—be clear and methodical. He tried to remember what had been going on the morning after the shooting at Fairytale Town. He'd had a terrible night's sleep. Yes. He got to work a little early and...

Then it hit him. He got to work early that morning, but Joe and Eddie were already there. They had the place mostly set and ready to open. On the morning that somebody made that phone call to the cops from inside the deli, Joe must have gotten there really, really early. He remembered that clearly. *Damn. Damn. Damn.*

Sid reached down and circled Joe's name again. The pen went round and round repeatedly, making the line darker, threatening to break through the paper. There were a few more names on the list, but this one was the odds on favorite. *Quadruple Damn.*

The timing for the cheeseburger was excellent. It arrived as Sid was ready to stop being Joe Diaz' judge and jury, but didn't know how to move on. He put down his pen and took a minute to arrange the burger just right and load up a reservoir of ketchup next to the fries. Sid put away about a third of the burger before resuming his task.

The next name on his list was Eddie Davis. Poor Eddie. He had really freaked out earlier when he saw Sid being worked over by Jock's thugs. Who'd have guessed he could make a sound like that? Maybe Yvonne the blonde social worker was right. Maybe the deli wasn't a good place for him. On the other hand, he seemed fine the rest of the afternoon.

So did Eddie's name stay on the list? It still seemed ridiculous. Everything he knew about Eddie Davis told him there was no way the guy could have played any part in the Capital Shooter story. But Sid certainly couldn't eliminate him based on what Woody had said an hour ago. Eddie had a key. For now, he stayed.

Could Joe and Eddie be in this together? Again… ridiculous.

Sid took a few more bites of the burger and ate a few

more fries. Then he glanced at the remaining names on the list and almost laughed.

Below Eddie's name he saw the words, "Maybe a cop." Yes, Sid had had his reasons for writing that two days ago, but now it seemed even more ridiculous than having Eddie's name on the list. As much as Sid disliked Det. Stokes, there was no reason the guy would want to set it up to make it look like he was the Capital Shooter. And, based on what Woody had said, there was no way Stokes could have been the one that made the phone call. He didn't have a key to the deli.

Sid put a line through "Maybe a cop."

The last name was Jackson Dexter. Nope. No key to the deli. Another slash.

Ten minutes later the burger was gone and the last fry had wiped up the last drop of ketchup. He'd been staring at the paper, trying to think of something else— something new—but it remained unchanged since he'd crossed Jackson Dexter's name off. There was no getting around the fact that only two names were left. Sid shook his head, picked up the pen, and did what he knew all along he was going to do. He put a big "X" over Eddie Davis's name. That left only one. It had to be Joe Diaz.

Sid was sitting in front of Amy's apartment, leaning back against her front door when she got home just before ten o'clock. It was too dark for her to see the tape across his nose, but she could make out the familiar outline. She rewarded him with a smile.

"If I'd known what was waiting for me, I wouldn't

have stopped for Chinese food."

"Got any leftovers?"

Amy held up a couple of little white cartons with wire handles.

They sat at her kitchen table as Sid polished off the General's Chicken and Pork Chow Fun. He wanted to tell her about the call coming from the payphone inside the deli, but he'd promised Woody that he would keep the secret. Nevertheless, between bites he did treat her to the story of his fight with Jock Bell that afternoon. She gasped when he told her about first seeing Mr. Moustache. She grimaced when he told her about getting his ears pulled. She covered her mouth with her hands and said "Oh my!" when he told her about Jock Bell busting his nose. She cheered when he told her about his ultimate victory. She listened and she cared. And over the course of their conversation, she vanquished any lingering doubts he may have had about his love for Amy Solomon.

Then they curled up on her couch together, and she gently kissed his nose.

CHAPTER 33

Sid woke up in the morning determined that, before the day was over, he'd have some answers. It was long past time to confront Joe Diaz. And even though he was increasingly convinced that everything pointed to Joe, he was also feeling pretty certain that he didn't need to be afraid. He had several reasons for believing that. First of all, if Joe had wanted to physically harm him, he would've done it already. Joe was huge. Secondly, he still thought that the Capital Shooter never really wanted to hurt anybody. The crimes were flashy, sure, but never deadly. And finally, whatever Joe Diaz was, he was Sid's father's best friend. He was Sid's own godfather. Yes, Sid was sure there was no real danger. So as he headed to work on Tuesday morning, May 27th, he never would have guessed that someone was going to die in the deli that day.

Sid got to work and unlocked the door right at 6 a.m. just as Eddie was rolling up on his bike. His nose was dramatically more sore this morning than it had been at any point yesterday. And it was pretty swollen and puffy. He could actually see it occasionally below him in his peripheral vision. Weird.

Joe showed up about ten minutes later and everyone

busied themselves with the same jobs they did every morning before opening. By 6:45 the place was looking pretty good. Eddie was finishing setting the tables, Joe was heating up the grill, and Sid's heart was pounding in his chest. It was time to talk to Joe—now, before the door was open and customers started coming in. Sid sat down on a stool at the counter.

"Hey, Joe. I need to talk to you."

"Yeah?"

"Yeah. You got a minute?"

"Sure." Joe said it over his shoulder, half paying attention.

"No, Joe, It's really important. I need you to look at me."

That seemed to work. Joe turned and took a moment to size up Sid Bigler, Jr. It was clear the young man had something big on his mind. Joe wiped his hands on his apron, which may in fact have made them dirtier, and waited.

Now Sid had his attention, and wasn't sure what to do with it.

"Uh, a lot of crazy stuff has been happening the last couple of weeks."

Joe stared back at him from across the counter. Sid hadn't expected that opening line to cause Joe to spill his guts, and it didn't. No reaction at all.

"You know. The shootings. All the reporters and stuff. Me going to jail..."

Again Sid waited for some response, but Joe crossed his arms and said nothing.

"So, the thing is... I think you have something to do with all this."

Sid decided right then that maybe he should have worked up a little better speech than that. For some reason, he'd expected something much more clever to come out of his mouth. More convincing and forceful. It was definitely not the kind of thing that would provoke a big confession. But he'd said it, and so he waited.

Sid's attention had been focused intently on Joe, and so he was quite startled when he heard a small noise right next to him and turned to see Eddie Davis standing there. Eddie's face was calm and, of course, smiling. He was looking at Joe. And then Sid saw that Joe was looking at Eddie. Joe's expression was more unreadable than usual—warm but troubled. He actually returned a small smile back at Eddie, but it was tinged with something other than happiness.

"We need to talk about this later," Joe said, and he started to turn his back.

"No we don't, Joe!" This time Sid did sound forceful. And loud. He banged his fist on the counter and a nearby napkin dispenser fell over. "We need to talk about it now!"

Joe stopped in mid-turn, then turned back toward Sid. He didn't look angry, and yet there was something terrible in his calmness.

"We can't talk in front of Eddie."

"What?" Had Sid heard him correctly? "What d'you mean we can't talk in front of Eddie? Are you talking about *this* Eddie?" Sid pointed as he asked, with more than a little sarcasm. "Are you kidding? C'mon, Joe, It's not like Eddie can understand what we're…"

Sid didn't even see Joe move. All he knew was that he was suddenly being lifted up off his stool. Joe was leaning across the counter with the front of Sid's shirt in his fist and his face only inches away.

"I won't talk about this in front of Eddie. We'll talk after work. Do you understand?"

Sid nodded, but Joe didn't move. The only sound in the room was the sound of Sid struggling to catch a breath.

"After work," Sid managed to repeat it, half choking.

"Yeah. After work." Joe held him for a moment longer, then finally let go.

Sid dropped a few inches back onto his seat. To say that his conversation with Joe had not gone as planned would be a gigantic understatement—like saying Kennedy's trip to Dallas didn't go well. Sid sat dumbfounded, rubbing his neck with one hand and trying to figure out what had just happened. How could someone so big move so quickly?

And then everything was back to normal. It was surreal. Joe was back at the grill and Eddie had returned to placing the silverware on paper napkins at each table— knife and fork, side by side, always precisely the same, just like he'd been doing for ten years. And always smiling, seemingly never bored. For ten years.

Sid straightened out the front of his shirt, then slid off the stool and walked to the front door. The sun was just coming up. He turned the deadbolt and went out onto the sidewalk. There was no one in sight. He shoved his hands in his pockets and breathed in the cool air. He glanced at the spot across the street where he and Jock had ended their wrestling match yesterday.

What the hell had just happened? Joe said he wouldn't talk about anything in front of Eddie. What could that possibly be about? *"He understands more than you think."* The social worker's words came to him again. It never would have crossed Sid's mind to watch what he said in front of Eddie. What did Joe know that he didn't—about Eddie and about the shootings?

"Hey, Sid!" He turned and saw a familiar face approaching. It was Roy, one of the old guys who regularly hung out at the deli to play cribbage. "Sid, you open yet?"

Sid glanced at his watch. It was five minutes before seven. He decided he didn't want to be in there alone with Joe and Eddie.

"Yeah, Roy. We're open. Come on in."

A very odd vibe between Sid and Joe continued to make its presence felt throughout the morning. There had been plenty of days in the past where they found little reason to talk to each other. But today the silence was heavy and awkward.

Fortunately, there was plenty to talk to the customers about. Even without the puffy nose and the piece of tape, everybody seemed to know about the fight with Jock Bell. Somehow the word was already out among the regular customers. There was a lot of joking about it, but the consensus was that Sid's actions were heroic. Nobody really knew what the fight had been about, but most agreed that Jock Bell needed a good beating up. Happily for Sid, the age difference between combatants only came up a few times. One of the more obnoxious guys suggested they set up a televised match between Sid and Grandpa Jones from Hee Haw. If he won that one, maybe he could go after Walter Cronkite next. People laughed and Sid was happy for the distraction, although Joe's promise to talk after work was never far from his mind.

Just before lunch, Jackson Dexter wandered in and dropped the day's Metro section on the counter. How was it that nobody had shown it to Sid before this? There was Dexter's little photo alongside his "Talk of the Town" column, and the lead story was all about a street fight between two notable Sacramentans.

"Just wanted to say thanks," Dexter said. "It would've been a slow news day without you."

"Yeah. Happy to help." Sid gave the column a quick scan. It said nothing about what Jock's two thugs had done just before the fight got going. "You know I was outnumbered, right? A couple of Jock's goons really started it."

"I heard you took the first swing, but who cares? Stuff like this sells papers. I just wanted to come by and get a look at your nose."

"Beautiful, isn't it? So who told you I took the first swing? Jock?"

"Maybe."

"Wouldn't be the first time he called you, would it?"

"No." Jackson Dexter didn't smile, but you could tell that he wanted to. "He told me you two had a nice talk while you were sitting on his back."

"Who else called you, Dexter? Two weeks ago, right after the last shooting. Who was it?" Sid made no effort to keep his voice down. Joe Diaz was probably standing close enough to hear, and that was fine with him.

"Can't help you, Sid. Journalistic integrity, and all that. But if you've got anything to add to this," he tapped the newspaper on the counter, "I'd be happy to get a few quotes for tomorrow's column."

"No comment."

"If that's what you want. Call me if you change your mind."

The rest of the day was uneventful. Typical Tuesday. At 1:30 they still had four tables going and two guys at the counter. Most were eating, but there were a couple of orders on the ticket rack. Joe kept an eye on a grilled sandwich while he worked on his clean-up duties. Eddie had also started some of his closing chores—wiping down empty tables and collecting the salt and pepper shakers. Sid acted like he was starting to count up the cash drawer, but he wasn't really. He just needed something to do with his hands. They were perhaps forty-five minutes away from closing up. Eddie could ride off on his bike and maybe then he'd get some answers from Joe Diaz.

And then the payphone in the back room rang. Sid,

Joe and Eddie all looked up, but none of them made a move to answer it.

On any other day it would have been odd, but not ominous. It was fairly common for somebody to wander back there and use the old payphone to make a call. It probably happened two or three times a week. But it never, ever rang. Who calls a payphone?

It rang a second, then a third time before anyone moved.

"I got it," Sid said as he walked past Joe and into the back room. Joe followed him in, stopping halfway between the door and the back wall, watching.

"Hello?"

"Sid, is that you?"

Sid recognized the voice right away, and he could tell something was up.

"Woody?"

"Yeah. Sid, I've found something. I called the number in back because I didn't want anybody else around you when I talked to you. I hope that's okay."

"How'd you call this phone? I don't even know the number."

"My friend Linda works the 9-1-1 switchboard. I had her check the Caller ID log from two weeks ago. 4:30 a.m. There it was."

"Is that legal?"

"I don't think so, but Linda's crazy about me. Listen, Sid, I've got some big news for you. Are you alone?"

For the first time, Sid turned around and saw Joe

standing there. He was a good eight feet away, just watching, no particular expression. Sid thought about how to play it for a moment, then turned back toward the wall and answered very casually, "Everything's fine. Joe's here."

"Joe's there with you?" Woody asked over the phone. And he couldn't resist a follow-up question. "Did you ask him about last night—what he was doing at that house?"

Sid paused, thinking. "Uh, no. Not really." If it had not occurred to Sid before this that he had no future in acting, he knew it now.

"Well, look, I've come across something about the Capital Shooter case you need to know. It's important. Can I tell you now, with Joe there?"

"I don't know, Woody. Why don't you just come down here and talk to me."

"Sid, I'm calling you from Reno."

"Reno?" Sid said it too quickly and too loudly, and wished right away that he'd kept his mouth shut. He turned and looked, and saw that Joe was still his old, emotionless self. What to do? He already had enough trouble with Joe and didn't need to add anything new, but he was dying to know what was so important.

"So... what's going on in Reno?"

Definitely more bad acting on Sid's part, but it didn't matter. Woody's answer would make Sid forget where he was and who was listening.

"Sid, I took the day off. I drove over here to do some snooping around for you. I just talked to the gun shop owner whose name was on your Dealer Record of Sale. The one who is supposed to have sold you the gun from the shootings. I asked him if he remembered selling a .25 caliber Raven revolver to someone named Sidney Bigler a few months ago. And he said he did. So I asked him if he could describe the guy to me, and you know what he said?"

Sid didn't respond, and a moment later Woody said the most surprising and unexpected thing he'd ever heard in his life.

"Listen to this, buddy. He told me that I must have made some mistake. It wasn't a guy that bought the gun, it was a woman."

"A woman?" The words jumped from Sid's mouth involuntarily, before they had a chance to register. He stared straight ahead at the wall, not willing to risk another look at Joe.

"Yeah, that's what he told me. Sidney Bigler was a woman."

CHAPTER 34

Everything felt familiar but everything was all wrong. Sid walked to the deli in the dark every day. But it should be cool out and the streets should be empty. Now as he hurried up L Street and turned onto 11th, it was hot. Maybe still in the nineties. And there were cars on the street and people on the sidewalk. It was after 9 p.m.

Sid reached for the door and gave the knob a twist. Still locked, just like he'd left it over six hours earlier. He fished the key out of his pocket, looked up and down the street for some reason, then let himself in. He closed the door and twisted the deadbolt to lock it. Then he paused, thought for a moment, and unlocked the door. He let his hand slide up the wall until it found the switch, and flipped the lights on. He was alone.

Sid dropped the keys on the counter as he walked around and got himself a Coke. Then he circled back and sat on the end stool, by the cash register. The drawer was open and empty, like it should be. The blinds looked like they were mostly shut, but he got up anyway and went around to twist the little rod on each one to make sure. The place was closed, and he didn't want to be unintentionally inviting anyone else in. It was just going to be him and Joe.

Sid had gotten a good shot of adrenaline when Woody called earlier in the day to drop the *"Sidney Bigler was a woman"* bomb, and he'd had a steady drip going ever since. The rest of the afternoon and evening had been a collage of conversations and clues that ultimately left him frustrated. He was struggling to put together a puzzle, and one big piece was still missing. Now, as he sat at the counter waiting for Joe to arrive and knocking back his Coke with no ice, he tried to think through it again.

He thought about the woman who bought the gun. His mind had returned to her again and again that day. Based on the description that the guy at the gun shop had given to Woody, there was no doubt about who it was. But it made no sense. Why *her*? Why would *she* want to hurt him? He caught himself staring blankly at a spot on the counter, no specific thought in his mind, waiting for an answer to come. And for perhaps the hundredth time that day, there was nothing. No answer. How could it be *her*?

And what had happened to Joe? He'd been standing there listening to Sid's end of the conversation with Woody, and then he was gone. Not just gone from the room, but gone. When Sid finally got off the phone, he'd found Joe's apron laying on the floor behind the counter and a patty melt still sizzling on the grill. But Joe had vanished. Sid did his best to finish up the two final orders, but had so little faith in his culinary skills that he didn't charge the last two customers.

What was the last thing Joe had heard him say when he was talking to Woody on the phone? Sid couldn't recall exactly, and was a little disgusted with himself for having such a lousy poker face. He definitely remembered that Joe was still in the room when he got the surprising news that the gun buyer was a woman. But then he hadn't looked for the minute or two that it took to finish his conversation. And when Sid finally turned around for the last time, Joe was gone. What had he heard that spooked him?

Sid thought about Woody's last words to him over the phone. *"This whole thing's getting too weird,"* he'd said. *"Maybe you should call Det. Stokes and talk to him."* Sid asked Woody how he was supposed to do that without getting him in trouble. Stokes might be a little bit upset to find out that some beat cop had been feeding information to one of his suspects. *"Yeah,"* Woody had said. *"I know."*

Once Sid had gotten the place closed up and Eddie had jumped on his bike and pedaled for home, he had run to his car and made the drive to Gloria's office. Her firm had taken over a beautiful converted Victorian in midtown. He showed up unannounced just after three o'clock and was told she was with a client. He told the receptionist it was an emergency, and Gloria had come out of her office to see him briefly. They ended up talking for almost half an hour, concluding with Gloria insisting it was time to call Det. Stokes and tell him everything. Sid had promised her that he would, but he didn't.

At 4:15 he'd pulled into Joe Diaz' driveway, then banged on the front door until Theresa opened it. Sid had always liked Joe's wife. She said that Joe had come home a little early, made a phone call, then he'd left. She had asked if everything was okay, and Sid had told her it was. *"You know, Sid,"* she had said to him, *"he hasn't gotten over losing your dad. It's been six months. I worry about him."*

Sid had just driven around for a while after that. There was no reason to go home, and he didn't know where else to go. So he drove and he thought, and after more than an hour, the driving and the thinking had both taken him nowhere.

Then he'd stopped by Pancake Circus on Broadway. Sid couldn't remember when he'd eaten anything that day, so he went in and ordered a BLT. He ended up eating less than half of it, and it was somewhere mid-sandwich that his frustration peaked. *Dammit!* He should be doing something. He hadn't figured everything out, but he knew plenty. Yet he had to admit to himself that he didn't know what to do next. He hated how that felt. He was suddenly mad at himself for sitting there picking at a sandwich when he should be doing... whatever it was he should be doing. On top of everything else, it was obvious that a couple other tables in the restaurant had recognized him from the news. Some kid in his late teens had come up and asked him something about the shootings, and Sid said a few things that weren't very nice. Then he got up, dropped some money on the table, and left.

Back at the car, Sid had reached up to rub his eyes and inadvertently sent a stabbing pain shooting through his nose. He yelled and banged the steering wheel with his hands, then lay his head back and closed his eyes, waiting for the ache to stop. At some point after that he must have dozed off, because he woke from a fitful sleep and the sun was down. There was still some light in the western sky, and it took him a moment to figure out where he was and how he got there. He started the car and drove to his mom's house, thinking about Joe and his father... about the series of shootings that had changed his life... about the woman who bought the gun.

His mother had jumped up off the sofa as soon as he opened the front door. Laverne & Shirley was on the TV behind her.

"Have you talked to Joe?" she had asked him. No greeting. Those were the first words out of her mouth.

"No, I've been looking for him."

"He called about two hours ago. He said he wanted you to meet him at the deli."

"When?"

"Tonight. At nine o'clock. Sid, what's going on?"

Rose's question remained unanswered as Sid sat and waited in the quiet deli. His glass was empty. He finally noticed how warm it was, and was just thinking about getting up and flipping on the A/C when the door opened and Joe Diaz stepped in. The clock on the wall said it was 9:17.

"You got my message," Joe said.

"Yeah." Sid tried to read his face. As always, it yielded nothing. "You're late."

"Anybody else here?"

"No. Should there be?"

Joe closed the door behind himself, then walked past Sid and stood behind the counter. Everybody's got their place in this world, and that was Joe's. He'd spent more time in that four foot by eight foot space over the last thirty years than anywhere else. He wasn't the kind of person that would stop to think about a thing like that— the sentimental type. The type that would do the math and discover that he'd stood over that grill for over 60,000 hours of his life. Sid realized for the first time that there wasn't one personal item of Joe's back there. Not a photo of his wife, not a coffee mug from Disneyland. His eyes searched the back counter. Nothing.

"I got to tell you something," Joe said. "Something about your father."

Sid looked at Joe, wanting to hear anything that could help him make sense of his life, but afraid of what it might be. He had visions of their last conversation here in the deli—the strange, rambling story of the day Joe first met Big Sid. He shifted his weight on the stool in an effort to get more comfortable. He didn't know exactly what to expect, but he figured it would be slow and awkward.

But Sid was wrong. As it turned out, Joe could tell a pretty good story when he wanted to.

CHAPTER 35

"Some people talk a lot but they got nothin' to say. Not Big Sid. He was talking all the time and still didn't say half of what he was thinking. I'd never met anybody with so many ideas, and who was so sure things were gonna work out. One of the reasons I wanted to be his friend was that he just flat out knew he was gonna get through that damn war and make something of himself. I wanted to be a part of that. I woulda gone and done whatever he wanted after the war. Didn't matter what it was. God, he talked about some crazy ideas, y'know?

"Me and your dad opened this place in 1947. The food's good, but the food's not why customers kept coming back. It was your dad. People didn't notice he was busting his ass because he was always having fun, but it was him that made this place what it was. Your dad was like that from all the way back to when we were in the Navy."

Joe paused there only for a moment, enjoying some particular memory. Sid was floored. He'd never heard Joe say more than four or five sentences in a row in his entire life.

"When we were on the Texas in the Pacific, a guy came on board. Maybe a year or two younger than us. Walters. Scared shitless all the time. Whenever something bad was happening, if we were coming under fire or the weather was really rough, your dad would always find Walters, make sure he was okay.

"Did you know that over the years there was probably ten or twelve guys that your dad fed for free down here at the deli? Everyday. Veterans, guys on the street, people he knew just couldn't take care of themselves. He made a good living for himself here, but he sure as hell made life a lot better for a lot of other people while he was doing it. I bet there's thirty guys that would've told you that Big Sid was their best friend. Maybe a lot more. And they would've been telling the truth. He was the best man I ever knew. But everybody makes mistakes, Sid. Your father made some mistakes."

Joe rubbed a hand across his face, and the only sound in the deli was the scratchy noise of his beard. Then he grabbed a cup, filled it with water at the sink, and took a long drink.

Something Joe had said was still echoing in Sid's head. *"He was the best man I ever knew."* Sid was pretty sure Joe had said the same thing that day last week when he'd been waiting in the deli and emptying a few Budweisers. Only this time he was stone sober. And this time he added something. *"Your father made some mistakes."*

"I know something about your dad, Sid. He made me promise I'd never tell a living soul. I've kept that promise a long time, but I'm going to tell you now. I think Big Sid would think it was okay. You need to know. I should've told you before this."

The next minute passed in silence. Joe stared blankly

out at the empty deli, seeing something from his past. Sid hadn't spoken a word since Joe started talking and was determined to keep his mouth shut. But as the seconds ticked by the wait was becoming unbearable. What could his father have done? And what could it have to do with what had happened over the past two weeks? Finally, Sid couldn't wait any longer.

"Joe."

The man remained motionless for a few more seconds. Then he let out a long breath, turned and looked at Sid. It looked like it required a great effort.

"1965. The deli had been open about eighteen years. It was really a great time for everybody. Business was good. Me and Theresa had been married a few years. You and Gloria were just kids in school.

"I don't know if you remember, your dad used to drink a lot more back then. He wasn't no drunk, right? He just liked to have fun. What was he then, forty years old? Maybe forty-one? He and some guys were out at a couple of bars one night, weren't doing nothing wrong. And when he went to drive home he was pretty lit up. People didn't think so much about that at the time. He was driving that butter yellow Cadillac you guys had, remember? It was late—after one in the morning—and Big Sid was driving down Riverside, heading toward home, going right by the cemetery. He was only a mile or so from your house when two people ran out into the street. I don't know why they didn't see Big Sid's car coming, but I know that he didn't see them. He hit 'em, Sid. Woman and a boy. I guess he stepped on the brakes, but not soon enough because he hit 'em."

"Did he kill them?" Sid hadn't intended to speak, but it came out.

"There's a neighborhood on the other side of the cemetery, I don't know if you've ever even seen it. It ain't like your neighborhood. It's government housing. Maybe it used to be nice, but it didn't stay that way. This woman and the boy, they were from over there. I don't know what they was doing running across Riverside, and I guess it don't matter. They were there and your dad hit 'em with his car and he'd been drinking."

Now Joe fixed his eyes on Sid to make sure he was paying attention. It wasn't necessary. Sid was all but holding his breath.

"The woman got up pretty quick, looked like she was okay. But the boy didn't look good. Hit his head, either on the car or the road when he went down. I never heard. But the boy didn't get up. Big Sid thought he was dead. They couldn't tell if he was breathing. His neck was at a funny angle and his eyes were glassy. Had blood coming out his ear. Terrible, terrible thing.

"Big Sid told me later there was something odd about the way the woman acted that night. Like I said, it was late. Just some closed up businesses across the street. No other cars came by, nobody else around. And here was this boy laying in the street, and the woman wasn't all that upset. Oh, she was mad, like it was a big, damn inconvenience. But not worried about the boy. Not like her baby was hurt.

"I want you to understand something about your

dad, Sid. Besides you and your mom and your sister, this deli was his whole life. It ain't just a place to get breakfast or a sandwich. He made this place a part of Sacramento. Important people come here. God, your dad was so proud that he built a place that governors came to. Governors and TV stars sometimes. And sports heroes. That's Willie Mays' picture right there. George Blanda and Ken Stabler both come in here once, too.

"When he hit that boy with his car, your dad knew it was all over. That was it. He was gonna lose everything. Famous people and their reputations don't have lunch at a place that's run by a drunk who kills little boys."

Sid had spent almost every waking moment of the last two weeks trying to solve a puzzle. But by the time Joe called his father 'a drunk who kills little boys', he'd completely forgotten about the Capital Shooter. He'd forgotten about Det. Stokes and Jock Bell and Jackson Dexter. He was utterly lost in this story about his father. It was like he was living a moment in Big Sid's life with him.

"How come I didn't know about all this? How come everybody doesn't know?" Sid asked.

Joe shook his head. "Because Big Sid did something else stupid that night. And he spent the rest of his life living with the mistake. He just couldn't lose this place. It was his whole damn life. He couldn't go to jail, couldn't stand the thought of what it'd do to Rose and you kids. And he'd always been able to talk himself out of whatever trouble he got into in the past. So he did something that he never should've done. He asked the woman to keep quiet. He asked her not to tell on him. And he offered her money."

"What?"

"Your father said he'd give her money if she'd let him go and then lie to the cops about what happened. He told her to say that she didn't get a look at the driver. To say it was a dark colored Ford or something. He gave her a business card and promised he'd pay her $10,000 if nobody found out about the accident. Ten grand in 1965. That was a lot of money back then. Especially where she came from."

"She took it?"

"She did. Yeah, she took it. Big Sid said he could get it to her in cash pretty quick and she said yes. Your dad got back in his car and drove away. Left her standing there with the boy laying in the road."

Then Joe said two more words, like an afterthought. He spoke them so quietly, almost under his breath. But Sid heard what he said.

"Beautiful boy."

Beautiful boy. And that's when Sid figured it out. Everything. It all fell together in an instant. And the funny thing was, when it all became clear, it wasn't a shock or a surprise. It was more like a relief. Like putting on a warm coat. Like coming home.

"Eddie," said Sid.

"Eddie," said Joe.

CHAPTER 36

"So Eddie didn't die, and the woman didn't go away, right?" Sid had a pretty good idea where the story went from here.

"Your dad gave her some of the money just a couple of days later. Took him about a month to get it all without it being noticed. Eddie was in the hospital, and I guess nobody thought he'd live. He's sort of a medical miracle.

"At first she didn't ask for more than the ten grand. But you're right. One day she comes walking into the deli. I didn't know nothing about all this at the time. She comes walking in and I saw your dad get this look on his face. I'd never seen him scared before that. He told me he had to go and he just walked out with this strange woman. It was the middle of lunchtime and he just took off. He came back later on after I got the place closed up—it was just the two of us—and he told me what had happened. This was maybe two months after the accident when I found out, and it started to look like Eddie might get better. The woman told him there were medical bills and she needed more money. So your dad started giving it to her every month."

"Mom does the books, Joe. How could mom not know about this?"

"It's a cash business, Sid. Easy to pull a little out of the drawer every day. Your mom didn't notice the money was light very often."

"And if she did," Sid said, "dad would tell her that he lost it gambling."

It was a guess, but it must have been a good one. Joe smiled for the first time that night.

"I never saw your dad bet on a horse or a card game in my life. But, yeah, that's what we'd say. Big Sid's gambling problem. It sorta became a joke."

Joe's smile lingered for a moment, then vanished as a pleasant memory was replaced by a different one.

"Your dad was giving that woman $500 a month. I told him she was lying. Medi-Cal or something like that was paying for Eddie's doctor bills. She was just playing him. But what was your father gonna do? She had him by the balls and she knew it. Any time I said something about it, Big Sid would say that the money was going to help the boy. Neither one of us believed it."

"So what happened? This didn't just go on forever, right? Eddie's a grown man now."

"He's twenty-seven," Joe said. "Exactly four days older than you. You know that?"

Joe paused. Maybe he'd reached some self-imposed limit on the number of words he could say at one time. Maybe he just needed to collect himself. But the break gave Sid a moment to soak up what he'd heard. For some reason, finding out Eddie's age—so close to his own—had a powerful impact on him.

Sid had never once thought of Eddie Davis as a

person. A person with a life and a future. Not for a second. He realized it now and it made him feel small. What would the man, Eddie Davis, be doing now if the boy hadn't run into the street in 1965? Or if Big Sid hadn't been drinking that night? In spite of the damage that had been done by the accident, Eddie was bright eyed and handsome. And while there was no way of knowing for sure, there was a quality about him that conveyed a thoughtfulness and intelligence. Twenty-seven. Eddie might have been a teacher now. An author. A doctor. Or maybe just some regular joe with a wife and kids and a mortgage, living a happy life and never knowing it might have been taken away by a drunk driver in 1965.

On the other hand, how many people from Eddie's old neighborhood went on to great things? How many found a way to avoid the temptation of an easy escape that drugs or crime seemed to offer? How many broke the chains of poverty and culture to find a prosperous life? Sid allowed himself to wonder for just a moment if perhaps his father's sin hadn't saved Eddie from something worse, but he recognized the rationalization for what it was. No, his father had done something terrible, and it wasn't his place now to decide what was best for Eddie Davis. If he were able, Eddie certainly wouldn't have chosen this life for himself.

Sid flashed on that high, peculiar scream that had stopped Jock Bell's boys from beating him up just the day before. Whether it was intentional or not, Eddie had really saved him. And for the first time he considered

that perhaps whatever had happened to Eddie Davis in
1965 hadn't so much affected his ability to see and
understand everything around him, as it had changed the
way he could react to it. Like someone wearing a mask
they couldn't take off. Sid's Uncle Bart had died of
A.L.S. in the sixties. Sid remembered vividly how sad it
was—his mom explaining to him that Uncle Bart was the
same inside as he always was, he just couldn't control his
body. He couldn't let what was inside of him out. Could
that be the life that Eddie Davis had been living since he
woke up in a hospital fifteen years ago?

"Your dad paid that woman every month." Joe
interrupted Sid's thoughts and picked the story back up.
"Eddie got better and better, and they put him in a special
school. His mother didn't seem to give a damn about
him, but Big Sid and I checked in on him some. About
the time he was through with school, your dad had the
idea that we could hire him to work here at the deli, and
that's what we did. Your dad knew somebody with the
County who got him into a program where he had a place
to live, and we got him away from that woman."

"And dad stopped paying her?"

"No. I wish that was true. Once Eddie was out of
her house, the bitch made your dad keep giving her the
money. Said she'd tell everybody what had happened if
he didn't. That's who she was all along. Five hundred a
month."

"For fifteen years?"

"Until he died. He was stuck and didn't know what
else to do. Your father loved that boy. Felt guilty every

day of his life. Guilty for what he'd done, and guilty for paying that woman all those years. I thought maybe that was part of why he shot himself, but I couldn't say anything at the time. I'd promised him."

Tears had begun to roll down Joe Diaz' cheeks, and Sid discovered that a lifetime of opinions that he'd formed about the man were being washed away.

"We just gave Eddie the job to keep an eye on him. Turned out he was a real fine worker. He's a good boy."

It felt like Joe had reached an end of some kind, and Sid desperately wanted to leave him alone with his sadness. Wished he could say something comforting and just go. But the story wasn't over, and he couldn't let it end here.

"Joe, where'd you go this afternoon?"

The room was silent for a moment, then Sid watched as the big man realized he'd allowed himself to appear weak. Joe pushed away from the bar, sniffed a couple of times and turned his head away. He grabbed a towel off the back counter and ran it over his face.

"I hadn't seen that woman for years before Big Sid died. I knew he was still paying her, but there was no reason for her to come around. And after your dad was gone, I didn't even give her a thought. I figured it was all over.

"And when the shootings started up I didn't think nothing of it. No reason to think it had anything to do with me or you. Then the cops started coming here and they found that gun, I figured maybe the bitch was back. Two nights ago I went to her house, and she said she didn't know anything about what was going on."

Sid didn't feel the need to tell Joe he'd seen him there. But he couldn't resist tying up a loose end.

"You still thought she might be involved, even though you called her about ten days ago from the payphone in back and told her to stay away?"

Joe looked legitimately surprised. "How'd you know that?"

"You think you're the only one who can stand in the back room and listen to other people's phone calls?"

Joe managed his second smile of the day, and Sid returned it.

"Yeah, I heard you talking to Woody this afternoon," Joe said. "I could tell it wasn't just a friendly call. Figured it had something to do with the shootings. And then I heard you say something about a woman and that was it."

"Did you go see her?"

"I tried. I went home and called her place and got no answer. Then I drove over there myself and nobody was home. I waited a couple of hours, then left a note for her to call me and went back to my house."

That made sense to Sid. Joe must have been away at the woman's house when he had stopped by to talk to Theresa.

"Then she calls just before seven o'clock, and I tell her that it's all over. No more secrets. Whether or not she's got anything to do with the shootings, I told her I was gonna tell you about everything."

"What'd she say?"

"She said that was just fine with her. Said she wanted to talk to you, too. And I told her we should just meet up here at the deli tonight."

That caught Sid by surprise.

"Here? She's coming here tonight?"

Joe nodded. "Gonna get it all out in the open. No sense running from something your father did anymore, Sid. She can't hurt you."

Sid wasn't given to hunches or intuition, but a shiver went down his spine. He was pretty sure Joe was wrong about that. Suddenly the deli was feeling like a very dangerous place to be. Sid thought for a moment, then asked a question he already knew the answer to.

"Joe, this woman—Eddie's mother—she's got blonde hair and big boobs, right?"

Joe was about to answer when a female voice surprised them both.

"I'm so flattered that you noticed."

The two men turned to see that the front door was wide open and Yvonne Wilcox was standing just inside. She had a shiny gold purse on her shoulder and a flat black pistol in her hand.

CHAPTER 37

"You like them?" She gestured to her breasts with the pistol. "I had them improved a few years ago. Not something a lot of girls in my neighborhood can afford, but I had a nice steady income for a long time."

"How long have you been standing there?" Sid asked.

"Long enough to hear Joe call me a bitch."

The woman took a step further into the restaurant and looked around, like she was making sure they were alone. Then she threw a nervous glance out the open door and said, "Get in here."

Eddie Davis stepped into the deli and the door closed behind him. He smiled at his mother. The same as always.

"Sorry I'm late. I had to stop by and pick up Eddie on the way. Thought I might need his key to lock up when I'm done." She put a hand on her son's back and gave him a little push. "You get in the back room, Eddie. And you stay there 'til I come get you."

Eddie Davis looked into Sid's eyes as he passed behind the counter. Sid searched for some understanding, some change in his expression. He wanted to see something new there, but didn't. He watched Eddie disappear into the other room and the door close behind him, then he turned back to the woman and they held each other's gaze for a moment.

"Oh, Sid, you looked at me so differently when you thought I was a nice social worker."

She must have seen some reaction in Joe's face, because she turned to him and said, "Yes, Joe. Sid and I know each other. I came down and said hello that afternoon the cops found the gun. I waited 'til you were gone. Wanted to see how little Sid here was doing. And I've been to his house, too. Haven't I, Sid?"

She gave Sid a wink. "He thinks my name is Yvonne." Then she laughed that same, charming laugh he'd found so attractive once before. It washed over her, and for a moment she didn't seem threatening at all. "*Yvonne.* I always liked that name."

"Things don't have to be like this," Sid said.

Now the laugh was gone. Completely. It was odd how her mood changed so quickly. She wagged a finger at him. "No, no, no, Sid. You don't get to tell me what things are like. You have no idea. Neither one of you do."

She walked about halfway from the door to the counter and dropped her purse on one of the tables. Now Sid was seven or eight feet away, Joe a little further as he stood behind the bar. She held the gun casually at her waist, but generally pointing in their direction.

"How about I tell you what things are like in the real world, hmm? Would you like to know what it's really like?"

Sid assumed the question was rhetorical, but she

stopped and seemed to be waiting for an answer. Despite the chilling effect of the pistol in the room, he felt surprisingly calm as he took a moment to survey Eddie's mom, whatever her name was. She'd been dressed fairly professionally in their first two meetings. Not this time. White halter top over a skirt that ended well above her knees. Hair pulled into a ponytail and four inch heels. A top-heavy, middle-aged Angie Dickinson playing a hooker.

"Sure. Tell me what the real world is like." Sid figured as long as she was talking she wouldn't be shooting, and that was a good thing.

"Pregnant at sixteen is the real world, Sid. Being the top student in your class in high school, but then discovering that you're having a baby. And it just wasn't cool to be a knocked up teenage girl in 1953. Not nearly so glamorous as today. I got expelled. My parents freaked out. My dad especially. And then Eddie arrived and it was pretty tough to convince my father that I hadn't had sex with a black boy. He slapped me around and told me to get out of his house. That's the real world."

The corners of her mouth went up, but it wasn't a smile. It was something else. Something cynical. Her eyes went a little glassy.

"Years go by, the girls who weren't as smart or as pretty as me went to college or got married. And I end up living with Eddie in a crappy apartment on public assistance. That's the real world."

"Are we bitter?" Sid couldn't resist.

"This may not be the best time to decide you're a smartass, Sid!" The woman was suddenly focused and very loud—screaming—and she took a step closer. It was another quick, crazy flip in emotions, but this time it was big. Like a bomb went off. "I won't be judged by a white bread kid who has no clue what my life has been like! My life ended at sixteen! You have no idea what I gave up!"

She stared intently at Sid, fuming. It had been just a short outburst, but it left her breathing hard and shaking, and the halter top was putting on quite a show. The glare continued as her breathing grew slower, more steady. Sid studied her face, deciding after a while that she wasn't really looking at him anymore, but at something else. Something far away. When she spoke again, the words came slowly and her voice had grown quiet.

"Halfway through my junior year and I hadn't gotten one single B. All A's. I was really good at math. Mr. Santos said I was. I used to lean over his desk on purpose. Give him a little peek. Dances. Lunch with my friends. Sneaking cigarettes behind the gym…"

The woman took a deep, slow breath, then let it out.

"My goddamn drunk father," she said. "And that damn black baby. "

The gun hung down at her side now, pointing at the floor, and she was speaking almost in a whisper. Elvis had left the building.

Under different circumstances, Sid would have felt sorry for the woman. But the gun in her hand seemed to preclude any pity.

"So when my dad hit you guys with the car, you saw a way for Eddie to pay you back for what he made you give up."

In an instant the light returned to her eyes. "What a nice, self righteous way to put it, Sid." The melancholy was gone, and she was once again the woman Sid had met in this very same place less than two weeks earlier. The gun barrel slowly came back up. "Anyway, I eventually got sick and tired of watching Big Sid's perfect life. So happy and successful. And you wanna know what the worst thing was? He took Eddie. He had a family of his own—had his own son—but that wasn't enough. Big Sid, so compassionate, hiring the retarded boy. He took him away, and nobody knew what he'd done to me. Last year I told him I was sick and tired of what my life had turned into here. I was all done with him and Eddie and that shitty apartment I was living in. Told him I wanted a hundred thousand dollars and I'd leave town and never come back."

Sid remembered Gloria telling him that their father had been making as much as $5,000 a month disappear not long before he died.

"He started to pay you, didn't he?"

"Yeah, the old man was making a real nice effort. And then for some reason he called it all off. Came right to my house, said there was no more money and told me he was going to stop paying. Told me I could call the newspapers or call the cops, but he was through covering up something he did fifteen years ago. Very impressive. Stupid, but impressive."

Abruptly and without warning, the woman sat in a chair, crossed her legs and began rubbing a foot with her free hand.

"God, these shoes hurt like a mother! Don't ever wear heels, Sid. They're not worth it."

Sid almost laughed, and it was at that moment he decided for sure that the woman was a complete and total nutcase.

"I shouldn't be the only one sitting, Joe. Why don't you come out from behind there and you two boys can have a seat together on a couple of those stools?"

Joe didn't say a word, but turned and walked around the counter. For a moment Sid thought the big man was going to make a move towards Yvonne—or whatever her name was—but he didn't. The two sat down, facing the woman. Her skin was shiny with perspiration and Sid noticed how thick the air had become.

"After your father was gone I decided to get the hell out of here. Just pack up and go somewhere else. Someplace that's not so damn hot in the summer. But I couldn't do it. I just couldn't leave things here the way they were. And you know why? Because of you, Sid. Because your life was too damn happy. Your father ruined my son. And I decided that, even if your bastard old man was dead, I was going to ruin his son, too.

"I thought about killing you, Sid. I really did. But that just didn't seem right. Didn't seem fair, y'know? I decided to send you to prison instead. I mean, that's sort of what Big Sid did to my Eddie, right? Took him away. Put him in a place where he couldn't talk to anybody.

Couldn't live life like the rest of us.

"So I just started watching your predictable life, little Sid. Going to the pretty girl's apartment every Saturday night. Going to work and going home the same time every day. Going out running the same nights every week. I think running's bad for you, Sid. It could get you killed."

The woman grabbed a paper napkin from the table, dabbed her forehead and then her neck. She leaned back in her chair.

"But, God, it was fun. I got a great black leotard. You should see it. Looked like Catwoman." She raised her eyebrows and gave Sid a look that was probably intended to be provocative. "I waited for you to go by each time, then Bang-Bang-Bang! I watched you stop, look around. And on that last night when you ran off at Fairytale Town… Oh, it was perfect. I came down here early the next morning with Eddie—It was so nice of Big Sid to give him that key— and I stashed the gun in your back room and called the cops. Too easy."

"Why'd you register the gun in my dad's name?"

"Yeah, that was a mistake on my part. Sloppy. I probably shouldn't have used that same fake I.D."

"Fake I.D.?"

The woman looked at Sid like he was ten. "Jesus, where have you been? Remember the phony drivers licenses everybody used to buy beer with when we were kids? This was a really good one, though. Got it from a guy who actually works at the DMV. Then I just put on a low cut top, drove up to Reno, and bought a gun from one of the nice men. Simple. But it was stupid to use that same drivers license that I used last year. Don't know what I was thinking..."

When she said it, Sid could sense Joe Diaz tense up next to him. He had heard it, too.

"Last year?"

"Yeah. When I bought the gun that killed Big Sid." She said it so casually. "You know, he was very helpful. The note was his idea. He wanted to say goodbye. Thought that would make it easier on everyone."

The woman smiled, and looked almost wistful.

"You know what your dumbass father said to me? He said he was sorry for everything. Like that made a difference. He told me he was sorry and he started to cry."

"But you pulled the trigger," said Sid.

"Yes. Of course."

Then three things occurred in such rapid succession, they seemed to happen all at once. Joe jumped to his feet and took a step toward the woman. The woman stood and raised the gun, leveling it at Joe's head. And Sid reached out with both arms to stop his father's best friend. All three froze for a moment. Sid had his arms around Joe Diaz, and could feel the powerful rise and fall of his chest with each breath.

"You should have left it alone, Joe. You should've waited one more day." She held the gun at eye level, steady. "I've got a flight tomorrow to San Diego, and I would've been out of your hair. But when I found that note you left on my door this afternoon, I knew I couldn't just leave you two like this. Somehow you'd figured out it was me. I couldn't let you talk to the cops."

Sid had no experience with handguns, and was transfixed by the sight of the end of the barrel. So perfectly round, and bigger than he would have expected. A gaping black hole only six feet away. He held Joe tightly, unsure now if he was trying to save the man or simply clinging to him for security. He studied the gun, trying to decide if it was pointed at Joe, or pointed at him.

He was surprised by the tremendous roar that filled the deli. Sid Bigler had no idea that guns were so loud.

CHAPTER 38

It's an odd thing, and he had never admitted it to anyone. Ever since his father's death, Sid had thought repeatedly about what it must have been like to have a bullet go through his head. Maybe the seed had been planted a few years earlier when Sid first saw the Zapruder Film. He was too young at the time to have his heart broken by the death of Jack Kennedy, but he was old enough to be morbidly fascinated. What must that be like? Standing in Sid's Deli on the night of Tuesday, May 27th, 1980, he got quite an education.

It was a big bullet. Bigger than the ones Eddie's mom had fired at the Capitol and all the other landmarks. Bigger than the one that had taken Big Sid's life. It was a .38 caliber slug and when it first struck something warm it was moving at over five hundred miles per hour. That's still below the speed of sound, so if you ever have the misfortune to be shot in the head, you might hear the bang before you feel the thud. It's just a fraction of a second difference, of course, but maybe it's enough time to think, "uh-oh."

And make no mistake about it, five hundred miles per hour is plenty fast to do the job. A projectile moving at less than a quarter of that speed will break the skin. A third of that speed and it'll break a bone. So the bullet barely slowed down as it passed through scalp and skull on its way to the brain. And once it reached the brain, the .38 slug made remarkably short work of a human life.

A lesser bullet—a .22—might have actually done more damage. The smaller piece of lead can fracture as it hits bone. The energy dissipates more quickly, and the bits of bullet can bounce off the far wall of the skull and rattle around in there for a little while, whisking the brain into a milk shake.

And a more powerful round—a high velocity rifle bullet—would have done more damage, too. A projectile racing through a brain at over two thousand miles per hour pushes tissue away from its path with such violent force that it actually creates a cavity—a surprisingly large air space that's several times the diameter of the bullet. Unfortunately, that rapid expansion can't be contained inside the skull. The forensics crowd refers to the end result as a "bursting injury." The head pops like a grape and gray matter rushes out any available hole. Not pretty.

But the bullet that flew through the air that night in Sid's Deli was a .38—a fat piece of lead moving relatively slowly.

The brain is essentially a collection of wires that carry electrical impulses. Tenuous, fragile wires made of human tissue. Whether it's from a high school biology class or a bad experience in a Turkish restaurant, people have a rather rubbery image of the brain. Cold and squishy, yet firm enough for a creepy game of catch. But that's not right. A living brain at 98.6 degrees is something much different. Think Jello pudding. Cottage cheese. Refried beans. There's a nice, fine membrane that holds everything in place, but if you could reach in there you'd have no problem swishing your fingers around.

When the .38 slug passed through the brain that night, it took a perfectly straight path from one side of the skull to the other. And as it passed through, it sent ripples of energy out in all directions, like a pebble dropped in a pond. The immediate path of destruction wasn't that impressive, but the ripples were, quite literally, killers. Moving at terrible speed, the waves of energy pulled apart the brain tissue from wall to wall, unplugging the living wires that control every aspect of life. Lights out. No time for pain. Adios. Au Revoir. Auf Wiedersehn.

On its way out of the skull and towards the back wall of the deli—once its killing work was done—the bullet managed to take a lot of stuff with it. Wet stuff that, along with splinters of bone, hung for a moment in the air like a veil. Like somebody sneezed with a big mouthful of SpaghettiOs.

Fortunately for Sid, the head through which the bullet had passed was not his own.

The woman's body fell to the floor like a marionette with its strings cut, and Det. Benjamin Stokes walked the rest of the way through the doorway into the deli, a finger of smoke climbing out of the barrel of his gun.

"Who'd I just shoot?"

Sid stood there, mouth wide open, taking in the scene. He tried to make sense of the patchwork of images that randomly caught his eye. A photo of some politician on the wall had a hole in the corner, and broken glass tinkled onto the floor below it. One of the woman's shoes had come off somehow, and was laying on its side next to her tiny, still foot. A spatter of blood and bits left a shiny path across at least four tables. The clock read 9:41, and the jerky second hand kept clicking and clicking.

Sid had no idea how much time had gone by. It might have been only a few seconds, but it seemed longer. His ears were still ringing from the blast of the gun, but it did finally sink in that Stokes had asked a question. Something about the woman. He let go of Joe Diaz and took a step towards the body on the floor.

"This woman… she was the shooter." He struggled to gather his thoughts. "She blackmailed my father… she was trying to…"

"Yeah. Yeah, I caught the end of your conversation," said Stokes. "I got all that. But what's her name? I'm gonna have a pile of paperwork to fill out." If the cop was rattled, he wasn't showing it.

"Oh. I don't know." Sid made a conscious effort to focus. "I don't know her real name."

"It's Joyce," said Joe. "Joyce Davis."

Stokes slid his weapon into a holster somewhere underneath his jacket and squatted down next to the woman. It was a waste of time, but out of habit or professionalism, he put a hand on her neck, feeling for a pulse.

"I thought for sure you were the shooter." Stokes was looking at Sid. "Thought you were a certifiable crackpot. Never would've guessed this."

"How'd you know what was going on?" asked Sid. "How did you know to come down here tonight?"

Stokes stood, found a paper napkin and wiped his hand off. "You can thank your friend, Officer Woody Carver. He called me this afternoon, gave me a heads-up that there was new information about the Capital Shooter. So I was working late, going over my notes on the case when I got a call from the switchboard."

One final, unexpected piece of the puzzle fell into place.

"They said they were getting 9-1-1 calls from this address," Stokes continued. "From your payphone back there. There was no answer when the emergency operator responded, but someone kept ringing from this number again and again. I figured maybe I should come down and check the place out."

Few moments in Sid Bigler's life would be as memorable as the one that followed. With the rattle of a knob and the creak of a hinge, the door to the back room opened. Sid, Joe and the cop turned to see Eddie Davis' face appear. His mother had once told Sid that he was good with numbers.

CHAPTER 39

People just expect the Fourth of July to be scorching hot in Sacramento, and they're seldom disappointed. But it turned out to be a surprisingly mild summer day that the weatherman said would top out in the eighties. It was coming up on lunch time, and forty or fifty people clogged the sidewalk at the corner of 11th and K, some of them spilling out onto the street. There were no TV stations, but Jackson Dexter was in the crowd with his camera in hand.

It had been almost five weeks since Det. Stokes had shot Joyce Davis in the deli. The dramatic climax of the Capital Shooter story was national news for a day or two, and managed to keep the interest of the locals for a little longer.

The cops had insisted that nobody touch anything in the deli the entire weekend following the shooting. The place had been crawling with investigators and technicians and a variety of official strangers. Once they got the okay, Sid and Joe had the deli cleaned up and ready to open the next day, but decided to keep it closed for the rest of the week. It just seemed respectful. When they finally did open the doors the next Monday, it was more crowded than ever. Credit the media attention and the return of the Brown Sugar Rolls.

If Eddie had been troubled by what he saw when he came out of the back room that night, it didn't show. The Mona Lisa smile never left, although Sid thought maybe he saw a sadness in his eyes. Maybe. Sid didn't want to read more into it than there was, but even awful mothers are still mothers, right? Joe had taken Eddie home with him that night, and he'd been staying with Joe and Theresa ever since. Joe hadn't said anything, but Sid was guessing that was going to be a permanent arrangement.

"Okay! Okay! Okay! Can I have everybody's attention?" Sid called out and most of the crowd complied. Gloria and her husband managed to corral Nicky and Nellie. Rose was beaming, proud of her son and happy with the decision he'd made. Joe Diaz stood by the door with his apron on and spatula in hand, looking like he wanted to get back to work. Amy was happy to hang around on the outskirts of the crowd. She'd have Sid's full attention later.

A sharp whistle pierced the air. "C'mon people, let's quiet down!" Officer Woody Carver turned on the cop voice. His cruiser sat in the street with the lights flashing, blocking a lane to make room for the crowd. The large blue tarp that was temporarily hung up above the doors to the deli caught a slight breeze and flapped just a little, then settled back down.

"Most of you are here today because you're a part of the family," Sid began. "And I don't mean just my mom and my sister. I mean the family of people that loved Big Sid." He searched the crowd for an unfamiliar face and couldn't find one. "Or maybe you're just a little early for lunch."

A polite chuckle made its way through the people standing outside the deli. Sid Bigler put his arm around Eddie Davis and he heard the whir of a camera as Jackson Dexter clicked off a half dozen shots.

"Nothing's really changed about this place since Dad and Joe opened it in 1947. The prices went up through the years and the walls got covered with pictures, but that's about it. I want you to know that what we're doing here today—it's not gonna change the things everybody loves about this place. Same people, same coffee machine, same tables and chairs."

"Same food!" It was big Pete with the suspenders over his white t-shirt as usual.

"Same food," said Sid. Then he reached up and grabbed the end of a rope that hung above the door. "All we're changing is the sign."

With a pull, the blue tarp fell from the front of the building, and for the first time, red and white plastic letters proclaimed a new name for Sacramento's Best Deli (as voted by the readers of both major newspapers). The sign said 'Sid & Eddie's.'

A cheer of approval rose from the crowd accompanied by an impressive round of applause. After ten seconds or so, the applause began to fade as applause always does. The sound of celebration diminished until only one pair of hands could be heard clapping. Eddie Davis was looking up, smiling, still applauding. Every eye in the crowd was on him.

Standing next to Eddie, Sid turned and looked again at the sign. He smiled, too, and joined Eddie again in clapping. An ovation of two. Aside from the obvious differences, they might have been brothers.

ACKNOWLEDGMENTS

I have many people to thank for making this novel possible (though none are to blame for any mistakes you may have found). Ian Cornell, in particular, is my favorite guy to bounce a plot twist off of, and a ruthless catcher of manuscript errors. His time and efforts on my behalf were heroic. Connie Neal's keen eye and thoughtful comments were also much appreciated. I shared many happy hours of story tweaking with Joe Cipov (cop buddy) and Phil Cowan (generic buddy). Dr. Mike Robbins is my favorite Brain Surgeon, and was generous with not only his time and wisdom, but wonderful encouragement, too. Ken Rosenfeld provided valuable legal insight, as did my son-in-law, Stephen, who abandoned a Harvard Law degree to pursue a career in fine wine (a decision that makes me proud). Thanks to Rich Hanna and Marty Inouye and my many running companions— they're all faster than I, but only Rich is faster than Sid. And a special 'Thank You' to Helen Robins because… well, because boys should always thank their mothers.

ABOUT THE AUTHOR

Paul Robins is a successful broadcaster, an avid reader, a slow but devoted runner, and a writer of mystery novels. His morning radio resume includes brief stops in Detroit & Dallas, and a wonderfully long one in Sacramento, California. In TV-land, Paul appeared for several years on The Discovery Channel as one of "The Answer Guys" and is currently seen on PBS's "America's Heartland." He can also be found anchoring the news weekday mornings on KTXL FOX40 in Sacramento.

Paul has been married to Bridget Robins for 33 wonderful years and has three lovely daughters, two handsome sons-in-law, and three delightful (and exceptionally smart) grandsons.

24219290R00178

Made in the USA
Charleston, SC
15 November 2013